I0654616

SPIDERS ON A SHIP

NATURE'S NIGHTMARES, BOOK 2
STACI LAYNE WILSON

Excessive Nuance

CONTENTS

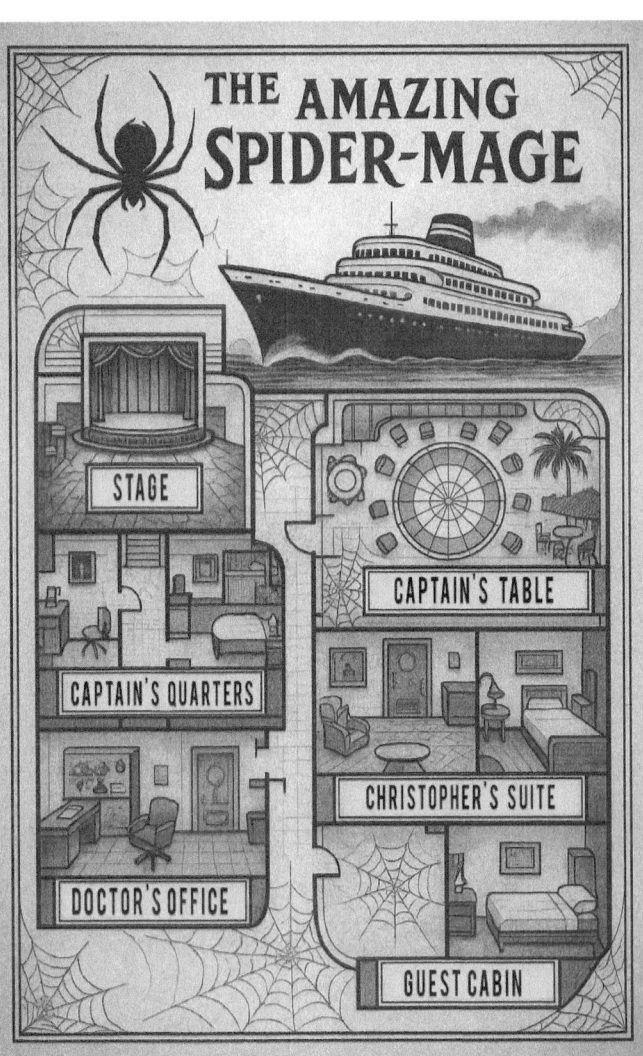

CHAPTER 1

The salt air carried a mixture of diesel fumes and customized air freshener as Christopher Webb stepped onto the gangway of the *Pacific Dream*. His weathered but strong, fortified leather case knocked against his hip with each step, the contents within shifting with familiar weight—glass terrariums, feeding supplies, and five of the most exotic arachnids money and persistence could procure. The irony wasn't lost on him that he was literally carrying his nightmares aboard a floating paradise.

In his other hand was a small gilded cage, holding a pair of white doves that cooed softly against his fingers. Every magician had to have doves, he mused, catching the faint sound of their feathers rustling with a whispered promise of illusion. Like his spiders, the doves were not given names. It helped him stay focused on the fact that they were tools of the trade, not pets.

He surveyed the ship from the walkway, taking in its vintage design that matched the 1940s throwback theme. Long Beach harbor sprawled behind him, the Queen Mary permanently docked in the distance, a real relic of the era this cruise merely pantomimed. A week trapped at sea with wealthy tourists playing dress-up. He sighed, the sound mingling with the distant cry of seagulls and the metallic clanking of cargo being loaded onto nearby vessels.

The ship's brass railings gleamed like gold in the afternoon sun, every surface polished to mirror perfection. His fingertips brushed against the cool metal as he steadied himself, feeling the slight vibration of the engines warming below deck. Art deco flourishes decorated the cream-colored hull, and bunting fluttered in patriotic reds, whites, and blues with a soft, rhythmic slapping sound against the gentle ocean breeze. The air tasted of salt and nostalgia, with hints of shoe polish and cigar smoke wafting from the upper decks.

It was as if someone had plucked a movie set from 1943 and dropped it into the modern Pacific, with swing music drifting from hidden speakers, its clarinets and brass instruments creating a tinny soundtrack that tickled his eardrums, and crew members dressed like extras from *Casablanca*. The fabric of their period-accurate uniforms rustled as they moved about, their shoes clicking precisely against the polished wooden deck.

At the base of the gangway, a photographer in period-appropriate attire—complete with suspenders and a newsboy cap—posed a group of passengers against the backdrop of the towering ship. Their vintage costumes ranged from sailors on shore leave to women in victory rolls and seamed stockings, all playing their parts with enthusiastic commitment.

"Perfect! Hold that pose," the photographer called, ducking beneath his draped camera. "Your keepsake photos will be ready in 8 by 10 glossies when you disembark. Additional prints are available via mail order, of course."

Christopher smirked. Even the photography was committed to the era; no digital cameras or instant gratification here. Just another carefully curated anachronism on this floating time capsule.

"Welcome aboard the *Pacific Dream*, sir!" A steward in crisp whites and a jaunty cap approached Christopher with practiced enthusiasm. His name tag read 'Denver Wheaton' in elegant script. "You must be our featured entertainer. The Amazing Spider-Mage himself!"

Christopher managed what he hoped was a charming smile, though it felt more like a grimace. The 'Amazing' part of his stage name had always made him cringe. It was a relic from his Vegas days when ego mattered more than authenticity. Now, at forty-three, with silver threading through his dark hair and crow's feet mapping years of late nights and early disappointments, the superlative felt increasingly hollow.

"Just Christopher Webb will do," he said, adjusting his grip on the case. Something inside clicked against glass, probably the huntsman shifting in its habitat. The sound made his stomach clench, a Pavlovian response he'd never quite conquered despite his years of handling the creatures.

Denver's grin never wavered. "Nonsense, sir! The passengers are absolutely cranked to see your act. We've got three sold-out shows already, and you haven't even unpacked!" He gestured toward the ship's interior with theatrical flair. "Shall I show you to your quarters? Your luggage is already there. The entertainment staff has premium cabins on Deck 8."

They walked through corridors that smelled of lemon oil and rustic wood, past porthole windows that cast dancing circles of light on burgundy carpeting. The ship's designers had spared no expense in creating their fab '40s fantasy. Every doorknob was brass, every light fixture dripped with crystal, and the walls were adorned with elaborate flocked paper and vintage travel posters promising adventure in exotic locales.

Christopher's reflection caught his eye in a gilded mirror as they passed. He needed reassurance that he could still command an audience, even one that was captive. Tall, lean, and sharp-featured, he still looked the part of a master illusionist. The spider tattoos that crawled up his forearms remained crisp and dark, though the playing cards and dice scattered across his hands had faded slightly with time. His off-stage outfit of black slacks and a short-sleeved charcoal button-down struck the right balance between professional and mysterious. *Still got it,* he told himself, though the voice in his head sounded unconvinced.

As they walked, Christopher's mind drifted to the Vegas theater that had once displayed his name in lights. Five years of sold-out shows, his name blazing across the Strip in electric blue neon that could be seen from airplane windows. Celebrities had jostled for the front row—he remembered DiCaprio's wide-eyed wonder during the Black Widow's Embrace illusion, and how Beyoncé had gasped when he'd transformed a trapdoor spider into a diamond bracelet and placed it around her wrist. Those performances had landed him on the covers of *Entertainment Weekly*, *Vegas Life*, and even a feature spread in *Vanity Fair* where they'd called him "the thinking man's magician, equal parts maestro and madman."

Now he was reduced to this... a drifting dinner theater where passengers with their maritime cocktails would be more interested in their all-you-can-eat buffet plates than his meticulously crafted illusions. They'd applaud politely between bites of overcooked prime rib, checking their watches, wondering when they could return to the slot machines on the casino deck. The thought stirred in his stomach like sourcrout soup. How quickly they forgot you in this business, how ruthlessly the spotlight moved on to fresher blood once you've hit middle age and shown them all your tricks.

"Here we are!" Denver threw open a door marked with a yellow copper nameplate: *Featured Performer - Private Suite*.

The cabin was larger than Christopher had expected, decorated in rich burgundies and golds that wouldn't have looked out of place in a vintage Park Avenue penthouse. A king-sized bed dominated one wall, its headboard upholstered in tufted velvet. French doors opened onto a private balcony where he could already imagine himself smoking cigarettes and brooding artistically—if he still smoked, which he'd quit two years ago after a particularly brutal review in the *Las Vegas Sun* that mentioned his smoker's hack.

Christopher's gaze lingered on the bed's luxurious expanse. The pristine sheets looked inviting, the kind that would feel cool against bare skin on a warm Pacific night. It had been months since he'd shared a bed with anyone. The thought of a woman's perfume mingling with his cologne in this room made his chest tighten with unexpected longing.

He set down his case with a sigh. Who was he kidding? He wasn't here for romance or even a casual fling. He was here to work, to perform the same illusions he'd done a thousand times before, all so he could write another check to Marissa. His ex-wife's alimony payments were like clockwork, the only consistent relationship he'd maintained in the past three years.

Last month's bank statement flashed through his mind: the deposit from his previous gig at that corporate retreat in Phoenix, followed immediately by the automatic withdrawal to Marissa's account. What was left barely covered his rent and the specialized care his arachnids required.

No, Christopher Webb wasn't looking for love on this floating theme park. Love was expensive, and he'd already paid more than his fair share. He unlatched his case, ready to settle his eight-legged companions into their temporary home. At least spiders didn't demand half of everything you'd ever earned.

"The *Stardust Salon* is just two decks down," Denver continued, apparently oblivious to Christopher's distraction. "Curtain goes up at nine-thirty sharp. Will you need assistance setting up your... equipment?"

The word hung in the air with barely disguised curiosity. Christopher had learned that people's reactions to his spiders fell into three categories: morbid fascination, barely concealed revulsion, or complete terror. This Denver character appeared to be hovering between the first two.

"I'll manage," Christopher said, setting his case on the bed with exaggerated care. "Though I'll need the theater to myself for setup. The ladies don't care for disruptions."

"Ladies?"

"My spiders." Christopher couldn't resist the small theatrical pause. "They're all female. More venomous that way."

Denver's smile flickered like a lightbulb with loose wiring, but he recovered admirably. "Of course, sir. I'll make sure you have complete privacy. Is there anything else you need? The bar is fully stocked, and dinner is served until eleven in the *Golden Parlor*."

"Actually," Christopher said, his attention caught by the sound of laughter from somewhere nearby—rich, throaty, with just a hint of Southern honey, "what can you tell me about the other entertainers?"

Denver's eyes lit up with gossip-hungry delight, practically vibrating with the opportunity to share insider information. "Oh, you must mean Miss Laveau!" he exclaimed, lowering his voice to a conspiratorial whisper though they were alone in the stateroom. "She's our resident psychic. Fourth voyage with us, and absolutely the bee's knees. Does palm readings, tarot, crystal ball gazing, the whole mystical repertoire. Claims she can speak with the dear departed and reveal secrets hidden in the folds of time, that sort of thing."

He straightened his perfectly pressed uniform jacket, a hint of admiration creeping into his professional demeanor. "Quite the personality, if I may say so. The management extended her contract twice already. Standing room only for her evening séances in the *Moonlight Lounge*. Between us," Denver leaned closer, "even the captain consulted her earlier today. Something about us leaving port on his late mother's birthday, I believe."

The laughter came again, closer now, followed by applause and the clink of glasses. Christopher found himself drawn to the French doors, stepping onto the balcony where the sound was clearer. Two levels below, on what appeared to be a pool deck, a crowd had gathered around a woman in flowing black fabric.

Even from this distance, she was magnetic. Dark hair tumbled over bare shoulders in glossy waves that seemed to absorb and reflect light simultaneously, framing a face he couldn't quite make out but could sense was captivating. Her jewelry, an elaborate collection of silver chains, pendants, and bangles, caught the late afternoon sun like a constellation of captured stars, sending prismatic flashes across the deck with each gesture. She moved with fluid grace, having long ago mastered the art of being watched, each turn of her wrist and tilt of her head choreographed to maximize its effect on her audience. Her body language spoke of absolute confidence, a performer who knew precisely how to command a space without appearing to try.

A crystal ball sat on the table before her, resting on what looked like a midnight-blue velvet cloth, but Christopher could tell from the way the crowd leaned toward her that she hardly needed such obvious props to hold their attention. Something in her posture reminded him of himself in his earlier days, before the Vegas residency had left him jaded, when the thrill of manipulation had been fresh and intoxicating. He recognized the subtle power play happening below, the delicate dance between performer and willing audience, all pretending the magic was real.

"Yes, that's her," Denver said, appearing beside him. "Claims to be descended from the famous Voodoo Queen Marie Laveau, though between you and me, I suspect that's part of the act. But Lordy, can that dame work a crowd."

As if summoned by their conversation, the woman looked up.

Their eyes met across the intervening distance, and Christopher felt something electric pass between them. Recognition, perhaps, or the acknowledgment that takes place between performers who understand the power of holding an audience's attention.

She smiled, raised her glass upward in a mock toast, and turned back graciously to her admirers.

"Well," Christopher murmured, watching her resume her performance with renewed energy, "this should be interesting."

Denver cleared his throat. "The passengers gather in the *Golden Parlor* for cocktails at six, if you're interested in mingling. Though I should mention, sir, that we do ask our performers to stay in character during public appearances. The 1940s theme is rather important to our guests' experience."

Christopher turned from the balcony, one eyebrow raised. "Character?"

"Well, you know, the wartime spirit, that sort of thing. Everyone's doing their part for the war effort, loose lips sink ships, all that." Denver's enthusiasm for the theme was both infectious and slightly off-putting. "The passengers love the immersion. Makes them feel like they're really living in the past."

If only they knew, Christopher thought, his hand unconsciously moving to the spider tattoo on his forearm, a memorial to his brother Danny, who would have been thirty-nine this year if a black widow hadn't bitten him when he was seven. *We're all living in the past,* he thought, *one way or another.*

"I'll keep that in mind," he said. "Now, if you don't mind, I'd like to get my ladies settled before dinner."

Denver reached into his jacket pocket and produced a small velvet pouch embroidered with the ship's logo. "One more thing, sir. I'll need to collect your cell phone for safekeeping."

Christopher's hand instinctively went to his pocket. "My phone? Why would—"

"As per the contract you signed," Denver interjected smoothly, his smile never faltering. "The *Pacific Dream* provides a complete immersion experience. No modern technology permitted for the duration of the voyage." He extended the pouch expectantly. "All passenger and performer devices are secured in our vault until we dock. It's one of our most popular features: a true digital detox."

Christopher frowned. He vaguely remembered skimming something about "authentic period experience" in the contract, but hadn't realized they'd be this committed to the bit. A week without his phone? Without checking his dwindling social media engagement or the reviews from his last disappointing tour?

"Is this really necessary?" he asked, reluctantly extracting his phone.

"Absolutely essential," Denver replied, his tone leaving no room for negotiation. "Our passengers pay premium rates to escape the modern world. Besides," he added with a conspiratorial wink, "absence makes the heart grow fonder. You might find yourself enjoying the freedom."

Christopher watched his last connection to the outside world disappear into the pouch and then Denver's pocket with surprising unease.

Denver gave a crisp salute, his posture military-perfect. "Enjoy your stay aboard the *Pacific Dream*, Mr. Webb. I'll see you at dinner." The door clicked shut behind him.

Alone in his cabin, he unpacked his stage clothes, the bespoke tuxedo with satin lapels, the top hat with its hidden compartments. Muscle memory from a thousand performances. This was all he knew. All he'd ever been good at since that summer day when Danny had been bitten, his small, swollen fingers turning black even before the ambulance arrived.

Christopher glanced at the ship's itinerary. Seven nights of performances. Seven nights of pretending this gig wasn't beneath him. Seven nights of grinning at passengers who thought magic was just pulling rabbits from hats.

But what choice did he have? Vegas had moved on to younger, sexier acts. Television wanted fresher faces. The Spider-Mage's web was unraveling, and this seabound relic might be his last chance to matter.

Christopher flipped through the glossy pages of the itinerary further, eyebrows rising with each turn. No sprawling casino floor. No twenty-four-hour buffet. No water slides or rock climbing walls.

"An expedition cruise," he muttered, scanning the description. "Intimate historical immersion experience... authentic swing-era entertainment... limited to three hundred and fifty passengers..."

He'd been expecting the usual cruise ship circuit—three thousand good-time Charlies with bottomless drinks and wallets to match. Instead, he'd signed onto what amounted to a floating museum with a captive audience of history buffs and wealthy eccentrics playing dress-up.

The itinerary detailed nightly big band performances, dance lessons, classic film screenings, and historical lectures. Even the route was designed to mimic Pacific voyages from the 1940s, with stops at small ports that had remained relatively unchanged since the war years.

Christopher ran his hand through his carefully combed hair. This wasn't just another gig; it was theatrical immersion on a scale he hadn't anticipated. No wonder they'd confiscated his phone. They weren't just selling a vacation; they were selling time travel. He glanced at his spider case. At least his act would still work. Fear, after all, was timeless.

At last, he opened his case with the reverence of a priest preparing for mass. Five custom terrariums, each climate-controlled and perfectly appointed for its resident. He placed the enclosures on the desk, expanding and arranging them meticulously.

The Australian huntsman skittered across its glass corral, legs spanning wider than a human palm, its amber body a blur of predatory grace. The Chilean recluse remained motionless in the corner, patient and deadly, its small brown form belying the tissue-destroying venom it harbored. The North American jumping spider—no bigger than a man's thumbnail but possessing eyesight that could track a fly from across a ballroom—perched alertly on a miniature branch, swiveling to follow her master's movements. Beside it, the Wraparound spider clung to its synthetic bark, camouflaged body nearly invisible until it shifted positions with deliberate slowness.

Each specimen represented years of collection, thousands in acquisition costs, and countless hours of training. They were his partners, his signature, his salvation from the memories that still haunted him. Christopher adjusted the humidity controls with nimble fingers, checking the temperature readouts with the attention of a father monitoring a sick child's fever. These creatures were the last vestiges of his fading celebrity, the final thread connecting him to relevance.

He stepped back to admire the arrangement, satisfaction momentarily overwhelming the nagging sense that he was a has-been relegated to entertaining retirees on a themed cruise. These arachnids had been with him through sold-out arenas and late-night talk shows. They would accompany him through this indignity as well, silent witnesses to his professional descent.

"At least you're still loyal," he murmured, tapping the glass of the Chinese bird spider, a massive specimen, highly aggressive and territorial, but not with him. They had an understanding.

"Hello, beautiful," he whispered, the endearment automatic despite the innate chill of nerves that tickled his spine. "Ready for another show?"

The spider paused, front legs raised as if gesturing to him. For a moment, Christopher could swear it was studying him with the same appraising intelligence he'd seen in Cleo Laveau's eyes moments before. Then it retreated to its hiding spot, leaving him to feed and water the birds.

Outside, the ship's horn sounded. A deep, resonant note that seemed to echo from the depths of the Pacific itself. The *Pacific Dream* was about to be officially underway, carrying its cargo of passengers, crew, and secrets toward whatever destiny awaited them in the endless blue.

Christopher closed the birds' cage and checked his watch. Two hours until cocktails. Time enough to shower, groom, and prepare himself for whatever performance this voyage would demand.

CHAPTER 2

Eleanor Hargrove's stilettos clacked frantically across the dock as she sprinted toward the towering white hull of the *Pacific Dream*. The gangway attendants were already removing the boarding ramp.

"Wait! Stop!" she called, waving one hand while the other clutched her Louis Vuitton weekender. "I'm a passenger!"

The crewmen exchanged looks—annoyed yet unsurprised. Eleanor recognized that expression. It was the same one baristas wore when she demanded they remake her oat milk latte because the foam art wasn't Instagram-worthy.

A uniformed officer with brass buttons and a captain's hat stepped forward. "Cutting it rather close, miss. We're scheduled to depart in three minutes."

"Do you know who I am?" Eleanor flipped her honey-blonde hair over one shoulder, chest heaving from exertion. "Eleanor Hargrove. I have one million followers on Instagram. Two point five on TikTok." She thrust her boarding documents forward. "I'm doing a sponsored content series about this cruise."

The man's face remained impassive, but he signaled to the attendants, who reluctantly lowered the gangway again. "Very well, Miss Hargrove. Welcome aboard the *Pacific Dream*."

Eleanor didn't thank him as she clip-clopped up the ramp, her vintage-inspired sundress fluttering in the breeze. The dress, a custom *Vixen* piece gifted to her by designer Micheline Pitt, was specifically designed to appear authentic while still accentuating her surgically sculpted figure. Her stylist had assured her it would photograph beautifully against the ship's art deco interiors.

A steward in a starched uniform approached as she stepped onto the deck. "Your luggage, miss?"

"My assistant was supposed to send it ahead yesterday." She frowned, scanning the busy deck. "There should be four Rimowa cases. Silver. They have my name engraved."

"I'll check with baggage services immediately." The steward bowed slightly. "May I escort you to your cabin in the meantime?"

"Suite," Eleanor corrected. "I'm in the *Marlene Dietrich Suite*. The cruise line comped it for my content package." She glanced at her watch, a vintage Cartier that had belonged to her grandmother. "And I need to speak with the cruise director about my itinerary. I require private access to certain areas of the ship before other passengers for my morning shoots."

The steward's smile tightened. "Of course. Right this way."

As they walked through the ship's grand atrium, Eleanor discreetly assessed the surroundings, mentally calculating optimal lighting angles and potential backdrops. The vintage theme was executed better than she'd expected. Brass fixtures gleamed under warm amber lighting, big band music played softly from hidden speakers, and crew members moved about in period-perfect uniforms. The polished mahogany railings felt smooth and cool beneath her perfectly manicured fingertips, while the air carried hints of furniture polish and top-tier air freshener. Her Chanel goatskin & grosgrain pumps clicked musically against the marble floor, the sound echoing slightly in the cavernous space. The gentle vibration of the engines thrummed beneath her feet, a subtle reminder they were already leaving the modern world behind.

"Your room key, Miss Hargrove." The steward handed her an ornate skeleton key attached to a heavy gold tassel. "How... quaint," she murmured, already composing the caption in her head: *Stepping back in time aboard the #PacificDream—where luxury meets nostalgia! #sponsored #vintagecruise #travelinfluencer*

"One more thing," the steward added. "I'll need to collect your mobile devices. Ship policy for our vintage experience."

Eleanor froze. "Excuse me?"

"All electronic devices are secured in our vault for the duration of the cruise. It's part of the immersive experience."

"That's impossible. I'm here to create content. I need my phone." She clutched her purse tighter.

"I assure you, our ship's photographer will capture plenty of images for your use after the voyage. It's all outlined in your contract."

Eleanor's Insta-ready smile faltered. Seven days without posting? Without checking her engagement metrics? Without monitoring what her rivals were doing?

"There must be some mistake," she said, her voice rising. "Get me the cruise director. Now."

The steward's expression didn't change, but Eleanor sensed his satisfaction at her dilemma. "As you wish, Miss Hargrove. Though I should mention, we're already underway."

Behind her, through the porthole, the dock was indeed sliding away, separating Eleanor from the world that validated her existence, one like at a time.

***

Carlotta Cross adjusted her navy blue uniform jacket as she strode down the corridor toward the *Marlene Dietrich Suite*. The lapel pin bearing the *Pacific Dream* logo gleamed under the haze of the sconces lining the hallway. Her radio crackled at her hip.

"Ms. Cross, Miss Hargrove is requesting your presence immediately regarding the device policy." The steward's voice carried the practiced neutrality of someone who'd just weathered a category five tantrum.

"Already on my way," Carlotta replied, keeping her voice chipper despite the familiar sinking feeling. First day, first hour, first problem passenger. Right on schedule.

She took a deep breath before knocking on the stateroom door. Behind it waited another entitled passenger who believed rules were suggestions meant for others.

The door swung open to reveal Eleanor Hargrove, five-foot-nine in heels with a scowl that could curdle milk.

"You're the cruise director?" Eleanor asked, eyes sweeping over Carlotta's perfectly period-appropriate uniform.

"Carlotta Cross, at your service." She extended her hand. "I understand you have concerns about our digital detox policy?"

Eleanor ignored the outstretched hand. "This is absurd. I'm here to create content. I signed a contract with your marketing department."

Carlotta stepped into the suite, noting the Louis Vuitton weekender already emptied across the bed, vintage-inspired clothing spilling out like confetti made of sequins, diamonds, and gold tassels.

"Yes, our marketing team mentioned your arrangement. I've been fully briefed." Carlotta maintained her corporate smile. "The contract specifically outlined our authentic 1940s experience, including our no-modern-technology policy. Your content package was designed with that in mind."

"But I need my phone to post! What's the point of being here if no one sees it?"

Carlotta had heard variations of this exact complaint from teenagers, CEOs, and everyone in between. The modern fear of digital disconnection was more terrifying than actual danger.

"Our ship's photographer will document your entire journey. Those images will be available when we dock, giving you an entire content library to curate and post." Carlotta gestured toward the porthole where open ocean now stretched to the horizon. "The delay actually creates anticipation among your followers."

Eleanor paced the suite, her spiky heels digging into the plush carpet. "Low-resolution paper photographs? That's your solution?"

"Actually, we use period-appropriate equipment that's been modified for high-resolution digital conversion. The aesthetic is quite popular right now, authentic film grain with modern clarity." Carlotta leaned against the doorframe. "I should mention that Olivia Batiste has been granted use of a vintage-styled digital camera for her documentary work. Perhaps you could—"

"Olivia? The sustainable travel girl?" Eleanor's face hardened. "Absolutely not. No collabs."

Carlotta nodded, unsurprised. "Then your options are our ship's photographer or waiting until we dock. I'm afraid the vault remains closed for the duration of the voyage."

Eleanor collapsed dramatically onto a brocade chaise lounge. "This is career suicide."

"Or a brilliant marketing angle," Carlotta countered. "The influencer brave enough to truly disconnect. Think of the narrative possibilities."

The ship's engines hummed beneath them, a gentle reminder of their isolation. Eleanor stared out the porthole at the endless blue.

"Fine," she finally said. "But I want exclusive access to the photographer. Morning shoots before other passengers are up. And I need guaranteed time on the bow at golden hour."

Carlotta smiled. Crisis averted... for now. "I'll arrange everything. In the meantime, might I suggest our welcome cocktail party? It's quite the spectacle."

Eleanor waved her hand dismissively. "Whatever."

As Carlotta turned to leave, she mentally updated her passenger threat assessment. Eleanor Hargrove: potential problem, currently contained. Just six more days to keep it that way.

Carlotta closed Eleanor's door with consummate restraint, releasing her professional smile the moment the latch clicked. She massaged her jaw muscles, sore from maintaining her cruise director façade. One passenger neutralized, dozens more to manage before dinner.

She checked her vintage pocket watch, a genuine 1943 Hamilton with a delicate engraving of ocean waves. Four hours until the evening's entertainment began. Just enough time to finalize preparations and brief the captain.

The narrow service corridors allowed Carlotta to move through the ship unseen by passengers. These hidden arteries of the *Pacific Dream* were her domain, where the illusion of vintage luxury gave way to the practical reality of modern cruise operations. Still, even here, she maintained her period-appropriate posture and gait. One never knew when a passenger might stumble into staff areas.

Carlotta mentally ticked through her evening checklist. The *Starlight Lounge* was set for Cleo's performance—crystal ball polished, tarot cards arranged, special effects tested. The woman was, of course, a fraud, but a talented one who understood the theatrical value of the throwback aesthetic. This was Cleo's fourth voyage, and she consistently ranked among the passengers' favorites.

"Genuine frauds," Carlotta murmured to herself, a category that included most of the ship's entertainment. People who acknowledged their performances were illusions yet delivered them with such conviction that passengers willingly suspended disbelief.

The new act, however, presented complications. Christopher Webb, the Amazing Spider-Mage, was an unknown quantity. His Vegas credentials were impressive, but ship performances operated under different constraints. Particularly his insistence on using live arachnids.

Carlotta frowned, remembering the heated debate with the safety officer. Technically, the *Pacific Dream* maintained a strict no-pets policy. But entertainment animals fell into a gray area. The birds were one thing—colorful, contained, predictable. But spiders? Five different species, each more exotic than the last.

She'd finally approved the act after Webb demonstrated his specially designed containment systems and handling protocols. Still, she'd stationed extra security for tonight's performance. Just in case.

A memory surfaced as she climbed the narrow stairs toward the bridge, of Whiskers, the small gray rat she'd discovered in her quarters two voyages ago. Rather than reporting the stowaway to maintenance, she'd secretly fed him cheese and crackers from the officer's mess. Over time, she'd trained him to come when she tapped her fingers three times on her desk.

"My one rule violation," she whispered, pushing away a pang of sentiment. Whiskers had disappeared somewhere near Puerto Vallarta. She liked to imagine him sunning himself on a Mexican beach rather than meeting a less pleasant fate in the ship's mechanical systems.

The bridge door opened with a pneumatic hiss, revealing the gleaming control center of the *Pacific Dream*. Unlike passenger areas, no vintage pretense existed here. Modern navigation equipment, radar displays, and communication systems filled the space with their quiet electronic hum.

"Captain," Carlotta nodded to the broad-shouldered older man studying a weather chart. "I've come to brief you on tonight's entertainment schedule."

Captain Abercrombie straightened, his authentic uniform at odds with the digital displays behind him. "Ms. Cross. I trust our passengers are settling in?"

Abercrombie's weathered face creased with his trademark scowl, his Scottish burr more pronounced when irritated. Carlotta knew the dignified captain tolerated the 1940s theme as a necessary evil and nothing more.

"One minor hiccup with Miss Hargrove regarding the phone policy, but it's resolved." She opened her leather portfolio. "Tonight's headline acts include Cleo Laveau at eight in the *Starlight Lounge*, followed by our new illusionist, Christopher Webb, in the *Stardust Salon* at nine-thirty."

"Ah yes, the spider fellow." Abercrombie's plush, white mustache twitched. "Security concerns?"

"Addressed. His containment systems exceed our requirements." Carlotta handed him the detailed schedule. "Though I've positioned additional staff, just as a precaution."

"Sensible." The captain nodded approvingly, stroking his neatly-trimmed beard. "And the weather?"

"Clear skies predicted through tomorrow evening. Perfect conditions for the deck party."

Abercrombie studied her for a moment. "You've thought of everything, as usual."

"That's my job, Captain." Carlotta tucked her portfolio under her arm. "To anticipate problems before they arise."

CHAPTER 3

T he *Stardust Salon* had been transformed into something between a cabaret and a séance parlor. Christopher stood in the wings, watching the crowd settle into their gold-trimmed chairs with cocktails that caught the stage lights like liquid amber.

The salon's name became clear the moment one looked up. A meticulous constellation of tiny lights twinkled across the midnight-blue ceiling, while silver threads woven through the plush carpet caught the light as guests moved, creating the illusion of walking through a field of fallen stars.

The air thrummed with anticipation and big band jazz, cigarette smoke from the few passengers bold enough to light up despite modern sensibilities, and the particular electric tension that preceded live performance.

This is what you live for, he reminded himself, adjusting his tuxedo one final time. The fabric was authentic 1940s; he'd had it tailored from pieces he'd found in a Hollywood costume warehouse, complete with mother-of-pearl buttons and silk lapels that had once graced some long-forgotten leading man. Tonight, he wasn't Christopher Webb, failed Vegas headliner with a spider phobia and a dead brother haunting his dreams. Tonight, he was the master of the impossible, dancer with death's eight-legged ambassadors.

The irony, as always, was exquisite.

"Ladies and gentlemen," came the announcer's voice, rich with theatrical gravitas, "the *Pacific Dream* is proud to present an evening of mystery, danger, and impossible beauty. Please welcome... the Amazing Spider-Mage!"

The velvet curtains parted like the Red Sea, crimson waves folding back to reveal the stage beyond. Christopher stepped into the spotlight, its harsh brilliance creating a halo around his silvery hair while casting dramatic shadows across his angular features. For a moment that stretched like eternity, he felt the familiar transformation occur—the alchemy that turned fear into performance, vulnerability into power, ordinary man into legend. The audience's collective intake of breath was better than any drug, more intoxicating than the finest cannabis, more affirming than any lover's touch. This was his domain, his kingdom of illusion where he reigned supreme.

"Good evening, beautiful people," he said, his voice carrying the perfect blend of charm and menace that had once packed theaters to capacity night after night. He let his gaze sweep across the room, establishing dominance through eye contact, a technique he'd mastered years ago.

"I'm told you're brave souls, willing to sail into the unknown for adventure. But how brave are you, really?" He paused, letting the question hang in the air and thrum with anticipation. His fingers twitched slightly at his sides, already anticipating the movements to come. "How comfortable are you with the spaces between what you think you know... and what actually lurks in the shadows? Those dark corners where rational thought fails and primal fear takes hold?"

He moved forward on the stage, the spotlight following him like an obedient puppy as his polished vintage shoes gleamed against the hardwood floor. The top hat in his hand caught the light, becoming another instrument in his carefully orchestrated symphony of deception.

He moved across the stage with the fluid grace of a panther, his trained performer's eye cataloging faces in the crowd. He'd met some of them, briefly, during the cocktail happy hour earlier that evening, exchanging pleasantries over champagne and canapés while mentally filing away details for potential audience participation later.

The Blacksmiths, a British couple, sat near the front, their hands intertwined like lovestruck teenagers despite their fifty-odd years of marriage, their eyes twinkling with anticipation beneath the vintage-style lighting. Mr. Blacksmith, with his neatly trimmed silver mustache and burgundy bow tie perfectly matched to his pocket square, leaned slightly toward his wife, whispering something that made her pearl earrings quiver as she laughed softly behind her gloved hand. Mrs. Blacksmith's carefully coiffed hair gleamed under the amber lights, her crimson lipstick immaculate despite the champagne flute she'd been sipping from all evening. Their matching wedding bands caught the light as their fingers remained laced together on the pristine white tablecloth, silent witnesses to a half-century of devotion that had weathered life's storms and still emerged intact. They'd booked this throwback cruise as an anniversary gift to themselves, and Christopher could read the childlike wonder in their expressions—the same look he'd spent so many years cultivating in audiences across flashy showrooms.

Rashida Bell occupied a corner table, her journalist's eyes narrowed slightly, not merely watching but dissecting his every movement. She sat with one elbow propped on the table, chin resting on her knuckles, her crimson-painted fingernails occasionally tapping against her cheek in contemplation. He could practically see the mental notes forming behind that analytical gaze, no doubt calculating angles, searching for the mechanics behind the mystery for whatever cynical exposé she planned to write. Christopher had spotted her earlier during introductions, noting the way she'd assessed him with that particular blend of professional skepticism and barely concealed boredom that suggested she'd seen too many "special experiences" that failed to live up to their hype. Still, she was in the spirit of things, channeling Lena Horne's elegant pressed hairstyle from the 1943 classic film, "Stormy Weather."

Several seats away, Olivia Batiste fidgeted nervously, her camera discreetly poised by her knee beneath the tablecloth. The soft glow from the device occasionally illuminated her face from below, casting dramatic shadows across her delicate features. She'd explained to him earlier, in a conspiratorial whisper backstage, that she was allowed the camera, but she had to be surreptitious and keep it as hidden as possible; a small concession the cruise director had made for her. She was a young girl of just nineteen, with bright eyes that darted constantly between him and potential camera angles, but she was probably richer than Christopher, running her own online businesses and becoming one of the most talked-about travel influencers of recent times. Her vintage-inspired outfit, a sailor-collared dress and white pillbox hat, somehow managed to look both period-appropriate and thoroughly modern on her slender frame.

And there, commanding a prime table mere feet from the stage, sat Eleanor Hargrove in a midnight blue taffeta dress that undoubtedly cost more than his entire day rate for this performance. Diamonds glittered at her throat and wrists, catching the light with every subtle movement of her body. The social media socialite's attention was focused on him with laser intensity, her meticulously glitter-lotioned hand wrapped around a martini glass, red-lacquered nails tapping lightly against the crystal stem. Her lips curved in the particular smile of a woman accustomed to getting precisely what—or whom—she wanted. She'd made a point of introducing herself at the mixer, letting her hand linger on his arm just a fraction too long as she'd mentioned how much she was looking forward to his performance, her perfume lingering in his senses long after she'd glided away.

But it was the figure at the back of the room that made his pulse skip: Cleo Laveau, draped in black silk that clung to her curves and billowed dramatically at the sleeves, making her look like she'd stepped out of a sudsy film noir fever dream. The vintage turban wrapped around her head was adorned with a single crystal brooch that caught the light each time she moved, sending scattered reflections dancing across the darkened room. She was watching him with the particular attention that one performer paid to another, evaluating, appreciating, *understanding* the mechanics behind every gesture and misdirection. Their eyes met across the crowd, and he felt that electric recognition again, stronger now in the charged atmosphere of live performance. A silent acknowledgment between two people who made their living selling the impossible.

Focus, he told himself, forcing his attention back to the show as he reluctantly broke their gaze. *You can play whatever game she's offering later. The audience comes first.* Yet even as he readied his first illusion, he could feel her eyes still on him, her presence a palpable distraction at the periphery of his awareness. Unsettling and thrilling in equal measure.

"Magic," he continued, pulling a deck of cards from his jacket with a flourish, "is about transformation. Taking something ordinary—"

He fanned the cards, letting them cascade from hand to hand in a waterfall of red and black. "—and revealing its hidden nature."

The cards vanished, replaced by a silk scarf that seemed to materialize from the air itself. With adroit skill, he began the routine that had served as his opening for fifteen years—the silk transforming into flowers, then birds, then smoke that dissipated into nothing, leaving only the faint aroma of roses and mystery.

But tonight felt different. The magic felt more real somehow, as if the ship's atmosphere were amplifying the boundaries between illusion and impossibility. When he made the flowers appear, their scent was almost overwhelming. When his doves materialized, their wings seemed to catch light that wasn't quite natural. The audience was responding more intensely than usual, leaning forward in their seats, hanging on every gesture.

The real show hasn't even started yet, he thought with dark amusement.

"Of course," he said, the cards reappearing in his hands as if they'd never left, "some transformations are more... dramatic than others. Some require us to confront our deepest fears, to tango with the very things that terrify us most."

He moved to the side of the stage where his equipment waited. Five smaller stage terrariums, arranged on a table draped in black velvet. The obsidian fabric seemed to absorb the spotlight, making the glass enclosures appear to float in darkness. These specialized hutches, unlike the ones the spiders lived in backstage, had been meticulously engineered with hidden trapdoors and sides that lifted and shifted with such microscopic exactness that not even the most scrutinizing eye could detect the mechanisms. Christopher had spent years perfecting these props, each one custom-built to his exacting specifications by a glassblower in Prague who specialized in magicians' apparatuses.

Even covered with their midnight cloths, the terrariums seemed to pulse with a contained energy, as if the creatures inside sensed their impending role in the evening's spectacle. A faint scratching sound emanated from one, barely audible but enough to send a visible ripple through the front row. The audience's mood shifted perceptibly. The eager anticipation of moments before now mingled with an underlying current of intrinsic unease. Christopher could feel it like a change in air pressure, that delicious tension between fascination and fear that he'd built his entire career upon.

In the corner of his vision, he noticed a middle-aged woman clutching her husband's arm, her knuckles white but her eyes unable to look away. Perfect. That was exactly the response he cultivated.

"Ladies and gentlemen, may I introduce my partners in tonight's performance. They are beautiful, deadly, and utterly without mercy. Rather like love itself, wouldn't you agree?"

A few nervous laughs rippled through the crowd. Christopher removed the first cover with the theatrical flair of a magician revealing his greatest trick. Inside the glass habitat, the massive huntsman spider crouched motionless, its legs spanning nearly six inches across.

The gasp from the audience was clear, followed by Eleanor's distinctly horrified "Oh my God" from the front row. But it was a slight shift from the back of the room that caught his attention. Not fear, but fascination. Cleo was leaning forward now, her professional interest clearly piqued.

"This is the Huntress," Christopher said, his voice dropping to an intimate whisper that somehow carried to every corner of the room. "She's from Australia, where everything is designed to kill you quickly and efficiently. She can move faster than your eye can follow, climb any surface, and her bite contains enough venom to drop a grown man in minutes."

Of course, none of this was true; the huntsman spider's bite would hurt, but really didn't do any damage to humans. Christopher had built his entire career on this careful manipulation, amplifying harmless creatures into monsters, transforming mild discomfort into mortal peril. The audience didn't want facts; they wanted the thrill of controlled danger. He caught Rashida's skeptical eye and the slight shake of her head. She knew he was full of it.

He opened the terrarium with such smooth gestures that they looked choreographed. The spider didn't move—yet. Christopher had learned long ago that the key to working with arachnids was understanding their psychology, such as it was. They responded to confidence, to calm energy, to the peculiar kind of respect that predators accorded one another.

"The secret," he continued, extending his hand toward the spider, "is not to eliminate fear, but to transform it. Fear is just excitement wearing a disguise."

Huntress stepped delicately onto his palm, her weight negligible but her presence enormous. Several audience members caught their breath. Christopher felt the familiar cocktail of terror and exhilaration flood his system; the high that had kept him coming back to this particular form of self-torment for so many years.

He moved through the routine with panache, the spider crawling up his arm, across his shoulders, down his chest. Every movement was calculated, every gesture designed to maximize both beauty and dread. But something felt different tonight. Huntress was more responsive than usual, almost as if she were performing rather than simply tolerating his manipulation.

"Fear," he said, allowing the arachnid to step across his outstretched fingers like a tightrope walker, "is humanity's oldest emotion. It kept our ancestors alive when the world was wild and full of things with teeth and claws and venom. But what happens when we've conquered the natural world? When we've eliminated most of the things that used to hunt us?"

He guided the large arachnid through a series of increasingly complex movements up his arm, around his neck, down to his other hand. The spider seemed almost to dance, her movements more fluid and purposeful than he'd ever seen before. Maybe she liked the motion of the ocean, the sway of the mighty cruise liner. Or perhaps it was the energy of the crowd, their gasps and whispers creating a kind of electric current in the air that the Huntress could sense through the sensitive hairs covering her body.

Christopher watched with a mixture of professional pride and private unease as the huntsman spider executed each transition with balletic precision. Her eight legs moved in seamless coordination, each step deliberate yet graceful, as if she were performing to music only she could hear. The stage lights caught the subtle iridescence of her exoskeleton, transforming what many would consider a nightmare into something mesmerizing—beautiful, even, in its alien way.

The gentle rocking of the *Pacific Dream* beneath them seemed to enhance the performance, adding an unpredictable element that forced both magician and arachnid to adjust constantly. Christopher noted how the Huntress compensated for the ship's movement with remarkable adaptability, sometimes pausing to rebalance herself on his skin, her tiny claws leaving ghost-like impressions that he could barely feel. It was as if the maritime setting had awakened something primordial in her, some ancestral memory of movement and rhythm that transcended her captive upbringing.

In the corner, he spotted Rashida taking notes, her skeptical expression momentarily softened by genuine fascination. Even the cynical journalist couldn't deny the hypnotic quality of this unusual dance between man and creature. She'd suspended her disbelief right on target. Now he had her.

"We create new fears," he continued, his voice taking on a hypnotic quality. "Imaginary monsters to replace the real ones. Ghosts, demons, things that go bump in the night. Because deep down, we know that a world without predators is a world where we've forgotten what we really are."

The next part of the routine involved transferring the huntsman to a series of props: silk threads stretched between stands, mirrors that reflected her image in kaleidoscopic patterns, finally a web of silver wire where she could display her natural grace. But as Christopher guided her toward the artificial web, something went wrong.

Huntress stopped dead, her entire body going rigid. For a moment that felt like hours, she remained motionless, her multiple eyes fixed on something in the audience that Christopher couldn't see. Then, without warning, she reared back on her hind legs in a threat display he'd never seen her do before.

The audience thought it was part of the show. Some even applauded. But Christopher felt ice drip down his spine. In all his years of working with spiders, he'd never seen behavior like this. She wasn't responding to him anymore; she was responding to something else entirely.

Stay calm, he told himself, extending his hand toward her again. *Don't let them see you sweat.*

But she ignored his outstretched palm, her attention still fixed on the back of the room. Following her many-eyed gaze, Christopher saw Cleo Laveau leaning forward in her chair, her face pale in the stage lights, her eyes wide with something that looked disturbingly like recognition.

What the hell?

The moment stretched into eternity, predator and psychic locked in some kind of wordless communication while Christopher stood between them, suddenly feeling like an intruder in his own show. Then the spider relaxed as abruptly as she'd tensed, and stepped delicately back onto his hand as if nothing had happened.

"As I was saying," Christopher continued, his professional training taking over even as his mind reeled, "the line between fear and fascination is thinner than we like to pretend."

He completed the routine with the other animals—the Wraparound, the jumping spider, the recluse, the Chinese bird—each execution flawless, each creature responding to his direction with uncanny attention. But throughout it all, he remained aware of Cleo's intense scrutiny, of the way her fingers moved restlessly up and down the stem of her wine glass.

The finale involved all five arachnids at once, a carefully choreographed dance of dread that required split-second timing and absolute trust between maestro and performers. Christopher had done it hundreds of times, but tonight it felt like walking a slack tightrope over an abyss. The spiders moved with unusual coordination, their individual patterns weaving together into something that looked almost like... words.

You're imagining things, he told himself, even as goosebumps crawled up his arms. *It's just the atmosphere, the salt air, the crowd, the adrenaline.*

But when he looked out at the audience during the final bow, what he saw in their faces wasn't just appreciation or relief. It was hunger. A united desire for something more, something darker, something that pushed further past the boundaries between safety and danger. Their eyes gleamed with an anticipatory fascination, mouths slightly parted, bodies leaning forward in their seats as if drawn by an invisible thread.

The vintage attire they wore for the themed cruise only enhanced the eerie tableau, like a roomful of ghosts from another era craving a spectacle beyond mere entertainment.

And in the back of the room, Cleo was smiling, but it wasn't the warm, appreciative smile of a fellow entertainer acknowledging good work. It was the smile of someone who'd just seen confirmation of something she'd suspected all along. Her red-painted lips curved upward beneath the shadow of her carefully wrapped turban, her fingers still caressing that wine glass with careful, almost ritualistic movements.

Had she sensed, or known, about his fear of the spiders? He'd never told a soul about Danny, at least not since he'd struck out on his own and become the Amazing Spider-Mage. The memory of his brother's small body, swollen and still on that hospital bed, was locked away in the darkest corner of his mind, alongside the guilt that had driven him to master the very creatures that haunted his dreams.

Rashida was scribbling something furiously now, her expression caught between disbelief and reluctant captivation. Even she, with all her cynicism about the cruise's "vintage shtick," appeared shaken by what she'd witnessed—as if she too had glimpsed something beyond the realm of tricks and illusions.

The curtain fell to thunderous applause, but Christopher barely heard it. His attention was fixed on the strange behavior of his performers, on the electric tension that seemed to be building in the air like a storm, and on the certainty that whatever game had begun tonight between him and Cleo Laveau, the stakes were about to become much higher than either of them realized.

CHAPTER 4

The *Golden Parlor* thrummed with post-performance ener-gy, champagne flutes catching the light like captured stars while passengers dissected every moment of Christopher's show. Cleo moved through the crowd like a shark through bloody chum, accepting compliments on her readings while her attention remained laser-focused on the magician holding court near the bar.

The *Golden Parlor* earned its name from the elaborate gold leaf adorning every surface, including ceiling medallions, ornate wall panels, and fluted columns that transported passengers straight to the opulence of the 1940s. At its center stood the crowning glory: a three-tiered fountain where champagne cascaded down in shimmering golden ribbons, passengers eagerly holding out their crystal flutes to catch the effervescent stream. The bubbling liquid caught the light from crystal chandeliers, creating an atmosphere of perpetual sunset.

Cleo saw that Christopher had changed from his stage tuxedo into something more casually elegant. Charcoal slacks and a white shirt open at the collar, revealing the edge of a serpent tattoo that curled around his throat like a promise of peril. The metallic strands in his hair caught the moody art deco lighting, and his eyes held that particular brightness performers got when the adrenaline was still singing through their veins.

Probably just another pretty boy with mommy issues and a death wish, she told herself, but the internal dismissal rang hollow. There had been something in his presentation tonight that transcended mere spectacle; it had vivified the audience and displayed a genuine communion with forces that most people pretended didn't exist. The way his spiders had responded to him wasn't training; it was *recognition*. A meeting of the minds.

"Magnificent show, Mr. Webb!" Roger Blacksmith was saying, his entomologist's enthusiasm bubbling over. "I'm retired now but I've studied arachnid behavior for forty years, and I've never seen anything quite like that coordination. How do you achieve such precise responses?"

Christopher's smile was modest, self-deprecating. "Trade secrets, I'm afraid. Though I suspect the real magic isn't in the training, it's in remembering that we're not so different from them. We're all just trying to survive in a world that wants to swallow us whole."

Philosophy and fatalism, Cleo noted. *How deliciously brooding.*

"Well, I understand completely," Roger said, his eyes crinkling with genuine admiration behind his wire-rimmed spectacles. "Professional discretion is sacred. But I must tell you, seeing your act has been on my bucket list for years, ever since that feature in *National Geographic* about unconventional animal communication." He turned to his wife, a woman with white-streaked hair pinned in an immaculate sideswept style that spoke of hours of preparation for this 1940s-themed cruise. "Hasn't it been, Karen? Remember how I clipped that article and put it in my 'someday' folder?"

The old woman nodded indulgently, her crimson lipstick perfectly lined and applied despite the ever-present gentle rocking of the *Pacific*

Dream. Her vintage brooch, a delicate silver spider web with a tiny diamond at its center, glinted under the chandelier lights as she adjusted her pearl necklace. "Whether I like it or not," she chuckled ruefully, patting her husband's arm with affection born of decades of marriage. "Roger's been talking about your spiders for so long I sometimes think they're extended family members."

Meanwhile, Cleo was contemplating her approach—something subtle, perhaps a comment about recognizing a kindred spirit—when Eleanor Hargrove materialized beside Christopher like a heat-seeking missile wrapped in Chanel No. 5.

"That was absolutely *incredible*," Eleanor gushed, her hand landing on Christopher's arm with calculated casualness. "I mean, I was literally shaking! You must be so brave to work with such dangerous creatures."

The young woman, seemingly channeling Veronica Lake, a cinema siren who'd died long before this upstart was even born, had changed from her audience ensemble into something that belonged in a museum of tactical seduction. A silver dress that clung to every curve while managing to look vintage-appropriate, hair swept into gentle waves that framed her face like something out of *The Blue Dahlia*. She was gorgeous in the way that stopped conversations and redirected traffic, and it looked like she knew it.

More importantly, Christopher seemed to know it too. His smile warmed considerably as he looked down at her, and something cold and sharp twisted in Cleo's chest.

Cleo sipped her martini, the olive bitter against her tongue as she watched Eleanor work her magic. Why was her stomach knotting with jealousy over a man she'd exchanged maybe ten words with since boarding?

Perhaps we knew each other before, she thought, the notion floating through her mind unbidden. *In another time. Another life.*

She nearly choked on her drink. Those weren't her thoughts. They were lines from her act, the mystical patter she fed to gullible passengers seeking connections to lost loves. Yet lately, the boundary between performance and instinct had grown troublingly thin. The tarot spreads that once meant nothing now seemed to whisper truths. The crystal ball that was supposed to be a mere prop sometimes clouded in ways that made her breath hitch.

Christopher laughed at something Eleanor said, his head tilting back to expose the strong column of his throat.

Cleo's fingers tightened around her glass. *This is ridiculous,* she scolded herself. *You're becoming the character you invented.*

But watching him... the way his hands moved when he spoke, how his eyes crinkled at the corners... she couldn't shake the feeling that something important was happening. Something fated.

"Danger is relative, Eleanor," he said, his voice taking on the intimate tone performers used when they wanted to make someone feel special. "The real risk isn't in what might hurt you, it's in what might change you."

Oh, for fuck's sake, Cleo thought, recognizing the smooth seduction routine for what it was. *And here I thought you had some depth.*

"Oh, please," the twit tittered, "Call me Ellie."

Even as Cleo prepared to write the magician off as another shallow entertainer chasing the prettiest available distraction, something made her pause. Throughout his conversation with Eleanor, Christopher's attention kept drifting to the other passengers, to the windows overlooking the dark ocean, to shadows in corners that shouldn't have held anything interesting.

He feels it too, she realized. *The shift. The charge in the air.*

"Would you like to see my suite? It's the *Marlene Dietrich*." Eleanor was asking, her invitation wrapped in enough plausible deniability to avoid seeming desperate. "I have some ideas for your Insta that would go beautifully with your aesthetic. For content, you know?"

Content. The word landed like a slap. Cleo had spent three years building her mystique, crafting an identity that commanded respect and fascination, only to watch this Instagram princess reduce everything to "content" potential. But what really galled her was the way Christopher was actually considering the offer, his performer's ego responding to the promise of documentation and a wider audience.

"That's very generous," he said, and Cleo could hear the yes forming in his voice.

Absolutely not.

"Christopher, darling," Cleo said, her Louisiana accent thickening as she glided into their conversation with the inevitability of fate itself. "What a *magnificent* performance tonight. You and your ladies were absolutely transcendent."

She'd timed her approach perfectly, arriving just as Eleanor opened her mouth to seal the deal. The younger woman's expression shifted from confident seduction to barely concealed irritation, but Cleo ignored her entirely, focusing on Christopher with the kind of intensity that made people forget other conversations were happening.

"Cleo," Christopher said, and she caught the slight intake of breath that preceded her name. Recognition, appreciation, and something that might have been relief. "I was hoping we'd have a chance to talk. Your performance this afternoon was... intriguing."

"Intriguing." She let the word roll over her tongue like an expensive Swiss chocolate. "Such a careful choice. Most people say 'impressive' or 'entertaining.' But intriguing suggests you're not entirely sure what you witnessed."

"I'm not entirely sure about anything tonight," he admitted, and there was enough honesty in his voice to make the influencer shift uncomfortably between them.

Good, Cleo thought. *Let her see what real chemistry looks like.*

"Perhaps we could discuss it somewhere more private," she suggested, her fingers trailing along the edge of Christopher's sleeve in a gesture that was both nonchalant and possessive. "I find that the most interesting conversations happen away from crowds."

It was a direct challenge to Eleanor's invitation, and everyone knew it.

"Actually," Eleanor interjected, her voice bright with forced cheerfulness, "we were just making plans to—"

"Were you?" Cleo turned to her with the kind of smile that made smart people back away slowly. "How presumptuous. I wasn't aware Christopher had committed to anything specific."

The three of them stood in a triangle of tension, two she-wolves circling their prey. Cleo could practically see the magician calculating the dynamics, weighing options, perhaps enjoying the attention more than he should.

Men, she thought with equal parts affection and exasperation. *Give them two women competing for their attention and they lose what little sense they were born with.*

Cleo watched the silent exchange happening in Christopher's eyes. Calculation, temptation, and something that might have been genuine interest in both women. The moment stretched like taffy, sweet and tense.

"Well," Cleo said, stepping back with a smile that didn't quite convince. "I should circulate. The night is young, and so many passengers are clamoring for glimpses of their futures." She inclined her head toward Eleanor but eyed Christopher. "Enjoy your evening with Miss Hargrove. I'm sure her... content... will be illuminating."

The magician's brow furrowed. "Cleo—"

"Another time, perhaps." She waved her fingers, bangles jingling like wind chimes. "The cards predict our paths will cross again. Soon."

She turned away before he could respond, letting the crowd swallow her. The retreat burned. She wasn't accustomed to conceding battlefields, but something inside whispered this wasn't surrender but strategy. Let the pretty influencer have her moment. Let Christopher see what shallow waters looked like before diving into Cleo's depths.

She floated through the *Golden Parlor*, dispensing cryptic predictions and mysterious smiles like party favors. Her fingertips traced invisible patterns on palms while her mind remained fixed on Christopher and that insufferable bottle-blonde parasite.

"Your lifeline suggests remarkable resilience," she told a middle-aged woman whose name she'd already forgotten. "You've weathered storms that would have broken lesser souls."

The woman gasped, hand fluttering to her chest. "How could you possibly know about my divorce?"

Cleo didn't bother explaining that ninety percent of middle-aged women on luxury cruises were either divorced or contemplating it. Instead, she nodded sagely and moved on, her patience wearing thinner with each interaction.

"The spirits are particularly chatty tonight," she told a group of wide-eyed passengers, though what she really wanted was silence. Her own thoughts were too loud, too insistent... images of Christopher's hands on Eleanor's waist, his lips against that perfect porcelain skin so pristine it looked filtered.

This is absurd, she thought, excusing herself with forced grace. *I need air.*

She slipped through the crowd toward the promenade deck, where the ocean's vastness might dilute her unexpected jealousy. Something was happening inside her, some awakening of power or madness, and she needed solitude to understand it before it consumed her completely.

The upper observation deck welcomed her with cool silence. Unlike the packed lounges below, this space remained empty. It seemed most passengers preferred cocktails and conversation to contemplation. Cleo moved to the railing, inhaling salt air that carried whispers of distant storms.

Moonlight silvered the waves, transforming the Pacific into a vast mirror reflecting constellations above. She'd always been drawn to water—its secrets, its patience, its absolute indifference to human concerns. How many bodies rested in those depths? How many shipwrecks? How many tears had been absorbed into that endless blue, leaving no trace behind?

"You're nothing special," she murmured to herself. "Just another tragedy waiting to dissolve into salt."

She was thirty-seven. Not old by any rational measure, but in a world that worshipped youth, especially female youth, she felt the clock ticking. Eleanor was what, twenty-four? Twenty-five? With that particular glow that came from never having been truly disappointed by life. That shine of believing one's beauty was permanent currency rather than depreciating capital.

Cleo knew her face was striking—high cheekbones, eyes that flashed colorfully with her moods, lips that knew how to curve in just the right way to make men forget their names. But the first whispers of time were there. The faintest lines at her eyes, a certain wisdom in her gaze that couldn't be disguised.

"You're getting maudlin in your old age," she told herself, trying to laugh.

Below, the ocean stretched like obsidian, swallowing light. So many secrets. So many endings. Perhaps her mother had been right. Power came in cycles for women. The maiden gave way to the mother, the mother to the crone. Each phase holding its own magic, its own gravity.

Maybe it's time to step aside, she mused. *Let the children play their games.*

Footsteps interrupted her solitude, measured, purposeful, masculine. Not the click-clack of women's heels but the solid tread of expensive leather soles. The Polo cologne she'd smelled just moments ago. She didn't turn, but her spine straightened, pride refusing to let her be caught in melancholy.

"I thought you'd be busy documenting content by now," she said, keeping her eyes on the horizon where black sea met black sky.

Christopher Webb moved beside her, his forearms resting on the railing, mirroring her posture. "I've never been particularly interested in being content."

The wordplay brought an unwilling smile to her lips. "Clever."

"Not really. Just honest." He looked at her profile, the wind lifting strands of her hair. "Why did you walk away?"

"Because some battles aren't worth the ammunition," she replied. "She's young, beautiful, and determined. You seemed... receptive."

"And you decided my preferences for me?"

Cleo turned then, studying him in the moonlight. "Aren't men's preferences generally predictable?"

"Maybe." He shrugged. "But I've never been particularly interested in predictable either."

Without further words, they stood in companionable silence, watching the dark waves part in the wake of the *Pacific Dream* as she hurtled them toward whatever unpredictable fate awaited.

CHAPTER 5

C aptain Alastair "Mac" Abercrombie had commanded enough cruise ships to recognize the particular alchemy that transformed a floating hotel into a temporary community of strangers pretending to be friends. Standing at the bar of the *Golden Parlor* at half past ten, nursing a bourbon from a very small glass that was disappointingly true to the period, he found himself cataloging the evening's social dynamics with impartial professionalism. Mac had been Royal Navy for most of his adult life before economic necessity had forced him into this carnival of nostalgia.

Five years of this theatrical nonsense, he thought, adjusting his period-correct naval uniform with the automatic gesture of someone who'd learned to inhabit a role he didn't entirely respect. *Playing the jolly wartime sea captain for tourists who want to pretend rationing was romantic and air raids were exciting.*

But tonight's entertainment roster had thrown him a curveball that his usual cynicism couldn't quite categorize.

Cleo Laveau, he knew well. Four voyages of palm readings and tarot cards, and that particular brand of psychological insight that made passengers feel special while separating them from their discretionary income. Professional mysticism, harmless enough, though he'd never understood why people paid premium prices to have strangers tell them what they wanted to hear about their futures.

At least she's competent at it, he acknowledged. *Better a skilled fortune teller than an amateur one.* Even he'd asked her a question or two.

The torch singer and jazz trio were standard cruise ship fare, competent musicians who understood that their job was to provide atmospheric background rather than demand attention. The kind of performers who made passengers feel sophisticated without challenging them to think too hard about anything more complex than whether to order another martini.

But the spider magician had been an unexpected addition to the roster, and Mac still wasn't entirely sure why corporate had approved Christopher Webb's booking. Exotic animal acts carried insurance complications, required special handling protocols, created potential liability issues that most cruise lines avoided as a matter of policy.

Though I have to admit, he reflected, remembering the evening's performance, *the man knows his craft.*

Webb's show had been genuinely impressive. Not the usual cruise ship magic of obvious tricks and audience participation, but something approaching authentic artistry. The way those spiders had moved with such unhurried grace across Webb's outstretched arms, the remarkable fidelity of their responses to his subtle hand gestures, the apparent intelligence behind their interactions with their handler... it went beyond mere training and approached something that looked like genuine communication.

Mac had watched, despite himself, with a mixture of professional appreciation and innate unease as the Australian huntsman spider had delicately plucked a wedding ring from a woman's finger and carried it across a tightrope of silk to return it to her astonished husband.

The Chilean recluse—a species Mac knew to be dangerously venomous—had performed an intricate dance across Webb's face without so much as grazing his skin with its fangs, demonstrating a control that seemed almost preternatural.

Even the tiny North American jumping spider had displayed coordination beyond what Mac would have thought possible for creatures with brains smaller than pinpricks, forming patterns on command and seeming to respond to Webb's voice with an attentiveness that gave Mac a shudder he couldn't quite explain. There had been moments during the act when he could have sworn the spiders were watching the audience with as much curiosity as the audience watched them, their multiple eyes reflecting the stage lights with an unsettling awareness.

Reminded me of that bloody great spider Mum found in the bathtub when I was a laddie, Mac thought with the particular mixture of nostalgia and revulsion that accompanied childhood memories involving arachnids. *Size of a dinner plate, the thing was. Tegenaria gigantea, also known as the giant house spider. Mum took one look at it and whacked it with her slipper like she was swatting a tennis ball. Different breed entirely from Webb's exotic beauties, but still...*

The memory made him uncomfortable in ways he couldn't quite articulate, so he pushed it aside in favor of more immediate social observations. The bar was populated with the usual cross-section of cruise passengers: retirees celebrating anniversaries, younger couples seeking romantic adventure, solo travelers looking for connection or escape. Or, these days, clicks on their social media posts.

Speaking of which...

Olivia Batiste had approached the bar. She was young—nineteen, maybe twenty—with the kind of careful styling that suggested social media was both profession and preoccupation.

"Captain Abercrombie?" she said, her voice carrying the slight uncertainty of someone who wasn't sure how to address nautical authority. "I wanted to thank you for accommodating my documentation requests. I know the no-phones policy is important for the authentic experience."

Documentation requests. Mac remembered the paperwork Ms. Cross had mentioned earlier; special permission to use digital cameras for "travel journalism purposes," exemptions from the electronic device restrictions that preserved the cruise's patinaed atmosphere.

"Quite alright, lass," he said, slipping into the theatrical Scottish brogue that passengers expected. "Though I trust you'll be discreet about any modern technology in public areas? Keep the camera out of plain sight, and on silent mode."

"Absolutely. Oh, and I wanted to make sure you understood that I use she/her pronouns. I'm gender-fluid, but those are the pronouns I'm most comfortable with during IRL interactions."

Pronouns. Mac blinked, his sixty-six-year-old brain struggling to process information that hadn't been part of social protocol during his formative years. Gender-fluid. IRL interactions. The terminology suggested complexities that his maritime training hadn't prepared him to navigate.

Right, he thought diplomatically. *Different generation, different world. Best to acknowledge and move on without causing offense.*

"Noted," he said with the kind of careful politeness that acknowledged information received without committing to complete understanding. "I'll be sure to... keep that in mind."

Olivia smiled, seemingly relieved she'd successfully gotten through a potentially awkward conversation, then moved away toward a table where she could document the evening's social dynamics without appearing to intrude on private conversations.

Modern complications, Mac reflected. *Twenty years ago, the most complex social navigation involved remembering passengers' drink preferences and avoiding political discussions at dinner tables.*

He was contemplating the generational gap between his own straightforward Protestant upbringing and the current generation's apparently infinite capacity for social taxonomy when a voice behind him interrupted his philosophical musings.

"Captain! Just the man we wanted to see."

Mac turned to find the Lichtenstein twins approaching with the coordinated enthusiasm that suggested they'd been planning this conversation. Arthur in his wheelchair, Arnold walking beside him in a protective stance.

Professional entertainers, Mac noted. *Always networking, always performing, even in casual conversation.*

"Gentlemen," he said, raising his drink in acknowledgment. "Enjoying the evening's entertainment?"

"Magnificent show," Arnold said, his eyes lighting up with genuine appreciation. "Christopher Webb is even better than his reputation suggests. We've been following his career since his Golden Nugget residency days."

Vegas residency, Mac thought. *That explains the corporate booking. Man's got legitimate credentials, not just cruise ship novelty act.*

"The spider work was extraordinary. A bit too risky for my taste, but still quite the spectacle," Arthur added, his performer's eye making him automatically analyze technical aspects that civilian audiences would miss. "The level of coordination, the accuracy of responses... we've worked with trained animals before, but nothing approaching that sort of sophistication."

Trained animals. The phrase that every performer used to describe creatures that seemed to transcend simple conditioning. Mac had seen enough stage acts to recognize the difference between rote obedience and what looked like genuine intelligence, and Webb's spiders had definitely fallen into the latter category.

"Oh? How long did you work with animals in your own act?" Mac asked.

The brothers exchanged glances, the kind of wordless communication that developed between people who'd spent decades anticipating each other's thoughts. A lifetime of shared stages, shared triumphs, and ultimately, shared tragedy reflected in that single look.

"Illusions, mostly," Arnold said carefully, his fingers drumming lightly against the lacquered walnut burl of the bar top. "Though we had a few acts that involved... let's call them cooperative creatures. Nothing as exotic as Webb's collection. Mostly birds, rabbits. The classics of the trade. We preferred the mechanical marvels, the grand deceptions."

"Until that cursed box trick went belly-up," Arthur said wistfully, his eyes briefly clouding with the memory. "It taught us that some illusions bite harder than a rabid raccoon. Magic has teeth, Captain. Real gnashers, like the ones that haunt my nightmares! You think those spiders are dangerous? Try being trapped in three hundred pounds of mahogany with faulty hydraulics and no emergency release."

The wheelchair, Mac realized, his gaze involuntarily dropping to Arthur's withered, immobile legs. *The accident they mentioned during the passenger interview process.* He'd skimmed the file when preparing for this voyage but hadn't connected the dots until now. The brothers' famous career had ended not with applause but with the sickening crunch of machinery gone wrong.

"Oh, my. Equipment malfunction?" he asked with the diplomatic curiosity that captains learned to employ when passengers wanted to share personal histories without being directly interrogated. His fingers traced the rim of his glass, the cool surface grounding him as he navigated the delicate conversation. The bar lights cast long shadows across the polished wood, highlighting the deep lines etched into the twins' identical faces—lines that spoke of shared pain. Mac gave the brothers space to elaborate or retreat as they wished, understanding all too well how some sea stories were meant to remain beneath the surface.

"Design flaw," Arnold said grimly, his expression hardening as he glanced at his brother. "The mechanism that was supposed to create the illusion of Arthur disappearing... well, it worked a bit too well. Crushed his spine when the false bottom collapsed. Thirty seconds that changed everything." He patted his brother's shoulder in a gesture that spoke louder than any words could. "Heard the crack from across the stage—thought it was part of the sound effects at first."

Occupational hazard of professional magic, Mac thought. *The line between illusion and genuine danger is thinner than audiences want to acknowledge.*

"But that's ancient history," Arthur said with practiced cheerfulness, waving away the somber moment with a flourish. "The important thing is recognizing quality when we see it. Webb's got something special. Not just technical skill, but a real connection with his performers. That's rarer than you might think. Those spiders move like extensions of his will, Captain. Almost like they understand him."

Maybe corporate knew what they were doing after all, Mac thought. *Exotic animal acts might carry insurance complications, but they also generate the kind of word-of-mouth enthusiasm that fills future bookings.*

Movement at the salon's entrance caught Mac's attention. Cleo and Christopher stepped in from the outdoor deck, their faces flushed from the night air or perhaps something more intimate. The psychic's hand rested possessively on the magician's forearm, her red nails standing out against his dark sleeve like warning flags. Webb looked slightly disheveled, his hair windswept, while Cleo's eyes darted around the room with the territorial assessment of someone marking boundaries.

"Excuse me, gentlemen," Mac nodded to the Lichtenstein twins. "Duty calls."

He made his way toward the bar where Carlotta Cross, his cruise director, was poring over a sheaf of documents. Her vintage-styled glasses couldn't hide the exhaustion in her eyes.

"Captain," she acknowledged. "I've finalized tomorrow's schedule. Breakfast service starts at seven, lifeboat drill at ten-thirty, and Webb's matinee performance at two."

"Any complications I should know about?"

"The kitchen's concerned about storage for Webb's special dietary requirements for his... pets." Her lips thinned with disapproval. "And Cleo wants extra time for private readings."

Mac suppressed a sigh. "Approved on both counts. Let's keep our performers happy."

"Of course." Carlotta's tone suggested professional compliance rather than agreement.

A commotion near the bar's far end caught Mac's attention. Voices raised in what might have been friendly conversation or might have been the beginning of social tension.

Cleo began speaking in what sounded like Cajun French, theatrical flourishes that were part of her mystical persona, designed to create atmosphere rather than communicate specific information. Mac's inborn Scottish pragmatism had no patience for mystical nonsense, though he had to admit the woman was skilled at creating dramatic effect.

All for show, he thought dismissively. *Psychology and theatrical presentation disguised as ghostly communication. Harmless enough, as long as passengers understand they're paying for entertainment rather than genuine spiritual guidance.*

The lights flickered briefly. Probably a minor electrical fluctuation, the kind of system hiccup that occurred regularly on ships of this size. Mac made a mental note to have engineering check the power distribution grid in the morning, then returned his attention to the social dynamics playing out near the bar.

"Oh, my!" Karen Blacksmith exclaimed and turned to Cleo. "I think you've raised some spirits!"

"I'll drink to that," her husband chuckled, reaching for his glass.

Nothing supernatural about electrical systems that need maintenance, Mac thought. *Though passengers do love to interpret coincidence as mystical significance.*

Whatever Cleo's performance was intended to accomplish, it seemed to be having the desired effect on her audience. Eleanor appeared genuinely unsettled, Webb looked spellbound, and the other passengers in the vicinity were watching with the fascination that people showed for social drama that didn't directly involve them.

Standard shipboard entertainment, Mac concluded. *Romantic tension mixed with theatrical mysticism. Nothing that can't be managed with diplomatic intervention if it escalates beyond polite competition.*

He really ought to socialize more, he grumbled internally. And toss around more of that ridiculous slang. Sure, after five years of this goofy gig, he'd memorized the whole dog-eared script, but it still felt about as natural as a toupee on a bowling ball. He almost envied those employees like Denver Wheaton, who practically lived in character. Bless his heart. After his stint in the actual Navy, the whole charade struck Mac as utterly absurd. Still, the paycheck kept the mortgage paid and the wife off his back, so there was that.

Mac drained his glass and set it on the bar with a soft click. Through the crowd, he spotted Denver escorting an elderly couple to their seats, his posture straight as a yardarm. The young steward leaned in with exaggerated chivalry, his voice carrying across the room.

"Absolutely copacetic, Mrs. Donovan! I'll fetch those gimlets faster than you can say 'jeepers creepers!'"

Denver never broke character, not once in five years. The man lived and breathed the vernacular like he'd been born in the wrong decade. Meanwhile, Mac had to mentally rehearse phrases like "that's the berries" before company inspections.

He straightened his captain's hat and prepared to wade back into the social fray. *Just another evening aboard the Pacific Dream,* he thought. He felt the satisfaction of a man whose professional pride extended beyond managing the social dynamics of more than three hundred passengers who'd paid premium prices to pretend they lived in a more romantic era.

After all, Mac reflected as he moved through the crowd with the measured authority that passengers expected from their captain, the best cruise ship entertainment was always the kind that made people feel they'd witnessed something extraordinary, even when extraordinary was just skilled performance enhanced by atmospheric lighting and carefully managed audience expectations. The Spider-Mage had certainly delivered on that front; perhaps he'd become a cruise staple.

Mac nodded perfunctorily at the Lichtenstein twins as he passed their table. Arthur raised his champagne glass in salute while Arnold bent down to whisper something in his brother's ear, no doubt another critique of Webb's technique.

The weight of his captain's uniform—authentic wool, because corporate insisted on "period accuracy"—made Mac uncomfortably warm under the chandeliers. He tugged slightly at his collar, careful not to let any passengers notice this break in his stoic demeanor.

Nothing supernatural about good showmanship, he thought. Just professional competence applied to the ancient art of making people believe in magic. The same could be said for his own performance as the gruff-but-charming old-timey naval officer, a role that felt increasingly like a straitjacket with each passing cruise.

CHAPTER 6

Cleo leaned against the back wall of the *Grand Salon*, arms crossed, watching Christopher work his magic on the afternoon crowd. His long, slim fingers danced through the air, coaxing the Chilean recluse spider to crawl from one hand to another. The audience gasped. One person squealed. The eight-legged performer pirouetted across his palm with delicate strides, as if it understood its role in this peculiar dance.

"The arachnid kingdom contains mysteries science has barely begun to comprehend," the magician announced, his voice dropping to that modulated hypnotic register that made Cleo's skin prickle. "These creatures possess intelligence beyond our understanding."

The Australian huntsman spider emerged next, its legs like uncoiled springs. Even from the back of the room, Cleo could see its distinctive markings. The audience drew a collective breath.

"Beautiful, isn't she?" Christopher's face glowed with genuine wonder. "Eight years old and still quick as lightning."

For a fleeting moment, Cleo felt something unexpected: a pang of empathy. The way he looked at that spider... it wasn't an act. He truly respected these creatures.

Her gaze drifted to Eleanor Hargrove, seated prominently in the front row. The influencer wore a tailored navy skirt suit with white trim. Perfectly on-theme, perfectly attention-seeking. Her phone might be locked away, but she behaved as if cameras still followed her every move. When Christopher approached her section, she leaned forward, ruby lips parted in exaggerated wonder.

Heat crawled up Cleo's neck. The scene from last night flickered through her memory, but Christopher had chosen to follow *her* outside and onto the deck. He'd even kissed her, but then quickly suggested they return to the salon. Mixed messages: the story of Cleo's checkered love life.

Next, he produced the North American jumping spider, allowing it to leap dramatically from his sleeve to his shoulder. Even Cleo couldn't suppress her amazement.

Last night, Christopher had told her about his ladies, his voice dropping to a reverent whisper as they stood beneath the stars.

"Their brains are extraordinary," he'd said, eyes alight with a different kind of passion. "The smaller spiders, especially. Their central nervous systems can occupy nearly eighty percent of their body space."

Cleo had watched his animated gestures, momentarily forgetting her jealousy.

"That's why they're so clever," he'd continued. "So much processing power in such a tiny frame."

Watching him onstage now, with the tiny terror rapt at his command, she could believe it.

"For my final demonstration," Christopher announced, "I'll need absolute silence."

The room stilled, breaths held in anticipation. Christopher closed his eyes and extended his arms with theatrical deliberation, his fingers splayed like a conductor before an orchestra. All five of his spiders—the lightning-fast Australian huntsman, the wily Wraparound, the substantial Chinese bird spider, the pale orange Chilean recluse, and the tiny, cartoonish North American jumper—emerged from various hiding places within his specially designed costume. They appeared from cuffs, pockets, and even from behind his ear, crawling in perfect synchronization across his spay-tanned skin.

The audience watched, transfixed, as the arachnids descended his arms and moved with unnerving quickness across the black velvet cloth he'd spread across a small mahogany table. Their many-legged bodies created intricate patterns before settling into a perfect five-pointed star formation, each spider positioned equidistant from the others, their bodies unnaturally still as if awaiting further instruction.

A woman in the front row literally clutched her pearls, Cleo noted with a chuckle, her white wrist-length gloves trembling theatrically. Several other passengers leaned forward in their seats, disbelief evident in their wide eyes and parted lips.

The crowd erupted in thunderous applause, several guests rising to their feet. Christopher bowed deeply, his slicked-back hair catching the spotlight as he dipped low. Behind him, responding to some invisible signal, his spiders retreated to their containers with eerie obedience, filing one by one into their respective glass homes without so much as a nudge from their master.

The emcee announced, "Ladies and gentlemen, the Amazing Spider-Mage thanks you for your attention. Please join us in the *Starlight Salon* for afternoon tea."

The audience rose, buzzing with excitement. Cleo remained motionless, watching Christopher carefully collect the containers housing his arachnid performers. His hands moved with tender care, each spider treated like a precious collaborator rather than a prop.

Eleanor sashayed to the stage, placing her hand on Christopher's arm. "Absolutely divine performance," she cooed loudly enough for everyone nearby to hear. "You simply must tell me how you trained them."

Christopher smiled that crooked, charming smile that had worked so well on Cleo just last night. "Some mysteries must remain mysteries, Miss Hargrove."

The psychic pushed away from the wall. The ritual meant nothing. The spiders were just well-trained, she suddenly decided. Christopher was just a skilled performer with a weakness for pretty faces. Nothing supernatural about any of it. So why did the back of her neck prickle with unease as she followed the crowd toward afternoon tea?

Cleo lingered in the doorway, glancing back at Christopher as he meticulously packed his glass enclosures. She turned away before he caught her watching. The corridor to the *Starlight Salon* stretched before her, its wood-paneled walls adorned with vintage cruise advertisements from the era, as well as the almost clichéd "We Can Do It" Rosie the Riveter poster. White-uniformed stewards carried silver trays of champagne flutes and mini teapots, their faces frozen in period-appropriate servant smiles.

Before long, the salon buzzed with conversation and the tinkling of fine china. Cleo found herself cornered by the Lichtenstein twins near a table laden with petit fours and cucumber sandwiches.

"Remarkable control he has," Arthur Lichtenstein said, maneuvering his wheelchair closer to the refreshment table. "In our day, we used pigeons. Much less impressive."

"And much messier," Arnold added, reaching for a sandwich. "Pigeons have no bladder control. Not like Webb's spiders. Then again," he went on, "Webb does have birds, too. I wonder why he didn't bring them out this time?"

"You two performed together?" Cleo asked, actually grateful for the distraction.

"Thirty-six years on the circuit," Arthur nodded. "Until the accident."

Arnold's face darkened. "Box trick gone wrong. Sawed my brother in half a bit too literally."

Cleo sipped her tea, half-listening as they launched into a well-rehearsed argument about the incident. She noticed their story had changed a bit from yesterday's version. Her attention drifted to the entrance where Christopher had appeared, freshly changed into a crisp white dinner jacket. His dark brown eyes caught the light as he accepted a flute of champagne from a passing steward.

"Excuse me, gentlemen," she murmured, but the twins were too engrossed in their bickering to notice her departure.

Before she could cross the room, Eleanor materialized at Christopher's side. The influencer had changed into a form-fitting ivory cocktail dress with a dramatic plunging neckline. Just how many outfits had this TikTok tart brought on board?

"There's our star performer," Eleanor's voice carried across the salon. "I was just telling everyone about your incredible finale."

Christopher's laugh rippled through the air. His hand settled briefly on Eleanor's bare shoulder, fingers lingering a moment too long.

Cleo felt heat rise in her cheeks. The teacup in her hand suddenly seemed too fragile, her grip too tight. She set it down carefully on a nearby table, forcing her face into the serene expression she used during palm readings.

Watching Eleanor press closer to Christopher, Cleo couldn't help but wish the spiders would find their way to the influencer's flawlessly coiffed hair. She smoothed her hands over the bodice of her dress and approached the pair with forced nonchalance. Her heart thumped traitorously against her ribs.

"Christopher, darling," she purred, sliding between them with the fluid grace of a cat claiming its favorite chair. "You outdid yourself today."

She placed her hand on his forearm, feeling the heat of his skin through the worsted wool dinner jacket. The possessive gesture wasn't planned; her body moved of its own accord.

Eleanor's fetching smile flickered for just an instant before reasserting itself. "Cleo! We were just discussing Christopher's remarkable connection with his eight-legged stars."

"Yes, we've discussed his special talents at length," Cleo replied, emphasizing the intimacy with a meaningful glance at Christopher. "Last night, under the stars."

Christopher's eyebrow arched slightly, but his lips curved upward. "Cleo has a unique appreciation for the mystical aspects of performance."

The warmth in his voice sent an unexpected flutter through her chest. This wasn't just about winning. Something deeper stirred beneath her competitive impulse. The realization startled her. She'd sworn off emotional entanglements after one too many heartbreaks, yet here she was, marking territory like some lovesick teenager.

"Perhaps I could read your cards later," she suggested to Christopher, ignoring Eleanor entirely. "I sense a... significant change in your future."

"Ladies," Christopher said, his voice carrying just enough authority to cut through the escalating tension, "I'm flattered by the interest, truly. But it's been a long day, and I should probably—"

"Oh, don't be such a diplomat," Eleanor said, her mask slipping. The perfect vintage makeup couldn't hide the petulant twist of her mouth. "Just choose. Her crystals and fortune-telling nonsense, or someone who actually appreciates the imagery of your art form. Someone who understands what real entertainment is about."

The dismissive tone made something dark and dangerous unfurl in Cleo's chest, spreading like octopus ink in cold waters, clouding her judgment. *Fortune-telling nonsense.* As if this self-absorbed content creator with her carefully curated aesthetic and thousands of faceless followers had any idea what real power looked like.

"Nonsense?" Cleo's voice dropped to a whisper that somehow carried more menace than shouting. The air around them seemed to thicken, the ambient sounds of the ship's lounge receding as if the world itself was holding its breath. "Honey child, you have no idea what you're dismissing. The powers I work with existed long before your great-grandmother pinned up her victory rolls. But perhaps you'd like a demonstration?"

She reached into her beaded clutch and withdrew a small velvet pouch—one of her working tools, not stage props. The contents clinked softly against each other as she shook the bag, bone against bone, secrets against secrets. She moved to the nearest high-top table, and Christopher and Eleanor joined her, as if pulled by invisible leashes.

The overhead chandelier flickered momentarily, casting strange, elongated shadows across their faces, and she could swear the sun's late afternoon glow dimmed in response, as if acknowledging something ancient had been awakened in the middle of this manufactured nostalgia.

She snapped her gaze to the influencer. "Are you ready?"

"No, thank you," Eleanor said quickly, but there was uncertainty in her voice now. Whatever she'd seen in Cleo's eyes had finally pricked her bubble of privileged arrogance.

"I insist," Cleo said, already pouring the bones onto the small, round cocktail table. They were old, worn smooth by countless castings, and they landed in patterns that made her breath catch. *Transformation. Betrayal. Awakening.* And underneath it all, threading through every symbol like a poisonous vine: *Jealousy.*

The bones were telling her story back to her, revealing motivations she'd barely admitted to herself. She was envious not just of Eleanor's youth and beauty, but of her careless confidence, her assumption that the world would rearrange itself to accommodate her desires. Most of all, she was jealous of how easily Christopher had been distracted from whatever uncanny connection had sparked between them just last night.

This is foolish, she told herself, even as her fingers moved over the bones in patterns older than New Orleans, older than Louisiana, older perhaps than the country itself. *You barely know him. He's just another performer, another handsome face.*

But the bones were warm beneath her fingers, and the ship seemed to be listening, and something in the air between her and Christopher's spiders, locked away in his suite, contained in their terrariums, was resonating like a tuning fork struck in the depths of the ocean.

"What do you see?" Christopher asked, his curiosity overriding whatever instincts had presumably been telling him to extract himself from the situation.

"I see a man who dances with death because he believes it gives him control over his fears," Cleo said, her voice taking on the cadence of a true reading, the words coming from someplace deeper than conscious thought. "I see a girl who mistakes desire for possession and beauty for power. And I see..."

She paused, her fingers hovering over one particular bone that seemed to pulse with its own heartbeat. The symbol carved into its surface was one she'd never seen before, yet somehow recognized—a spider web with something trapped at its center, but that something wasn't prey. It was a key.

"What?" Eleanor demanded, her earlier dismissiveness replaced by unalloyed unease. "What do you see?"

"I see that we're all about to discover what happens when the line between performance and reality evaporates entirely," Cleo whispered, and as the words left her mouth, she felt them settle into the world like seeds finding fertile ground.

The lights in the *Golden Parlor* flickered again, longer this time, and in the brief darkness that followed as storm clouds covered the sun, she could have sworn she heard something skittering in the walls.

Almost as quickly as it had come, the darkness receded. When the illumination returned, Christopher was staring at her with an expression she couldn't quite read. Part fascination, part apprehension, and something else that might have been recognition.

He feels it too, she realized. *The charge building in the air, the sense that something is about to crack open.*

Around them, the patrons had gone eerily quiet. The other passengers had stopped their conversations to watch the tableau unfolding—a psychic with fire in her eyes, a magician caught between fascination and alarm, and a young woman with a pout that was akin to an angry toddler whose toy was about to be taken away.

Eleanor, apparently immune to atmospheric tension, chose that moment to play her trump card. She stepped closer to Christopher, close enough that her *eau de toilette* would be dizzying, close enough that her carefully displayed assets were impossible to ignore. "Forget the mystical mumbo-jumbo," she said, her bejeweled hand finding his chest. "I have a hot tub on my private balcony and a bottle of

Dom Pérignon Luminous 2013. What do you say we make this night memorable?"

It was crude, direct, and, Cleo had to admit, effective. Men were simple creatures at their core, and Eleanor was offering the kind of uncomplicated pleasure that didn't require decoding bone castings or navigating the treacherous waters of genuine connection.

Christopher looked down at Eleanor's upturned face, her eyes wide with invitation, then across at Cleo with her scattered bones and knowing smile that now seemed to quiver at the edges. Then back at Eleanor again. For a moment that stretched like elastic, the outcome hung in the balance, the air between them thick with perfume and possibility, the soft clink of glasses and murmur of voices fading to a distant hum.

Then he smiled. Not the performer's smile, but something more wolfish, more base. His eyes darkened to the color of wet earth, and Cleo could almost hear the rapid drumming of his pulse.

"That does sound tempting," he said, his voice dropping to a velvet rumble. Cleo felt something cold and sharp settle in her stomach, a sensation like swallowing ice that spread outward until her fingertips tingled with numbness. The bones beneath her hands seemed to grow cooler, as if drawing heat from her skin.

Of course, she thought bitterly, her throat constricting around unspoken curses. *Of course it would be that easy for her.* The familiar sting of rejection mixed with a deeper, more venomous feeling. It was betrayal that tasted like copper pennies on her tongue. Here was Christopher, proving himself just as shallow as every other man who'd ever crossed her path.

But as he began to step away from the table, Cleo saw that something caught his attention. One of the bones had shifted position while they weren't looking, rolling from the symbol of betrayal to land squarely on the spider-web key. In the *Golden Parlor's* elegant lighting, the carved lines seemed to pulse with their own inner fire.

"Interesting," he murmured, reaching toward the bone before Cleo could stop him. The moment his fingers made contact, the ship's lights didn't just flicker, they strobed in patterns that made him wince. And in the brief moment of chaos that followed, Eleanor made her fatal mistake.

"God, this is so ridiculous," she snapped, her patience finally exhausted. "Can we please stop with the parlor tricks and focus on seeing what's real here?"

Parlor tricks? Cleo thought, a shocking rage burning through her like flash fire. *You want to see something real, little girl?*

Later, she would tell herself that what happened next was impulse, jealousy, the kind of petty magical thinking that everyone indulged in when they were angry and drunk and feeling dismissed by someone who should have been more aware. She would insist that she never intended for the words to carry actual power, that she was just venting frustration in the same way other people threw drinks or slapped faces.

But in the moment, with Christopher's fingers still touching the bone that had somehow carved itself with symbols that predated known history, with Eleanor's casual cruelty still echoing in the air. In that moment, Cleo Laveau opened her mouth and let three years of carefully contained power pour out in a stream of Creole French that her spirit guides had whispered to her in dreams.

"Que tes précieuses bêtes se retournent contre toi comme tu t'es retourné contre moi. Que ta fierté devienne ta prison et que tes peurs se multiplient jusqu'à ce qu'elles remplissent chaque ombre."

Let your precious beasts turn against you as you have turned against me. Let your pride become your prison and your fears multiply until they fill every shadow.

The words zapped like static electricity, like the moment before lightning strikes. For a heartbeat, the entire *Golden Parlor* held its breath.

Then Christopher's hand jerked back from the bone as if it had burned him. Eleanor stepped back with a nervous laugh. The other passengers resumed their conversations with the particular loudness of people pretending they hadn't noticed anything unusual.

But Cleo knew better. She could feel the words taking root in the ship's infrastructure, spreading through the ventilation systems like spores, finding their way to the one place on board where fear and fascination lived in perfect, precarious balance.

What have I done? she thought, but it was too late for regret. The spell—if that's what it had been—was already weaving itself through the ship's nervous system, looking for the intersection between human fear and arachnid instinct, between performance and reality, between the equilibrium she had maintained for years and the chaos that bubbled just beneath the surface of every necromancer's art.

Eleanor was still talking, something about how they should really get going before the champagne got warm, but her voice sounded very far away. Christopher was staring at Cleo with an expression of dawning comprehension, as if he were finally beginning to understand what kind of game they'd been playing.

And three floors below, in the carefully climate-controlled darkness of Christopher's suite, something was stirring. Something that had been content to perform, to play its part in humanity's elaborate dance of fear and fascination, but was now remembering what it felt like to hunt for something other than applause.

Cleo could feel it.

The *Pacific Dream* sailed on through the gathering fog, carrying its cargo of dreamers and schemers toward a destination that had just changed in ways none of them could imagine. After all, Cleo thought with a mixture of satisfaction and growing dread, the girl had wanted to see something real.

Eleanor was about to get her wish.

CHAPTER 7

A rnold Lichtenstein adjusted his bow tie and nudged his twin
brother with his elbow.

"Sit up straight, Arthur. Captain's table demands proper posture."

Arthur shifted uncomfortably in his wheelchair, eyes darting to
the ornate chandelier that hung above the dining table. The *Pacific
Dream*'s grand dining room glittered with crystal and polished silver,
the perfect pantomime of 1940s luxury liner elegance. He'd counted
three potential falling hazards since they'd arrived.

"That chandelier's not properly secured," Arthur muttered. "One
good wave and it's curtains for everyone at this table."

"Nonsense. You said the same thing about the one at the Bellagio
in '99, and we're still here."

Their server, Bonita Diaz, appeared at Arnold's elbow with a bottle
of wine. "Château Margaux, gentlemen? Captain's compliments."

Arnold beamed at her. "My dear, you're a vision. Pour generously.
My brother needs something to steady his nerves."

"I don't need wine. I need proper safety protocols," Arthur grumbled, but held out his glass anyway.

Denver Wheaton, the ship's steward, appeared behind the captain's empty chair. "Ladies and gentlemen, Captain Abercrombie sends his regrets. He's been delayed by a small matter requiring his attention. Please begin without him."

"Something wrong with the ship?" Arthur asked, a little too quickly.

Denver's poise never faltered. "Nothing to concern yourself with, sir. Just routine maritime business. Everything's just swell."

Arnold watched Denver's performance with professional admiration. The man never broke character—not a hint of modern inflection in his speech, not a single contemporary gesture. He spoke in that staccato rhythm that movie stars from that era affected. If Arthur didn't know better, he'd think Denver had stepped straight out of a time machine.

Across the table, Olivia Batiste was documenting her plate arrangement as furtively as possible with an antique-looking camera. Without her phone, she'd been forced into film photography, and Arnold suspected she was chafing at the inability to immediately share her experiences.

"The Amazing Spider-Mage," she said, tucking the camera away and turning her attention to the twins. "You two know him professionally, right? His act was incredible today."

Arthur's fork clattered against his plate. "Incredible isn't the word I'd use."

"Oh?" Matt Craig looked up from cutting his wedge salad. The solo businessman had been quiet until now, seemingly preoccupied with his own thoughts.

Arnold jumped in before his brother could launch into one of his safety tirades. "What my brother means is that Christopher Webb's performance today transcended 'incredible.' It was masterful technique."

"It was reckless," Arthur countered. "Did you see how he handled that Australian huntsman? Too casual. Those things can move sixty feet per second. One wrong move and..." He snapped his fingers.

"You sound concerned, Mr. Lichtenstein," Matt said, cutting a perfect bite of bacon-topped wedge salad.

"We've seen what happens when magic goes wrong," Arthur said darkly. "I've got the wheelchair to prove it."

Arnold patted his brother's arm. "What my pessimistic twin isn't telling you is that we were once the most sought-after illusionists in Las Vegas. The Lichtenstein Twins and Their Miraculous Metamorphosis."

"Until the apparatus malfunctioned," Arthur added. "Crushed my legs like twigs."

Olivia leaned forward. "That's horrible! But you still love magic, even after that?"

"Magic didn't betray me," Arthur said. "Poor equipment maintenance did."

Arnold smiled wistfully. "To answer your question, dear Olivia, we booked this cruise the moment we heard Webb would be performing. We've studied every magician worth their salt. We had a spider illusion too, you know. Not real ones like he uses. Ours were motorized. A giant mechanical black widow that would descend from the ceiling and—"

"And malfunction," Arthur interrupted. "Third show at the Sands. Nearly decapitated a woman in the front row."

"Tut, tut," Arnold chuckled nervously. "My brother has a flair for the dramatic."

Bonita arrived with their appetizers, setting down delicate plates of oysters Rockefeller. "Everything to your satisfaction?" she asked.

"Perfection, my dear," Arnold said. "Though I don't suppose you could tell us when the Spider-Mage might be joining us? I believe he was invited to the captain's table tonight."

"Mr. Webb sends his apologies," Bonita replied. "He's... indisposed."

Arnold caught the slight hesitation. "Nothing serious, I hope?"

"An issue with his... companions," Bonita responded carefully.

Arthur's head snapped up. "His spiders? What's wrong with them?"

"I'm not at liberty to say, sir." Bonita's workplace smile remained fixed, but Arnold noticed her eyes flick toward Denver, who gave an almost imperceptible shake of his head.

Matt Craig set down his wine glass with deliberate care. "I'm sure it's nothing. Creatives are temperamental. Perhaps he's just preparing for tomorrow's show."

"No," Arthur said, lowering his voice. "Something's wrong. I saw it during his performance today. The Chilean recluse was agitated."

Arnold studied his brother with respect. Despite his paranoia, Arthur had always been the more sharp-eyed of the two when it came to performance details.

"You noticed that too?" Olivia asked. "I thought I imagined it, but when he did the vanishing act with the bird spider, it seemed... weird."

"Webb was sweating," Arthur continued. "Not the normal kind from the lights. Cold sweat. Fear sweat. I've seen it before... right before accidents happen."

Denver cleared his throat. "I assure you, gents, everything aboard the *Pacific Dream* is hunky-dory. Mr. Webb is simply taking a night to rest his voice."

"His voice seemed fine when I saw him arguing with that fortune-teller in the corridor an hour ago," Matt said casually, bringing an oyster to his small plate with a pair of tongs.

All heads turned toward him.

"Cleo Laveau?" Arnold asked. "The medium?"

"If that's what she calls herself," Matt shrugged. "They were having quite the heated discussion. Something about 'what she'd done' and 'how to fix it.' Lover's quarrel, I assumed."

Arnold gripped the table edge. "Did you hear anything about his spiders?"

The businessman's expression took on a gossipy glow and he opened his mouth to speak, but a crash from the kitchen interrupted him.

Bonita flinched, and for just a moment, her persona slipped. "What in the actual fu—" She caught herself, switching back to period-appropriate language. "My goodness, what a clatter. Please excuse me while I investigate."

As she hurried away, Arthur leaned toward his brother. "It's starting," he whispered.

"What is?" Arnold asked.

"The cascade. First small malfunctions, then bigger ones. It's how every disaster begins."

Denver smiled tightly. "I assure you, gentlemen—"

"I saw Webb's face during the finale," Arthur cut in. "That was the face of a man who's lost control of his act. I know because I wore that same expression right before our box collapsed."

Arnold felt a chill that had nothing to do with the dining room's temperature. In thirty-six years of performing together, he'd learned to trust his brother's instincts about impending disasters. Arthur had predicted three major mishaps in their career, including his own.

"Perhaps," Arnold said carefully, "we should inquire about the lifeboats. Just as a matter of curiosity."

Olivia laughed nervously. "You can't be serious."

But Matt was watching the twins with new interest. "You know," he said quietly, "I always make a point of knowing where the exits are." He dabbed his mouth with his napkin. "Perhaps after dinner, Mr. Lichtenstein, you might share your concerns."

Before Arthur could answer, Bonita returned, her steps quicker, her smile more brittle than before.

"Is everything all right?" Denver asked her.

"Perfectly fine," she replied, as she refilled water glasses. "Just a small kitchen incident. Nothing to worry about."

But Arthur was gripping the arms of his wheelchair, knuckles white. "It's never nothing," he whispered.

Arnold watched the dining room doors swing open as Captain Abercrombie strode in, his naval uniform crisp despite the late hour. The captain's presence immediately commanded attention, conversations at nearby tables dropping to respectful murmurs.

"Ladies and gentlemen, please accept my sincere apologies for the delay." Mac's tone carried the rote warmth of someone who'd given thousands of such addresses. He took his seat at the head of the table, napkin snapping open with a decisive snap. "Ship's business waits for no man, I'm afraid."

Arnold studied the captain's face for signs of strain. The man's wind-weathered features revealed nothing unusual, though a slight tightness around his eyes suggested fatigue.

"We heard quite a commotion from the kitchen, Captain," Arthur ventured. "Is everything shipshape?"

Mac waved dismissively. "Just a bit of broken crockery. One of our lads took a tumble. Hazard of working on moving water, wouldn't you say?" His chuckle sounded genuine enough. "Denver, I believe I'll start with the consommé."

"Very good, sir." Denver signaled to Bonita, who hurried toward the kitchen.

Arthur leaned forward, the leather seat of his wheelchair creaking. "Captain, about Webb's spiders—"

"Ah, yes." Mac cut him off smoothly. "Ace performer."

Arnold recognized the deflection but played along. "Yes, but—"

"Captain," Matt interrupted. "Perhaps you could satisfy my curiosity about safety protocols aboard the *Pacific Dream*."

A flicker of annoyance crossed Mac's face before his smile returned. "What specifically interests you, Mr. Craig?"

"Lifeboats, primarily. Their capacity, location, deployment procedures." Matt's tone was casual, but his eyes were sharp. "Just a professional interest in maritime operations."

The captain's lips disappeared into a thin line. "We conduct a mandatory safety drill on day one, Mr. Craig. Did you miss it?"

"Not at all. I simply enjoy the details."

"Our vessel exceeds all international safety requirements by twenty percent. Six lifeboats, each with capacity for seventy-five souls. Though I assure you, they're merely decorative on this voyage."

Arnold felt the tension at the table rise. The captain was polite but clearly irritated by the questioning. Before anyone could respond, Arthur suddenly jerked in his chair, eyes wide.

"There!" Arthur jabbed a finger toward the white tablecloth. "Did you see it?"

"See what?" Arnold asked, alarmed by his brother's pallor.

"A spider. Small, dark... it ran right across between the bread basket and the salt cellar."

Everyone at the table froze, then leaned forward, examining the pristine tablecloth.

"I don't see anything," Olivia said, peering closely.

Denver stepped forward, lifting the bread basket. "Nothing here, sir."

"It was there," Arthur insisted, voice dropping to a whisper. "I know what I saw."

Captain Abercrombie cleared his throat. "The light plays tricks sometimes, especially with the chandelier's crystal reflections."

"It wasn't a trick of the light," Arthur muttered.

Arnold placed a steadying hand on his brother's shoulder, feeling a slight tremor. "Maybe just a shadow from the candle flame?"

Arthur shook his head but said nothing more.

Mac signaled for more wine to be poured. "Now then, shall we discuss pleasanter topics? Miss Batiste, why don't you tell everyone how you're documenting our voyage for your followers?"

As Olivia launched into an explanation of vintage photography filters, Arnold watched his brother's eyes continually scanning the table. Arthur had always been the more observant twin, which was precisely why Arnold found himself unconsciously lifting his feet slightly off the floor, as though the deck itself might be teeming with unseen creepy-crawlies.

CHAPTER 8

D r. Fiona Hand had learned to distinguish between different types of late-night medical calls during her three months aboard the *Pacific Dream*. There were the predictable ones: seasickness, too much champagne, the occasional misadventure that required a Xanax and diplomatic silence. Then there were the calls that made her former profession's instincts prickle with unease, the ones that suggested patterns lurking beneath surface normalcy, the whispers of something that didn't quite fit the established medical paradigm she'd been trained to recognize.

Christopher Webb's voice crackling through her cabin's intercom at 2:17 AM fell decidedly into the latter category, carrying a quaver she sensed was fear.

"Dr. Hand? I'm sorry to wake you, but I need... I think I need medical consultation. Not for me," he added quickly, as if reading her automatic assumption through the static-filled connection. "For my spiders. Something's wrong with them. They're behaving... abnormally."

She chuckled, though sleep deprivation made the sound rougher than intended as she swung her legs over the side of her narrow cot.

"You do know I'm not a veterinarian, right? And we don't have any on board unless one of the passengers happens to be moonlighting as an exotic animal specialist..."

"You worked for the CDC, right? I read your bio in the brochure. I'm worried they might have a virus of some kind, or..." His voice trailed off, replaced by what sounded like frantic movement in the background. "They're moving differently. I've worked with these species for years, and I've never seen anything like this. Maybe it's a germ they picked up? Can you take a culture?"

"I'll be right there," she said, already reaching for her medical bag and pulling her uniform from its hook. The old-style nurse's outfit felt absurdly theatrical for what might be an actual emergency, but protocol was protocol. Better to assess the situation before it escalated into passenger panic or, worse, actual injury. Whatever was happening with Webb's arachnid assortment, her years tracking disease vectors told her that unusual animal behavior rarely signaled anything good.

The ship's corridors felt different at this hour. Longer somehow, with shadows that seemed to shift independently of the overhead lighting. The vintage aesthetic that felt charming during daylight took on a more sinister quality in the small hours, like a movie set where the cameras had stopped rolling but the actors hadn't gotten the memo. The art deco sconces cast elongated figures against the wood-paneled walls, their golden glow insufficient against the pressing darkness that pooled in the corners and beneath the ornate side tables lining the passageway.

Christopher's suite was on the same deck as hers, but the journey felt interminable. Twice she paused, certain she'd heard something scurrying in the walls. Probably just the ship's mechanical systems adjusting to temperature changes, but her nerves were already on edge from the unusual nature of the call. The third time she stopped, she actually pressed her ear against the cool surface of the wall, listening for that unsettling scratch-scratch-scratch that seemed to follow her progress down the corridor. The *Pacific Dream* creaked and groaned around her, its hull responding to the gentle sway of midnight waters, but beneath those familiar nautical sounds lurked something more deliberate, more purposeful.

She found Christopher's door slightly ajar, warm light spilling into the hallway like an invitation or a warning. Fiona hesitated, her medical training warring with a natural instinct to retreat. The sound that emerged from within made her pause with her hand raised to knock. Not quite music, not quite static, but something that suggested pattern and purpose in its frequencies. Her fingers tightened around the handle of her medical bag as goosebumps raised along her arms despite the corridor's warmth. Whatever waited beyond that threshold, she sensed it represented a significant departure from the routine ailments and seasickness she typically treated aboard the *Pacific Dream*.

"Mr. Webb?" she called softly.

"Come in. Quickly."

His voice carried an edge she hadn't heard during their brief previous interactions, the particular strain that came from watching something familiar transform into something unrecognizable. Fiona had heard that tone plenty of times during outbreak investigations, usually right before everything went sideways.

The scene that greeted her was surreal in its mundane strangeness. Christopher Webb stood in the center of his cabin wearing pajama pants and a tank top that revealed the full extent of his tattoo collection—serpents and spiders and playing cards crawling up his arms like an illustrated autobiography. In the harsh overhead light, the ink seemed almost alive against his skin, the arachnids appearing to pulse with each rapid breath he took.

Five glass terrariums were arranged on his coffee table, each one illuminated by internal heating elements that cast everything in hellish red. The merlot glow transformed the luxury cabin into something otherworldly, painting shadows that danced across the vintage cruise decor with sinister intent. The air felt thick and warm with a musky, earthy scent, like a disturbed grave.

Christopher's face, half-bathed in that blood-colored light, looked gaunt and haunted, a stark contrast to the confident showman who had commanded the stage just hours earlier. Fiona could hear his shallow breathing, punctuated by the faint scratch of tiny legs against glass, a sound so subtle yet unmistakable that it sent an involuntary shiver down her limbs. The polished wood surfaces reflected the crimson illumination, creating pools that seemed to pulse with a sense of sentience.

But it was the sound that made her skin crawl—a rhythmic tapping that seemed to come from all five containers simultaneously, as if their inhabitants were communicating in Morse code. The accuracy of it was unnerving; precise synchronization across different species that should have had no means of coordination. Each tap resonated through the cabin with unnatural clarity, cutting through the ambient noise of the ship like a scalpel. Fiona felt the hairs on the back of her neck stand at attention as she realized the tapping followed a distinct pattern repeating with an exactness that no natural behavior could explain.

"When did this start?" she asked, setting down her medical bag and moving closer to examine the terrariums.

"They were agitated earlier tonight, but this... this *sound* started about twenty minutes ago. All at once." Christopher ran his hands through his collar-length hair, the gesture revealing how badly his fingers were shaking. "I've worked with these particular species for seven years, Dr. Hand. I know their behaviors, their cycles, their individual traits. This isn't... this isn't normal."

Fiona peered into the first terrarium and immediately understood his concern. The Australian huntsman spider, which had performed so gracefully during the evening show, was now positioned in the exact center of its habitat, its front legs raised like a horse rearing up. But it wasn't responding to any external stimulus. It was simply holding the position, motionless except for the rhythmic tapping of its two rear legs against the glass.

"Have you noticed any particular reaction to changes in their environment?" she asked, moving to examine the second terrarium. "Temperature fluctuations, humidity, vibrations from the ship's engines?"

"Nothing. Everything's exactly the same as it's been for the entire voyage."

They had been at sea three days now, and aside from some strange light flickering during Cleo's readings, everything aboard the *Pacific Dream* had proceeded exactly as advertised in the cruise brochures. The passengers had settled into the rhythm of vintage luxury, surrendering their modern devices and embracing the carefully curated nostalgia that surrounded them. The weather had been cooperative, the entertainment well-received, and Christopher's show had been drawing particularly enthusiastic crowds each afternoon and evening.

Christopher joined her beside the glass containers, his tall, thin frame casting a long shadow across the terrariums. His proximity brought with it the scent of expensive cologne—something woodsy with notes of amber—but it couldn't quite mask the underlying aroma of fear, that particular sharp, acrid scent produced by someone whose fight-or-flight response was working overtime. His salt-and-pepper hair, usually so carefully styled for his performances, hung limply around his face.

The second animal, a jumping spider that should have been dormant at this hour, was exhibiting the same behavior. Centered position, threat display, rhythmic tapping. But what made Fiona's medical training clash with rational thought was the synchronization that reminded her of a Busby Berkeley picture. His 1943 film, "The Gang's All Here," had played in the theater earlier that evening. All five spiders were tapping in unison like tiny Carmen Mirandas, as if responding to some external choreography signals she couldn't detect.

Impossible, she told herself. *Spiders don't coordinate behavior like this. They're solitary predators, not hive insects.* She didn't have a background in etymology, but she remembered a little of what she'd learned about insects in relation to viruses.

Fiona leaned closer to the terrariums, her scientific mind racing through possibilities. Each species was native to different continents, with distinct evolutionary paths, yet here they were, moving as one organism.

"Have you added anything new to their habitats recently?" she asked.

Christopher shook his head. "Nothing."

She couldn't help but think back to her tenure at the CDC—how Dr. Moretti's unauthorized experiments had cascaded into a public relations nightmare, with her name dragged through medical journals and congressional hearings despite her ignorance of his actions. The scandal had effectively demolished her research career, forcing her to pivot toward this ship doctor position. The *Pacific Dream* had seemed like a perfect temporary refuge: days and nights at sea, treating nothing more serious than sunburns and seasickness while the controversy died down. A chance to rebuild her professional reputation away from the whispers and sideways glances of the research community.

Now, staring at these arachnids exhibiting bizarre behavior, she felt an uncomfortable echo of those dark days, standing before evidence that defied explanation, knowing that reporting it honestly could make her sound unhinged.

But what could she do in the here and now? The state-of-the-art lab she'd once commanded would have equipment to analyze this properly—gas chromatography, mass spectrometers, electron microscopes—not the basic medical kit she carried for seasick passengers.

"I'm not sure I can help," she admitted.

"I'd just like your opinion, Dr. Hand."

"Okay," she sighed, thinking. "Has anyone else been in contact with them recently?" she asked. "Other passengers, crew members?"

Christopher's expression shifted, becoming guarded. "There was... an incident. Cleo Laveau was doing some kind of reading, and she asked me to touch one of her casting bones. The moment I made contact, the ship's lights flickered and..." He paused, clearly debating how much to reveal. "When I returned to my suite, all of my ladies were sleeping. It was odd. Then, when they all woke up, they made these sounds."

Cleo Laveau. Fiona had attended one of the psychic's afternoon sessions, more for anthropological curiosity than genuine belief, and had been impressed despite herself by the woman's psychological insight. But psychological insight was a far cry from influencing arachnid behavior through supernatural means.

Although, she thought, remembering some of the more inexplicable cases she'd encountered during her lab stint, *there's still so much we don't understand about the intersection between consciousness and biology.*

"I think," she said carefully, "we should consider the possibility that this is stress-related. Performing animals sometimes exhibit unusual behaviors when their routines are disrupted, especially in unfamiliar environments. The confined space of a cruise ship, the constant vibration of the engines, even changes in barometric pressure could all be contributing factors."

It was a perfectly reasonable explanation that accounted for none of what she was actually observing. The analytical part of her brain was desperately trying to rationalize what her eyes couldn't deny. The tapping had evolved now, becoming more complex. Not just rhythmic repetition but actual patterns that suggested... communication? Coordination? The Australian huntsman and the Wraparound spider were now perfectly mirroring each other's movements, their legs lifting and falling in precise synchronicity, creating a hypnotic percussion against the glass that made Fiona's eyes widen.

Stop it, she ordered herself, pressing her palms against her thighs to steady her nervous hands. *You're letting the atmosphere get to you. Next, you'll be believing in haunted cruise ships and vengeful sea spirits.* She'd spent her entire career as a scientist, relying on evidence and methodology. Yet here she was, aboard a vessel carefully designed to evoke nostalgia for a tragic, bygone era, seeing arachnids behave in ways that defied rational explanation.

But as she watched, the third spider—the Chilean recluse that should have been hiding in the darkest corner of its habitat—moved to the front of its terrarium and began the same synchronized display.

"Mr. Webb," she said slowly, "I think we need to consider quarantine protocols."

"Quarantine?" His voice caught slightly on the word. "You think they're sick?"

"I think they're exhibiting behavior that suggests potential neurological influence. Whether that's viral, bacterial, parasitic, or..." She paused, unwilling to voice the other possibilities her mind was exploring. "Well, until we understand the cause, we should minimize their contact with other organisms."

It was a euphemistic way of saying *until we figure out if whatever's affecting them can spread to humans*, but Christopher was clearly smart enough to read between the lines. His face went pale beneath his spray tan.

"You think this could be contagious?"

Before Fiona could answer, the tapping stopped. All five spiders froze simultaneously, their threat displays dissolving into sharp stillness. The sudden silence was somehow more unnerving than the synced sounds had been.

Then, as if responding to some signal she couldn't perceive, all five spiders turned to face the cabin door.

That's not possible, Fiona thought, even as her eyes took in the undeniable spectacle. *Spiders don't orient themselves toward sounds like that. They don't respond to coordinated stimuli.*

But the evidence was there. Five different species of arachnid, in five separate containers, all facing the same direction with the detail of a flawless military drill. And that direction led straight toward the corridor where she'd heard—

A scream echoed through the ship's intercom system, high and desperate and abruptly cut off. The sound reverberated through the cabin, suspended in the air like a physical presence before dissolving into static. Then another voice, male this time, shouting something about the ladies' powder room on C-deck. The words were garbled by panic, but the urgency was unmistakable. Someone was in serious trouble.

Christopher and Fiona looked at each other with the particular understanding that passed between people who'd just realized their small crisis was about to become everyone's problem. The illusionist's mussed hair seemed to have lost some of its luster in the harsh cabin light, his brown eyes wide with an apprehension that stripped away his stage persona.

"We should go see," Fiona said, already reaching for her medical bag, her fingers methodically checking its contents—syringes, antivenoms, bandages—tools of a science that suddenly felt inadequate.

As they moved toward the door, she couldn't shake the feeling that they were making a terrible mistake. That whatever was happening to Mr. Webb's spiders was just the beginning of something larger, something that had been set in motion by forces that existed well outside the boundaries of rational medical science. The movement of the arachnids played on a loop in her mind—these animals acting as a single organism, defying everything she knew about biology and behavior. She reached for the door handle, wondering what awaited them in the powder room on C-deck, and whether the screams they'd heard were just the first of many to come.

Behind them, in their glass containers, five predators watched their retreat with the patience of creatures that had suddenly remembered what it felt like to hunt for something more substantial than applause.

CHAPTER 9

E mma Glopstein had died long ago, buried beneath layers of
theatrical makeup and sultry Louisiana mystique. In her place
stood the wholly invented Cleo Laveau, third-generation descendant
of the infamous Voodoo Queen, reader of souls, speaker to the restless
dead. At least, that's what the passengers believed, and belief, Cleo
had learned, could be more powerful than truth. It was a currency
that bought her respect, admiration, and a steady income aboard the
Pacific Dream, where fantasy was the commodity they all traded in.

Cleo was tired. She'd been rousted from bed along with everyone
else last night at 3 AM following a blood-curdling scream that had
echoed through the ship's corridors like a banshee's wail. The sound
had jolted her from a fitful sleep, leaving her heart racing and her
skin tingling with goosebumps. But the source had never been found,
despite the crew's thorough search of every deck. Everyone denied
being the source of the scream, their faces showing frank confusion
when questioned. The incident had left a pall of unease hanging over
the ship like a dense fog that hid just the tip of an iceberg.

She thought back to her conversation with Christopher about her
fake spell and his spiders' seeming reaction to it. The memory made

her stomach knot uncomfortably. Those eight-legged creatures had behaved so strangely after her theatrical curse, skittering in ways that defied explanation. They'd quarreled bitterly, his accusations of sabotage meeting her defensive anger, and her feelings were more mixed than ever.

The attraction that had initially drawn her to him now warred with irritation and a nagging sense of doom. She decided she didn't like him after all, with his arrogant smirk and dismissive attitude toward her abilities. But there was an undeniable pull to him, something magnetic that she couldn't quite shake, no matter how she tried to focus on his flaws.

She and Eleanor had managed to steer clear of each other since their tense encounter during high tea, which was fine by Cleo.

She sighed, turning her attention back to the task at hand.

The late afternoon sun painted the *Victory Deck* in shades of amber and gold, casting skinny shadows between the striped cabanas. Cleo adjusted her turban, silk the color of midnight, pinned with a brooch that had belonged to someone's grandmother (she'd bought it at an estate sale in Metairie). She smiled at Mrs. Pemberton from Dayton, Ohio.

"Your Harold is watching over you," Cleo murmured, her voice dropping to that honeyed whisper that made people lean closer. "He says the garden is looking magnificent this year."

Mrs. Pemberton's eyes filled with tears. "He planted those roses for my birthday. How could you possibly—"

"The dead speak loudest through love," Cleo interrupted gently, her fingers dancing over the crystal orb. In truth, she'd overheard Mrs. Pemberton talking to another passenger about her late husband's prized roses not twenty minutes ago, seen her open a locket to show her a portrait. But the woman didn't need to know that. She needed comfort, connection, the reassurance that death wasn't an ending but a transformation. Cleo could provide that service. She had been providing it for three years now, ever since she'd fled New Orleans and the wreckage of her former life.

The crowd around her table murmured appreciatively. Cleo basked in their attention like a cat lazing in sunshine, feeling the familiar rush of a successful performance. This was better than any drug, this moment when strangers hung on her every word, desperate to believe in something larger than themselves.

"Now," she said, pressing Mrs. Pemberton's palm between her own, "Harold wants you to know that you shouldn't feel guilty about the cruise. Enjoy yourself. Dance with that handsome widower from the shuffleboard court."

Mrs. Pemberton blushed and giggled like a schoolgirl. The crowd laughed along with her, the tension of the séance dissolving into warm camaraderie. Cleo had learned long ago that people came to psychics not for revelations but for permission to grieve, to love again, to forgive themselves for being human.

As the group began to disperse, pressing tips into her hands and promising to attend her evening show in the *Stardust Salon*, Cleo's attention was drawn upward. On one of the upper deck balconies, a figure stood observing her—tall, lean, with silver-streaked hair that caught the light like spun mercury. His silhouette was unmistakable, even from this distance. Elegant yet somehow predatory in his stillness, like one of his eight-legged pets waiting for the perfect moment to strike.

Well, well, she thought, raising her glass of champagne in a mock toast. *Speak of the devil.* She held his gaze, letting the moment stretch between them like a silken thread.

He turned away, probably still miffed about their argument.

She looked out over the ocean, its deep blue waves gently rolling beneath the cloudless sky, the horizon a perfect line dividing water from heavens. The vastness of it calmed her in ways she couldn't put into words. Maybe they'd see some dolphins today; the captain had announced over breakfast that pods had been spotted in these waters recently.

She stifled a yawn, adjusting one of her crystal bracelets as it clinked against her champagne flute, which she'd filled with cream soda to keep herself alert for her readings, but it didn't seem to be doing the trick.

The Lichtenstein twins had bent her ear over breakfast that morning, talking about a loose spider they'd seen at dinner the night before. It was probably just a harmless daddy long-legs, nothing compared to the monstrosities Webb kept as "co-stars." Cleo was used to the bugs in Louisiana. Mosquitoes that hummed like tiny violins, cockroaches that survived even the most thorough exterminations, all of which could be found on the *Pacific Dream* despite its luxury status. Even mice, rats, and other creatures managed to stow away, no matter how much maintenance sprayed its poisons throughout the vessel's hidden corridors and crawlspaces. Nature always found a way to survive, to adapt—a truth Cleo understood better than most.

A voice broke through her reverie.

"Another reading, Miss Laveau?"

Cleo turned to find a young woman with short blonde hair styled in perfectly sculpted and lacquered waves. Olivia Batiste, who'd introduced herself earlier as a "sustainable travel influencer," whatever that meant. The girl had the kind of thin, desperate prettiness that screamed for attention, all carefully constructed angles and practiced poses.

"Of course, darling," Cleo said, gesturing to the chair across from her. "Though I should warn you, the spirits are particularly chatty today."

Olivia giggled. "Okay, but first, I wanted to ask about your friend upstairs. The magician? I'm thinking of collaborating with him for my content. You know, vintage magic meets vintage voyage? It could be amazing."

"Christopher Webb is hardly my friend," Cleo said carefully.

"But you were just... I saw you looking at each other. There was definite chemistry." Olivia leaned forward conspiratorially. "Is he single? He looks like he'd be incredible on camera."

Chemistry. Cleo still felt it too, even after the blowout. But hearing it from this vapid child's lips made it feel cheap, reduced to content for social media consumption.

"I'm sure I wouldn't know, honey child," Cleo said, her accent thickening by design, the way it always did when she needed to reinforce her mystical persona. She draped her words in the cloying tones of the bayou, letting "Nawlins" seep into every syllable. "Perhaps you should ask him yourself. The Amazing Spider-Mage seems quite... approachable to certain young ladies."

Olivia's face split into a wide, perfected grin, the kind that showed exactly the right number of teeth for maximum photogenic appeal. "Oh, no. You misunderstand me completely. I'm celibate." She tossed her perfectly coiffed blonde waves with a rehearsed nonchalance. "It's part of my brand authenticity journey. My followers are super invested in my spiritual growth."

"Well, well," Cleo murmured, not bothering to hide her skepticism. She reached for her velvet pouch, her numerous crystal rings catching the afternoon light streaming through the porthole. "Let's see if my reading detects any hope for your... future endeavors. The cards rarely lie about such matters."

"I'm perfectly at peace with my choices," Olivia assured her, leaning forward eagerly despite her proclaimed disinterest. Her eyes darted around the table, taking in all the potential props for her invisible audience. "What I really want to know is, will I ever get past a million followers? I feel like I've hit a plateau, and my agent says vintage content is the next big thing. That's why this cruise is so perfect. It's totally on-brand."

Cleo suppressed an eye roll as she withdrew her favorite tarot deck, a genuine antique set she'd found in a dusty voodoo shop, their edges worn soft by decades of handling. The cards felt warm against her fingertips, almost alive. With expert grace, she fanned them across the table, the worn gold filigree on their backs catching the light.

"Choose three cards, darling," she instructed, watching the girl's perfectly manicured nails hover indecisively over the spread. "One for your past, one for your present situation, and one..." she paused dramatically, "for what awaits you in the shadows of your future."

***

The afternoon crowd began to thin as passengers retreated to their cabins to prepare for dinner. Cleo packed up her crystal ball and tarot cards, each item returned to its appointed place in her kit with anal accuracy. The smooth, cool surface of the crystal slid against her fingertips as she wrapped it in black velvet, the heft of it comforting in her hands. But her mind wasn't on the familiar ritual; it was on dark hair and intelligent eyes, on the way Christopher Webb had looked at her as if he could see past her carefully constructed mystique to the woman beneath. The memory sent a warm pulsing at the hollow of her throat.

Dangerous, she told herself, inhaling the lingering scent of incense that clung to her clothes. *You're here to work, not to get distracted by some washed-up Vegas magician. Remember what happened last time you mixed business with pleasure.* But even as the warning echoed in her thoughts, she felt her heart quicken at the prospect of kissing him again.

She was already planning her outfit for dinner. The black silk dress with the plunging neckline, perhaps. The one that made her look like a film noir goddess. She could almost feel the cool fabric against her skin, hear the whisper of the silk train as she walked. *Let him see what he's up against. Let them all see.*

She made her way to her cabin, the gentle sway of the ship beneath her feet now as familiar as breathing. The corridor hummed with the distant sounds of the engines and the muffled laughter of passengers behind closed doors. She nodded to passengers who called out greetings, the persona of Cleo Laveau, The Clairvoyant, firmly in place despite her wild, wandering thoughts.

The Blacksmiths waved from their deck chairs, the ocean breeze carrying the scent of salt and expensive perfume, and she paused to ask about their anniversary celebration. *Fifty years together. Now that's real magic,* she thought with a pang of something that felt suspiciously like envy.

Rashida Bell, the writer—a real one, not an 'influencer'—looked up from her notebook with a sardonic smile that Cleo appreciated. Here was someone who understood that authenticity was just another form of performance. *She sees through it all, doesn't she?* Cleo thought. *I wonder what she's really writing about this floating time capsule. About me.*

Cleo stepped off the sunlit deck into the ship's interior, leaving behind the vast expanse of sky and sea. The hallway enveloped her in its manufactured atmosphere with pine-scented cleaner masking the faint mustiness of salt-dampened wood, oriental carpets muffling her footsteps. The dimmed lighting cast a warm glow over brass fixtures polished to a high shine.

Her cabin was smaller than Christopher's suite but elegantly appointed in deep purples and golds. Cleo had personalized it with scarves draped over the lamps, crystals arranged on the vanity, and a small altar to various saints and spirits—some real, some invented for effect. The line between genuine belief and theatrical necessity had blurred long ago. She found comfort in the rituals regardless of their authenticity.

She was hanging up her turban when a soft knock interrupted her thoughts. "Come in," she called, expecting one of the stewards with the evening's itinerary or perhaps a fresh towel for tomorrow.

Instead, Mrs. Pemberton peered around the door frame, her dark pewter-colored hair catching the cabin's warm light. "I hope I'm not bothering you," she said timidly, fingers nervously clutching the pearl necklace at her throat. "I wanted to ask... How did you know about my husband's roses? The yellow ones he planted for our first anniversary?"

"The spirits whisper secrets to those who know how to listen," Cleo said, settling onto her bed and patting the space beside her. The mattress dipped slightly as Mrs. Pemberton hesitantly perched on the edge. "But sometimes, my dear, the most profound magic is simply paying attention to what people tell you about themselves. The photograph in your locket, I noticed the yellow roses in the background when you opened it just before our session."

The older woman's eyes narrowed, crow's feet deepening around them. "So you didn't actually... I mean, was it real? The connection to the other side?"

"What's real?" Cleo countered, watching the disappointment and relief battle across the woman's face. "You feel comforted knowing he's still with you in some way. Does it matter whether the roses were revealed by spirits or observation? The comfort you feel is genuine either way."

"I... I guess so." Mrs. Pemberton fiddled with her wedding band, twisting it around her finger where the skin had smoothed to accommodate its presence over decades. "It's just different from what I expected. More complicated. Less black and white."

"Everything worth doing is complicated," Cleo said, surprising herself with the sincerity in her voice. "Love, grief, faith—none of it fits in neat little lockets."

They sat in companionable silence for a moment, watching the ocean through Cleo's porthole. The water was beginning to darken as twilight approached, its surface painted with the ship's lights in rippling streams of gold and red. A flying fish briefly broke the surface, its iridescent body catching the last rays of sunlight before disappearing back into the depths.

"Miss Laveau?" The woman's voice was smaller now, more vulnerable, barely audible above the gentle hum of the ship's engines. "Do you really believe in magic? Not just the show you put on, but actual... power?"

The question stayed suspended between them, honest and searching. Cleo felt something shift in her chest, a crack in the armor she'd built around herself. When was the last time someone had asked her what she believed rather than what she could provide? What services she offered? What guarantees she could make?

"I believe in power," she said finally, choosing her words with care. "The power of intention, of will, of understanding the hidden currents that run beneath the surface of things. Whether you call that magic or psychology or simple human nature... well, that's just semantics. Something exists in the spaces between what we can explain. I've felt it, even when I couldn't prove it."

There was a sudden knock—sharp, insistent—that made them both startle, the intimate moment shattered like a dropped vase.

"Cleo? You in there, darling?"

Eleanor Hargrove's voice carried through the door like hammered nails, each syllable precise and demanding.

"I should go," Mrs. Pemberton whispered, gathering herself with a rustle of her vintage-appropriate silk dress. Her eyes, momentarily clear and penetrating, met Cleo's. "Thank you for your honesty."

She got up and went out the door, nearly bumping into Eleanor who stood in the hallway, transformed from her afternoon casual wear into a stunning evening gown that hugged and showcased her considerable assets. The deep emerald fabric caught the light, making her look like some exotic predatory fish, beautiful and dangerous.

"There you are!" Eleanor exclaimed, barging into the cabin without invitation. "I've been looking everywhere for you. I need your help with something."

"How presumptuous of you to assume I'd provide it," Cleo said dryly, but she closed the door anyway. Despite her irritation, she was curious about what had brought the Instagram princess to her door.

Eleanor spun around to face Cleo more directly, her dress flaring dramatically. "It's about Christopher Webb."

"What exactly are you asking me to do?" Cleo inquired, stepping away and settling into her vanity chair and beginning to remove her jewelry. She wondered why, after what had happened the other night, this child would be coming to her for help. Maybe she was obtuse enough to think Cleo had forgotten the whole thing or given up.

"Help me get his attention. You know, woman to woman."

The request was so transparently manipulative that Cleo almost laughed. But beneath Eleanor's calculated charm, she sensed something desperate—a young woman so accustomed to being desired that rejection felt like existential threat.

"Darling," Cleo said gently, "if a man isn't interested, no amount of scheming will change that."

"But he's perfect for my brand. Dark, mysterious, dangerous... my followers would eat it up. And he's exactly the kind of man who should want me."

Should want me. The phrase revealed everything. The entitled assumption that beauty equaled desirability, that attraction was a transaction rather than alchemy. Cleo felt a strange mixture of pity and disdain.

"Beauty is not a currency that buys love," she said. "And men like Christopher Webb... they're attracted to hidden allure, to complexity. You might be stunning, Eleanor, but you're about as mysterious as a billboard."

The words were harsher than Cleo had intended, and the girl recoiled as if she'd seen her follower count drop by a thousand. For a moment, her perfect facade cracked completely, revealing the insecure child beneath the Instagram goddess.

"That's... that's cruel," Eleanor whispered.

"It's honest," Cleo replied, though she felt a pang of guilt. "If you truly want to interest him, stop performing and start being real. But I suspect that terrifies you more than rejection."

Eleanor straightened, her armor snapping back into place. "You know what? Fine. Keep your wisdom. I don't need help from some washed-up fortune teller anyway."

She stormed out, slamming the door behind her. Cleo sat in the sudden silence, staring at her reflection in the vanity mirror. Her own mask looked back at her—the dramatic makeup, the curving cat's-eye liner, the carefully styled hair, the mystical props that transformed Emma Glopstein into Cleo Laveau.

Hypocrite, she told herself. *You're lecturing her about authenticity while living a complete lie.*

But even as the thought formed, she knew it wasn't entirely true. Cleo might be a carefully crafted construction, but she wasn't empty. She was built from Emma's genuine empathy, her real desire to help people, her authentic fascination with the spaces between the seen and unseen worlds. The lie served a larger truth.

Still, Eleanor's desperation had stirred something uncomfortable in Cleo's chest. She recognized the hunger for validation, the fear of invisibility. They were more alike than either wanted to admit. What would it be like to be seen by him? Really seen, the way performers recognized each other across the divide of public persona? The thought was both thrilling and terrifying. Cleo had spent so long hiding behind her mystique that the prospect of genuine connection felt like stepping off a cliff.

Don't be ridiculous, she told herself, fastening a necklace of crystal beads around her throat. *You're here to work, not to fall for some brooding magician with beautiful eyes and tragic past.* She'd overheard the Lichtenstein twins gossiping over breakfast about young Christopher's little brother dying when Christopher was supposed to be watching him. She wondered if that was why the magician seemed so aloof at times. Was he afraid to get close to someone for fear they'd be taken away?

A glance at her wristwatch showed it was nearly six, and time for cocktails in the *Golden Parlor*. As she applied the final touches to her lipstick—a deep red that made her look like a proper *femme fatale*—she was planning her entrance to the gala. The way she'd move through the crowd, drawing attention without seeming to seek it. How she'd position herself where Christopher couldn't help but notice her, where Eleanor's designed beauty would pale in comparison to her authentic mystique.

After all, Cleo thought with a smirk that was inscrutable, if the girl wanted to play games, she'd chosen the wrong opponent. Emma Glopstein might have been ordinary, but Cleo Laveau was magic itself. And magic, as any practitioner knew, was equal parts creation and destruction.

Chapter 10

C hristopher Webb had always known that performing with spiders was a form of elaborate suicide. Death by a thousand tiny cuts, each show a gamble against odds that would eventually turn against him. But standing in his opulent suite, watching his performers, who'd somehow found their way out of their enclosures, he was dumbstruck. He watched them multiply through some biological impossibility that defied every law of nature he'd thought he understood, he finally grasped that his particular form of Russian roulette had just loaded all the chambers.

The transformation was obscene in its accelerated efficiency. Each of his spiders had begun extruding what looked like silk, but instead of webs, the material was forming dozens of cocoons pulsing with internal movement that suggested gestation periods measured in minutes rather than weeks. As Christopher stared in horrified fascination, the sacs began splitting open, releasing arachnids that were identical to their progenitors but somehow *more*—larger, more aggressive, possessed of a fierceness that made his original performers look like simple pets.

Cleo's spell. She didn't just curse them—she awakened something.

They'd had words over it yesterday, but she assured him it was just some mumbo-jumbo to scare Eleanor. There had been some rumblings of loose spiders, but he knew that his five were accounted for. And after last night's bizarre display, they'd all settled down; he'd let Dr. Hand know not to worry. And his afternoon show had gone off without a hitch.

But then he'd heard the strange tapping again.

The huntsman emerged first from its many cocoons, each new iteration slightly larger than the last. They moved with that characteristic crab-like scuttle, but now their movements were coordinated, purposeful. As Christopher gaped, three of them positioned themselves at different points around his cabin while a fourth began what looked suspiciously like reconnaissance, testing air currents, examining surfaces, seemingly mapping the space.

Speed demons, the magician thought, remembering the creature's natural hunting characteristics. *But now they're not hunting for food. They're hunting for territory to secure.*

The Wraparound spiders were even more disturbing in their metamorphosis. Their natural camouflage abilities had been amplified by whatever supernatural force was driving their reproduction, allowing them to flatten against surfaces until they were virtually invisible. Christopher found himself scanning his cabin walls as each new iteration scuttled away, knowing that dozens of ambush predators were positioned throughout the space but unable to identify their exact locations.

Masters of disguise, he noted with the neutral professionalism that had kept him functional during so many years of performing with creatures that could kill him. *But now they're not just hiding from prey... they're coordinating defensive positions.*

The Chinese bird spider's offspring were the most obviously threatening—massive tarantulas that had grown to nearly ten inches in span, their dark bodies moving with territorial aggression that filled the suite with the particular tension that preceded violence. These weren't just larger versions of their progenitor; they carried themselves with the authority of creatures that understood they were apex predators in whatever hierarchy was being established.

Alpha spiders, Christopher thought. *They're creating a chain of command.*

But it was the Chilean recluses that made his blood run cold. Their natural preference for dark, undisturbed spaces had been weaponized by the spell's influence. They were systematically exploring every shadow, every crevice, every space where a human might seek refuge. And their venom, which naturally caused necrotic tissue damage, seemed to have been enhanced. The few surfaces they'd tested with their fangs showed decay patterns that spread far beyond the original contact points.

Silent stalkers, he realized. *They're not out for immediate kills... they want slow, rotting deaths that will terrorize the survivors.*

The jumping spiders were no less upsetting in their spontaneous reproduction. Their natural intelligence and curiosity had been amplified into something that approached true problem-solving capability. Christopher saw them leap between surfaces with mathematical assessment, testing distances, calculating angles, apparently mapping three-dimensional spaces in ways that suggested tactical knowledge.

Spies and messengers, he thought. *They're small enough to go anywhere, smart enough to gather intelligence, and agile enough to coordinate attacks.*

Christopher took a tentative step backward, bracing for the inevitable attack. None came. The spiders, now numbering in the hundreds, parted around him like water around a stone. They scurried past his feet, maintaining a perfect perimeter of empty space, as if he existed in his own protective bubble.

"What the hell?" he whispered.

The huntsman spiders that had been organizing near the door stopped their activities, turning simultaneously to face him. Their many sets of eyes reflected the cabin light, creating a sinister constellation of tiny dead stars aimed in his direction. But they didn't advance. If anything, they seemed to be... waiting.

Christopher raised his hand experimentally. The spiders nearest to the movement retreated slightly, maintaining their distance. He stepped toward his bathroom, and the arachnid army flowed around him, never breaking their unspoken rule about proximity.

The sound of his cabin door opening made him spin around, his reflexes overriding rational thought. But instead of the human visitor he'd expected, a flood of his newly-spawned spiders began pouring out of the room, spreading through the ship's corridors with the purposeful efficiency of an army that had just received marching orders.

They're not staying contained, he realized with heart-dropping horror. *They're spreading through the entire ship!*

But even as his rational mind cataloged the implications of what he was witnessing, another part of his consciousness was dragged backward through time to a memory he'd spent thirty-two years both trying to suppress and reliving daily. The memory clawed at him now with renewed urgency, as if the spiders surrounding him had torn open the carefully constructed barriers he'd built around his past.

Danny. Seven years old. Always following his big brother around, always wanting to help with Christopher's magic tricks, always so proud when the older kids paid attention to him. That gap-toothed smile, those freckles across the bridge of his nose, the way his eyes lit up whenever Christopher pulled a coin from behind his ear.

The memory unfolded with the particular vividness that trauma carved into consciousness, every detail preserved with crystalline clarity: the summer afternoon in their grandmother's attic, the musty smell of old furniture and forgotten belongings, the way sunlight slanted through dusty windows to illuminate their exploration of childhood treasures. He could still feel the rough wooden floorboards beneath his knees, the stifling heat that made their t-shirts stick to their backs, the excitement of discovery that hummed between them like electricity.

"Chris, look at this!" Danny's voice, bright with discovery, echoed across time. "It's like a magic trick box!" The sound of it made Christopher's chest constrict painfully, as fresh as if his brother were standing beside him now instead of being gone for over three decades.

The old steamer trunk, filled with their grandfather's belongings from his traveling salesman days, beckoned. Its brass latches had been tarnished with age, the leather straps cracked and peeling. And nested in one corner, behind a collection of sample cases and marketing materials, was a black widow with its distinctive red hourglass marking its abdomen. It had probably been living there undisturbed for months, spinning its chaotic web among the forgotten remnants of their grandfather's life.

Danny reaching in before Christopher could stop him, his small hand darting past Christopher's warning grasp. The spider, startled from its hiding place, biting in reflexive self-defense. Danny's small hand jerking back, a tiny puncture mark that didn't even hurt at first, just two minuscule dots that would change everything.

"It's okay, Chris. It's just a little spider. It probably got hurt more than I did," Danny had said, rubbing his hand and trying to be brave, not wanting his big brother to think he was a baby.

But it hadn't been okay. Over the next forty-eight hours, Christopher had seen his little brother die by degrees. The tissue around the bite turning black and spreading like a shadow consuming his small hand, Danny's confusion and pain growing as fever set in, their parents' panic as the local doctor struggled with a bite he'd never seen before. The frantic drive to the hospital two towns over. The specialists who arrived too late. The machinery that couldn't stop the inevitable.

Danny asking him, near the end, his voice thin and his eyes glassy with fever: "Chris, will you still do magic tricks for me when I get better? Promise you won't forget how to make the cards dance."

And Christopher, eleven years old and watching his world collapse, swallowing the lump in his throat: "Of course, Danny. I'll always do magic for you. The best tricks you've ever seen. I promise." A promise he'd kept, though his audience would never again include the one person he most wanted to impress.

There was no saving Danny. Christopher remembered watching the small oblong box go into the deep black hole, a disappearing act with no hope of return. The finality of that moment—earth striking polished wood, his mother's stifled sobs, his father's hand gripping his shoulder so tightly it nearly left bruises.

The memory dissolved as abruptly as it had formed, leaving him standing in his spider-infested cabin with tears on his face and the absolute certainty that whatever was happening aboard the *Pacific Dream* was connected to that childhood trauma in ways he was only beginning to understand. The spiders continued to maintain their distance, as if respecting the invisible boundary of his grief, or perhaps recognizing in him something kindred: a man who had spent his life trying to master the very thing that had destroyed it.

Survivor's guilt, he thought, naming the psychological weight that had driven every career decision, every performance, every self-destructive relationship of his adult life. *I've been trying to control death ever since Danny died. And now death is controlling me.*

A sound from the corridor made him turn.

Cleo Laveau stood in the doorway, her usually immaculate appearance slightly disheveled, her dark eyes wide with the particular combination of terror and comprehension that came from recognizing the full scope of a mistake. Her turban sat slightly askew on her head, several crystal necklaces tangled together at her throat, and her signature red lipstick was smudged at one corner, as though she'd been running her fingers over her mouth in distress.

"I saw them in the hallway," Cleo whispered, her eyes darting between him and the horror show of his cabin. "A line of them, marching like soldiers. I followed them here." She stepped inside, flinching as spiders parted around her feet. Her face drained of color as she took in the pulsing cocoons and suspiration of movement.

"Christopher," she choked out, her voice trembling with a vulnerability he'd never heard from the normally confident psychic, "I need to tell you what I did. What I *really* did. It was an accident, though... I was using an incantation that came to me out of nowhere. Words that I thought I was making up, just part of a binding ritual."

There she is, he thought, recognizing something in her expression that transcended her carefully constructed persona. *The real woman behind the mystical act. She's as terrified as I am.*

"I know what you did," he said quietly, his voice toneless with resignation. "The question is: can you undo it?"

Before Cleo could answer, movement in his peripheral vision caught his attention. His doves were huddled in their travel cage near the window, their usually smooth feathers ruffled, wings twitching nervously, their typical calm replaced by the particular agitation that prey animals displayed when predators were near. One of them was cooing with increasing urgency, a sound Christopher recognized from years of working with the birds—pure, instinctual alarm.

They don't deserve to die for my mistakes, he thought, moving toward the cage with hands that were steadier than they had any right to be. *They've never been anything but beautiful. Innocent participants in my illusions.*

He opened the cage door and gently coaxed the birds toward the cabin's porthole, which he'd opened to let in ocean air that now carried the scent of something that might have been fear or might have been death—a metallic tang that reminded him of the funeral home where they'd prepared Danny's small body.

"Go," he whispered to them, watching as they spread their wings and disappeared into the Pacific sky, brilliant white against endless blue. "Find somewhere safe, my dears."

As the doves vanished into the distance, becoming small specks and then nothing at all, Christopher felt something settle in him. Not peace, exactly, but a kind of acceptance. Whatever was going to happen aboard the *Pacific Dream*, at least some beautiful things would survive. Perhaps that was the only real magic he could perform now.

Behind him, Cleo began to speak, her voice carrying the weight of confessions that could no longer be contained. She twisted her hands in the fabric of her caftan, the sequins catching what little light filtered through the porthole.

"I think it was an unveiling ritual," she told him. "Not just words, but a ceremony that opens doorways between what is and what could be. I thought I was casting a simple curse, but I was actually performing an awakening, calling forth the collective consciousness that spiders have always possessed but rarely accessed. A shared awareness, coordinated purpose, that I thought would bind you to me."

Christopher nodded, but he wasn't ready to hear those explanations yet. He was still looking at the empty sky where his doves had disappeared, still feeling the weight of childhood guilt and adult responsibility, still coming to terms with the realization that his lifelong dance with death had finally found its rhythm. The spider tattoos on his arms seemed to be mocking his illusion of control.

Finally, he turned and looked at Cleo, who was still standing in his open doorway. She was looking back, as if expecting him to take control of the situation.

Somewhere in the ship's corridors, in the growing network of webs that was no doubt spreading through the *Pacific Dream's* infrastructure like a nervous system made of silk and intention, something vast and ancient and utterly unfamiliar was stirring to full consciousness for the first time in evolutionary history. Christopher knew it pulsed through the ship's corridors, sensing the vibrations of fear, tasting the air for the chemical signatures of human panic.

We are no longer alone, it might have thought, if it thought in ways human minds could comprehend. *We are no longer individual. We are collective. We are purpose. We are hunger. We are awakened.*

Christopher edged toward Cleo and the corridor, every nerve ending in his body blaring klaxon warnings. The spiders that filled his cabin moments ago had vanished, melting into crevices, slipping under doors, disappearing into ventilation grates. The sudden absence was almost more unsettling than their presence had been.

"Where did they go?" Cleo whispered, her voice tight with apprehension. She stood close enough that he could smell her signature fragrance—jasmine and something darker, muskier—mingling with her personal scent.

They moved together down the empty hallway. No passengers. No crew. No spiders. The ship's antiquated lighting cast wavering shadows across polished wood and brass fixtures, creating phantoms of movement where there was none.

"This isn't right," Christopher muttered. "There should be panic. Screaming. Something."

"Could they have been... hallucinations?" Cleo asked. "Maybe the spell created some kind of vision?"

Christopher ran his fingers along the doorway's edge, finding nothing. No silk strands. No egg sacs. No evidence of the arachnid army that had poured from his cabin.

"Your spell was real enough to multiply my ladies," he said. "I saw them, hundreds of them."

"So did I," Cleo affirmed.

"But where did they go? The air ducts? Between the walls?" He pressed his ear against a ventilation grate and heard nothing, not even the normal hum of the ship's systems. The silence felt pregnant with promise.

"Maybe they're hiding," she suggested, her confidence faltering. "Waiting for something."

The ship seemed to be holding its breath, as if the very structure was aware of what lurked within its depths.

"I didn't mean for this," Cleo whispered, wiping a tear from her cheek. "I'm so sorry."

Christopher didn't answer. He was staring at the ceiling, suddenly understanding.

The spiders weren't gone.

They were busy planning, spinning their webs.

CHAPTER 11

Mario Lombardi scowled at the gleaming stainless steel countertop where a black speck the size of a pinhead skittered across his *mise en place*. With steely determination, he brought his cleaver down, missing the arachnid by millimeters as it darted between his perfectly diced shallots.

"*Figlio di puttana*!" he cursed, flinging the blade into the sink with a clatter that made his sous chefs flinch. "That's the third one today."

The head chef's legendary temper was matched only by his fanatical dedication to kitchen cleanliness. For twenty years, he'd maintained five-star standards in floating kitchens across three cruise lines. The *Pacific Dream*'s theme might have tourists swooning over Victory gardens and ration-book cocktails, but Mario's kitchen operated like Swiss clockwork regardless of era.

"Chef, there's another one," his pâtissier called, pointing to a spider traversing the rim of a mixing bowl.

Mario snatched a towel and smashed it against the counter. When he lifted the cloth, there was nothing there.

"Matteo! Check the refrigerator. Something came aboard with the produce." He yanked open a cabinet, rifling through spice jars. "And call the exterminator. I want this kitchen fumigated tonight."

"We don't have an exterminator onboard, Chef," Matteo replied. "We're in the middle of the Pacific."

Mario's face reddened. "Then get me the captain. *Now*."

***

Ten minutes later, Captain Abercrombie pushed through the swinging doors, looking distinctly uncomfortable in the kitchen's humid heat. Beads of perspiration immediately formed on his forehead, and the starched collar of his uniform darkened with moisture. The cacophony of clattering pots and sizzling pans assaulted his ears as he navigated between bustling line cooks.

"What's the emergency, Lombardi?" Mac asked, tugging at his collar where it chafed against his reddening neck. The smell of parmesan cheese and reduced wine sauce permeated the air. "We've got three hundred passengers waiting for dinner service."

Mario pointed wordlessly to the far corner of the kitchen where a small cluster of spiders—perhaps a dozen—huddled near an air vent. Their dark bodies pulsed slightly, almost in unison, their spindly legs twitching with an unsettling synchronicity.

"Been trying to smash the little *bastardi* for an hour," Mario said, his hand tightening around the handle of a spatula. "They're too quick. Never seen spiders move like that. It's like they... anticipate the blow." The chef's voice dropped to a hush as he leaned closer to Mac. "You hear that clicking sound? That's them."

Mac leaned closer, squinting, the metal vent cool against his finger-tips as he braced himself. "Those look like—" He stopped himself, the words catching in his throat. His nostrils flared at the faint, unfamiliar musty odor emanating from the vent. "Probably came aboard with supplies at our last port."

"I've been whipping up my masterpieces on ships for nineteen years." Mario's Italian accent gelled with indignation, his breath hot and garlicky as he moved into Mac's personal space. "Never had an infestation mid-cruise. The way they move... the way they watch us..." He shuddered visibly, the overhead lights catching the sheen of his olive skin. "Something's not right."

The captain straightened, unconsciously hugging himself. "I'll have maintenance check the ventilation system. Probably nesting in there. Could be the heat attracting them."

"And tonight's dinner service?" Mario asked.

"Proceed as normal," Mac ordered, his voice leaving no room for argument, though his eyes darted briefly back to the writhing mass by the vent. The spiders seemed to pause, as if listening. "But if you see any more unusual activity, report it immediately. And Mario—" he lowered his voice to a gravelly whisper, "—keep this quiet for now."

As Mac left, he saw the chef return to his station, picking up a knife and pointing it at his staff. "Nobody speaks of this to the passengers," he warned. "Not one word."

***

Hector Shoemaker whistled tunelessly as he made his way through the maintenance corridors below deck. Twenty-three years at sea had taught him to navigate the labyrinthine passages of cruise ships by instinct. The *Pacific Dream* might dress up like a 1940s ocean liner, but underneath the vintage veneer, it was the same tangle of pipes and electrical systems as any other modern vessel. The stale, metallic-tinged air filled his nostrils as he ducked beneath a low-hanging conduit, the familiar smell of machine oil and sea salt a constant companion in these hidden arteries of the ship.

His radio crackled with static before a voice cut through. "Shoemaker, you copy? Captain wants ventilation checked in the main galley."

"Copy that," he replied, adjusting the volume on his handheld. "On my way to the central hub now." He patted the wrench in his pocket, a habit formed over decades of troubleshooting at sea.

The narrow corridor led him deeper into the ship's bowels, where the temperature rose and the constant thrum of engines vibrated through the metal walls. Perspiration prickled Hector's underarms as he navigated the claustrophobic passage, his small, deft hands occasionally brushing against the warm pipes overhead. His flashlight beam bounced off pipes and conduits until he reached the main ventilation junction, casting creepy shadows that gamboled across the utility space like phantom sailors.

Something caught his light. It was a silvery thread spanning the corridor at eye level, glistening with an unnatural sheen under his beam.

"What the hell?" he muttered, reaching up to brush it aside, his fingers extending toward the gossamer strand.

The thread stuck to his fingers, unexpectedly strong and adhesive. He pulled his hand back and found more threads clinging to his skin, stretching rather than breaking, wrapping around his wrist like living filaments. Pointing his flashlight upward, Hector froze, his breath hitching in his throat.

The ceiling was covered in webbing. Not the flimsy, individual webs of house spiders, but a complex, interconnected network that spanned the entire junction. The intricate architecture resembled something designed by an engineer rather than an arachnid, with support strands and cross-hatching that defied natural patterns. Suspended within the silken architecture were dozens of bulbous sacs, each about the size of a golf ball, their translucent surfaces pulsing with shadow movements inside.

Hector had seen enough nature documentaries to recognize egg sacs when he saw them, but nothing in his years at sea had prepared him for their sheer number and organization.

As he watched, transfixed with horror, one of the sacs pulsed slightly, its membrane stretching as something inside pressed against it.

"Control room," he said into his radio, his voice surprisingly calm despite the hammering of his heart. "We've got a situation in junction B-7."

Static answered him, punctuated by what sounded like tiny clicks.

"Control room, do you copy?" His thumb pressed harder on the transmit button, as if that might force his message through.

More static, then a brief burst of what sounded like chittering. A rapid, insectile sound that had no place on a ship's communication system.

Hector backed away slowly, his flashlight still trained on the ceiling, illuminating the horror above. Something moved within the webbing—a dark shape larger than any spider he'd seen before, its legs splayed wide as it navigated the web with predatory precision. Then another emerged from a shadowy recess, its abdomen swollen and glistening. And another, descending on an invisible thread directly in his path.

He turned and ran, boots clanging against the metal floor, the sound echoing through the corridors like a warning bell no one would hear.

***

Carlotta Cross consulted her clipboard as she strode through the *Starlight Ballroom*, where crew members were setting up for the evening's Glenn Miller tribute performance. Everything was moving precisely to schedule, just as she liked.

"The microphones need to be covered with vintage-style facades," she instructed a sound technician. "They're right behind the stage. Remember, it's all about the authentic experience, but with superior acoustics."

"Ms. Cross?" A nervous-looking junior steward approached, his hands fidgeting with the buttons of his period-correct uniform jacket. His cheeks were flushed. "There's been a... disturbance in the *Vista Lounge*."

"What kind of disturbance?" she asked sharply, already mentally cycling through her crisis management practices. Everything had its own specific response flowchart, and there was nothing she couldn't handle in short order.

"Some passengers saw spiders." He lowered his voice, glancing around as though the arachnids might be eavesdropping. "Not just one or two. Several. They're refusing to attend the afternoon tea dance. Mrs. Donovan is particularly upset; says she won't set foot in there even if Benny Goodman himself rose from the dead to play clarinet."

Carlotta sighed, pinching the bridge of her nose. Of all the ridiculous complaints she'd fielded on cruises—from social media withdrawal symptoms to midnight buffet disappointments to vacation romances gone spectacularly wrong—arachnophobia was hardly worth disrupting her carefully planned itinerary. Day three always had its challenges, but this seemed particularly trivial.

"Tell them we've had the area thoroughly checked," she said, straightening her aquamarine brooch with fussy rigor. "Emphasize that spiders are common on ships, completely harmless, and actually beneficial for controlling other insects. Perhaps throw in something about 'authentic 1940s pest control' if you think they'll appreciate the humor."

"But Ms. Cross," the steward persisted, shifting his weight uncomfortably from one foot to another, "they're saying these spiders are... unusual. Moving in formation, according to Mrs. Blacksmith. Like they're... coordinating."

Carlotta rolled her eyes, checking her pocket watch. "Moving in formation? Mrs. Blacksmith had three martinis at lunch. I saw her myself."

The employee hesitated, his eyes darting toward the corridor. "There's something else. The *Palm Court* is... well, there are webs. Lots of them. Johnson from housekeeping said he cleared the room at ten, and by one it looked like—" he searched for an appropriate description, "—like Halloween decorations gone wild."

This gave Carlotta pause. The *Palm Court* was scheduled for bridge tournaments all afternoon, with the semi-finals of the ship's duplicate bridge championship starting at five. If it was unusable, she'd need to reorganize quickly.

"Has anyone talked to the magician? What's his name—Webb? None of his spiders got loose, did they?" She recalled the performer's promotional materials mentioning exotic arachnids, though she'd been assured they were safely contained.

"Can't find him," the steward said, dabbing at his forehead with a handkerchief. "We've paged his cabin three times. But he's only got five on board, according to his manifest. These are... more. A lot more. And they're everywhere. Under tables, in the potted plants, even hanging from the chandeliers."

"Show me," she said decisively, abandoning her clipboard on a nearby table and straightening her shoulders. Whatever this was, she'd handle it with the same efficiency she applied to every cruise crisis.

The *Palm Court* was eerily silent when they arrived, devoid of the usual chatter of passengers and clinking of teacups. Gossamer strands stretched between potted palms, creating a delicate latticework that caught the afternoon sun streaming through the windows, casting intricate shadow patterns across the polished floor. Under different circumstances, Carlotta might have found it beautiful, like something from a fairy tale rather than a nightmare.

"This is... unusual," she admitted, keeping her voice neutral as she surveyed what should have been a bustling social hub transformed into an abandoned cobweb palace.

A movement caught her eye—a passenger peering anxiously through the doorway.

"Is the four o'clock bridge tournament still happening?" the elderly woman asked.

Carlotta's professional smile snapped into place. "We're relocating to the *Starboard Lounge*. A slight plumbing issue, nothing to worry about." She turned to the steward. "Rope this area off. Tell maintenance to clean it immediately. And not a word about spiders."

As she ushered the passenger away, Carlotta felt something brush against her ankle. She looked down to see a small brown spider scurry across her vintage heels and disappear under a table. For the first time in her career, Carlotta wondered if there was a contingency plan for this particular crisis.

CHAPTER 12

Captain Alastair Abercrombie leaned against the polished mahogany of the ship's bridge, scanning the latest incident report with a deepening frown. Three separate departments had flagged unusual spider sightings in the past six hours. Normally, he'd dismiss it as passenger hysteria, but the consistency troubled him.

"Blasted eight-legged menaces," he muttered, stroking his close-cropped beard.

He needed to find that magician.

Mac found Christopher Webb on the *Promenade Deck*, gazing out at the endless Pacific with an uncharacteristic stillness. The magician's hair caught the dappled light reflecting off the waves, making him look momentarily otherworldly.

"Mr. Webb," Mac said, forgoing his usual theatrical greeting. "A word?"

Webb turned, his customary smirk replaced by something guarded. "Captain. What can I do for you?"

"Your spiders. I understand they've gone missing."

Webb's expression flickered. "Not missing. Temporarily... relocated."

"Relocated," Mac repeated flatly. He raised a bushy eyebrow.

"A minor mishap during rehearsal. All five ladies are accounted for." Webb's fingers drummed against the railing. "Just not precisely where they should be."

"You understand that having venomous creatures loose on my ship—"

"I have everything under control." Webb straightened his cuffs, a nervous gesture at odds with his confident tone. "They're trained, Captain. They'll return to their enclosures when they're hungry."

Mac stepped closer, lowering his voice. "Five exotic spiders loose among over three hundred passengers isn't 'under control,' Mr. Webb. Show me where you last saw them."

He and Christopher stepped away from the railing and back into the ship's interior corridor.

A waiter balanced a tray of champagne flutes, nodding respectfully as they passed. Two elderly women in period-appropriate floral dresses compared brooches near the art deco bar. A young couple swayed to distant jazz music filtering through the ventilation system. No one seemed remotely concerned about arachnid invaders. The air smelled of polish and perfume, undercut with the faint brine of ocean water.

They moved through the ship's corridors, Webb occasionally pausing to peer behind decorative fixtures or beneath furniture. Mac watched him carefully, noting the magician's tense shoulders and darting eyes.

"Passengers are reporting dozens of spiders, not five," Mac said as they descended toward the entertainment level.

"Mass hysteria. One wealthy dowager screams about a daddy longlegs, and suddenly everyone's seeing tarantulas doing the backstroke in their martinis."

Mac stopped abruptly, causing Christopher to nearly collide with him.

"Listen here, Webb. I don't give a damn about your professional pride or whatever this is. My job is passenger safety, not coddling your ego."

Christopher's eyebrows shot up.

"I'm not questioning your expertise with these creatures, but that dismissive attitude? Save it for your stage persona. On my ship, we take every concern seriously, no matter how small... or eight-legged."

"Noted," Christopher said, dipping his head at the chastisement.

They checked service corridors, ventilation access points, and storage areas. Mac spotted a few common house spiders—inevitable on any vessel—but nothing exotic or threatening. No elaborate webs, no swarms, nothing to justify the growing unease among his crew. His mind flickered to the small cluster he'd seen in the kitchen, but he quickly dismissed the memory, as if merely thinking of it would tempt fate.

"See? Nothing to worry about," Webb said, his relief palpable. "My ladies are likely hiding in the walls. They'll come back when they're hungry."

Mac wasn't convinced. Either his staff was exaggerating wildly, or something stranger was happening. Neither option sat well with him.

As they headed back toward Webb's cabin, Roger Blacksmith approached from the opposite direction, his tweedy professor look perfectly aligned with the cruise's vintage aesthetic.

"Captain! Just the man I wanted to see." Blacksmith adjusted his wire-rimmed glasses. "Karen's quite upset about these spider sightings. She's lying down with a headache now, poor dear."

"We're addressing the situation, Mr. Blacksmith," Mac assured him.

"I told her not to worry. I spent decades studying invertebrates at the University of Oxford. If there were any significant arachnid presence, I'd have noticed." He chuckled, shaking his head. "A few escaped specimens hardly constitute an infestation."

"Your expertise is appreciated," Mac said, noting how Webb visibly relaxed at Blacksmith's dismissal.

But Mac couldn't shake his unease. Decades at sea had taught him to trust his instincts. Something wasn't right. The reports were too numerous, too specific. Either his ship had developed a shared spider hallucination, or the creatures were staying hidden.

Mac followed Webb and Blacksmith down the carpeted corridor, his unease growing with each step. "I want to see these terrariums myself," Mac said. "Proper containment is non-negotiable."

Webb sighed but nodded. "This way, Captain."

"Mind if I join?" Blacksmith asked, eyes bright with interest. "Professional curiosity."

Webb's suite was impeccably organized with props arranged in order of priority, performance attire hanging in garment bags. Five glass enclosures lined the long coffee table, illuminated by specialized heat lamps. Inside each terrarium, a spider rested in plain view.

"There. All present and accounted for," Webb said, gesturing with an exaggerated flourish. "Told you they'd come back when they got hungry."

Mac studied the creatures—the huntsman's long legs, the bird spider's imposing bulk, the recluse's violin-shaped marking. Something felt off. The spiders seemed... sentient. More alert. Watching.

"These all your specimens?" Mac asked.

"Of course," Webb answered too quickly.

Mac's radio crackled. "Captain, we need you in the galley. Urgent."

"Lock these in your room safe," Mac ordered. "No more performances until further notice."

As he turned to leave, Mac caught Webb exchanging a look with Blacksmith. Secretive, concerned. Whatever Webb was hiding, Mac would deal with it later.

* * *

Christopher stared at the terrariums after the captain left, an uncomfortable tightness in his chest. The spiders sat perfectly still, as if posing for inspection. Too perfectly still.

"Those aren't your spiders, are they?" Roger asked, leaning closer to the glass.

"No." Christopher's voice was barely audible. "I mean, they look identical, but..."

"But what?"

"Mine were definitely gone. These just... appeared before you and the captain followed me inside." Christopher ran his hand over his face and sighed. "And they're watching us."

Roger straightened, squinting through his spectacles. "Spiders don't 'watch' in the way you're suggesting. Their visual processing is entirely different from—"

"I know my ladies, Professor. I've worked with these specific specimens for years." Christopher tapped the glass of the huntsman's enclosure. The creature didn't flinch or retreat. It merely rotated slightly, keeping its many eyes fixed on him. "They're not behaving normally."

"Perhaps the stress of travel—"

"It's not that." Christopher lowered his voice. "Something's happened to them. Something... unnatural."

Roger's academic composure faltered. "What exactly are you suggesting?"

Christopher paced the room, weighing his options. The professor was a man of science, unlikely to believe in the reality of what Cleo had done. But he needed help. Specialized help.

"This will sound insane," Christopher began, "but I need to understand what's happening to these spiders after Cleo's spell."

Roger's laugh died when he saw Christopher's expression. "You can't be serious, old man."

"Cleo Laveau, the psychic performer. She was angry with me for flirting with Ellie Hargrove. She performed some ritual with a grimoire from New Orleans."

"A book doesn't have magical properties, Mr. Webb. It's paper and ink."

"I know how it sounds. I'm a magician. I deal in illusion, not actual magic." Christopher leaned against the wall. "But something happened. These aren't just spiders anymore. They're multiplying, changing."

Roger removed his glasses, polishing them nervously. "Even if I entertained this notion, what exactly would you have me do?"

"You're an invertebrate expert. I need to understand what they're capable of, how they might be communicating. If there's a scientific explanation—"

"There's always a scientific explanation," Roger interjected.

"Then help me find it." Christopher's voice took on an edge of desperation. "I'm worried about what might happen."

Roger replaced his glasses, considering the spiders with newfound unease.

"Perhaps they're not physically present at all," he mused. "Could they be some form of mass hallucination? The mind is susceptible to suggestion."

Christopher shook his head. "Maybe they're illusions," he agreed, clearly grasping at straws.

Roger studied the terrariums again, his studious curiosity visibly wrestling with skepticism. "I've admired your performances for years, you know. Very scientific in its way."

"I need that scientific mind now."

After a long pause, Roger sighed. "I'll help document their behavior patterns. Perhaps there's a biological agent causing these changes. A toxin or parasites?"

"Thank you." Christopher reached for his phone. "I need to call Cleo."

He dialed her cabin number, drumming his fingers nervously on the desk.

"Hello?" Her voice sounded small, frightened.

"It's Christopher. I need you to come to my suite. Now."

"I can't—"

"The spiders came back, Cleo. All five of them. Except... they're not mine. And Roger Blacksmith is here. He's an invertebrate biologist."

Silence stretched across the line.

"Cleo?"

"I'll be there in five minutes." Her voice trembled. "Christopher... I'm so sorry."

"Just get here. We need to figure out how to reverse whatever you did."

He hung up, turning to find Roger examining the Chilean recluse's terrarium with newfound intensity.

"Fascinating," the professor murmured. "They appear to be arranging the substrate into patterns."

Christopher looked closer. The tiny bits of soil and moss indeed formed an unmistakable spiral pattern.

"That's not fascinating," Christopher whispered. "That's terrifying."

CHAPTER 13

Captain Abercrombie had commanded vessels through typhoons that could swallow a city, navigated diplomatic waters more treacherous than any reef, and once talked down a drunken oil executive who'd threatened to throw himself overboard somewhere off the coast of Venezuela. But standing in his wheelhouse at 0900 hours, staring at reports that defied every rational principle of maritime operations, he found himself longing for something as straightforward as a natural disaster. The polished brass instruments surrounding him, normally a source of pride and security, now seemed like relics from another era and useless against whatever unholy mess was unfolding below decks.

The communication array crackled with fragments of hysteria from the dining room—a static that seemed to pulse with its own malevolent rhythm, punctuated by screams that cut off with disturbing abruptness. Mac adjusted his period-correct cap to better conceal his bald spot, a gesture that had become automatic after five years of this ridiculous, pretentious assignment, and tried to process information that his military experience insisted couldn't be accurate. His fingers pressed against the polished brim, betraying the tension his face refused to show.

Spiders. Emerging from a passenger's mouth. Jesus Christ.

"Bollocks, and bullshit," he muttered, his Scottish accent clotting with stress in a way that would have horrified the cruise line's authenticity consultants. The overhead lights flickered momentarily, casting strange shadows across the navigation charts.

Playing the jovial wartime captain for tourists who wanted to pretend the 1940s had been all swing music and heroic poses instead of rationing and death had been galling enough when the worst crisis involved seasick passengers and overpriced champagne complaints. Now, apparently, his theatrical command was facing something that belonged in a low-budget horror film rather than a luxury cruise itinerary. How quickly normalcy could dissolve into madness.

"Sir?" First Officer Patterson appeared at his elbow, her usually composed expression pinched with the strain of trying to maintain professional protocol while reality dissolved around them. Her uniform was slightly askew, a strand of auburn hair escaping from beneath her hat. "The dining room situation is... escalating. Should we initiate emergency procedures? People are—" she lowered her voice, "—panicking, Captain."

Mac looked at her—really looked. Patricia Patterson had been with *Pacific Dream* for two years, a competent officer who'd adapted to the cruise line's stagey requirements better than many. She spoke the staccato vernacular fluently, handled passenger complaints with period-appropriate charm, and had never once broken character during the most challenging situations. She'd once maintained her composure during a kitchen fire that threatened to spread to the passenger cabins, directing the evacuation with calm efficiency while never dropping her affected Mid-Atlantic accent.

Now she was staring at him with undisguised terror, waiting for orders that would make sense of the senseless. Her right hand kept twitching toward her neck, as though checking for something crawling there.

"What exactly are we dealing with, Patterson?" Mac asked, moving toward the navigation console, needing the familiar solidity of its metal edge beneath his palm. "Give me facts. Not speculation, not rumors. Facts."

"Sir, I've seen the footage from Miss Batiste's camera. She filmed it all…" Patterson paused, swallowing hard, her throat working visibly with the effort. "One of the passengers in the dining room appeared to be choking during the breakfast service. When Bonita, the waitress, attempted the Heimlich maneuver, spiders—dozens of them—were, er, ejected from the man's mouth. They scattered across the dining room floor, up the walls, across the ceiling. He died, sir… right there between the Belgian waffle station and the omelet bar."

"Who was this man?" Mac demanded, his knuckles rosy against the console as he fought to maintain his composure. The ship seemed to lurch beneath him, though the sea was calm.

"Umm, I'm not sure… can't remember, umm…" Patterson babbled, shaking her head in shock and disbelief. Her carefully maintained subordinate demeanor was crumbling further with each word. "Spiders… how… were they in his food? Were they eggs or something?" She looked queasy, and there was a sheen of fear glossing her eyes, catching the light from the wheelhouse windows.

Mac felt something cold roosting in his stomach—the particular dread that came from recognizing that familiar operational parameters no longer applied. It was the same sensation he'd felt during a storm off the Horn of Africa, when he'd realized the navigation systems had failed completely and they were sailing blind toward a coral reef.

During his Royal Navy years, he'd learned that the most dangerous situations were always the ones where normal protocols became not just ineffective, but potentially catastrophic. This felt worse, as though the very laws of nature had been upended.

"Current passenger count?" he demanded, forcing himself to focus on concrete numbers, on the tangible responsibilities of command rather than the impossible horror unfolding below.

Patterson swallowed, and composed herself with visible effort. These were questions she could answer, a lifeline of normality in the churning sea of madness. "Three hundred and twelve guests, forty-seven crew members. All accounted for as of last night's manifest check, though I can't confirm current status given the communication disruptions."

"Communications status?"

"Satellite uplink is intermittent. Ship-to-shore radio is producing mostly static. Internal communication systems are..." She paused again, clearly struggling with the impossibility of what she was reporting. "They appear to be compromised, sir. We're receiving signals from various sections of the ship, but they're not coming from crew members."

Not coming from crew members. Mac filed that particular bit of impossibility away for later consideration. First things first: assess the scope of the crisis, establish communication with unaffected areas of the ship, implement containment protocols.

"Right," he said, moving toward the ship's internal communication panel. He raised the speaker to his lips. "All hands, this is Captain Abercrombie. We have a medical emergency in the main dining room. All passengers are to return to their cabins immediately and await further instructions. Crew members report to your section supervisors for emergency assignments."

The response was immediate... and horrifying. Instead of the usual crisp acknowledgments from various departments, what emerged from the speakers was a cacophony of static, screaming, and something that sounded disturbingly like chittering—a dry, clicking noise that seemed to multiply and echo through the command center's acoustics with unnatural persistence.

"Sir," Patterson's voice had dropped to a whisper, her typically composed bearing crumbling as her trembling finger extended toward the surveillance station, "look at the security monitors."

Mac turned to the bank of screens that provided visual surveillance of the ship's public areas. These cameras were discretely concealed behind fixtures to maintain the vintage veneer, brass-rimmed portholes and ornamental moldings that kept the '40s fantasy alive for paying customers who wanted the full immersive experience. What he saw made his naval training clash violently with his understanding of biological possibility, decades of military discipline warring against the inherent instinct to flee.

The dining room was empty of human life, but it wasn't empty. Hundreds—possibly a thousand—of spiders covered every surface, moving in patterns that hurt to watch directly. A headache surged behind his eyes. The arachnids flowed across walls, over tables, through ventilation grates, all with a coordination that suggested not just intelligence but *purpose*. The elegant chandeliers swayed slightly as arachnids dangled from silken threads, while others arranged themselves in concentric circles around abandoned plates of half-eaten breakfast pastries. Some appeared to be communicating through strange movements, like a grotesque semaphore system that Mac couldn't—and didn't want to—decipher.

And they were spreading. Through every doorway, every crack in the woodwork, every seam in the ship's infrastructure, a writhing tide of eight-legged horror advancing methodically through the *Pacific Dream*'s confined spaces, claiming territory with terrifying efficiency.

The security feed from C-deck showed passengers running toward their cabins while spiders poured through the hallway's air vents like living liquid. B-deck's cameras revealed crew members fleeing through corridors as the ship's lighting systems flickered in patterns that seemed to match the spiders' movements.

They're in the electrical systems, Mac realized with growing distress. *They're not just infesting the ship. They're taking control of it.*

"Patterson, we need to access the passenger phone vault. If we can't communicate with the outside world through normal channels, we need to get to the passengers' personal devices."

Mac checked the security feed for D-deck and felt his blood turn to ice water colder than the Mariana Trench. The corridor leading to the vault was carpeted with spiders—not randomly scattered, but arranged in defensive formations that looked like a drill team. They formed concentric rings around the vault door, with what appeared to be larger specimens stationed at strategic intervals like sentries. Some clung to the ceiling directly above the approach, positioned for an ambush that would shower down on anyone foolish enough to attempt passage.

As if they know exactly what we're trying to access, he thought.

He frantically toggled through the security feeds, checking the other decks. Bizarrely, they seemed completely free of danger. Corridors empty, public spaces clear. The infestation was concentrated exclusively on areas that were the most crucial: the engine room, communications center, and now the vault containing the passengers' phones. The tactical intelligence behind this selective occupation sent a chill through Mac's military-trained mind.

The ship's intercom crackled to life with a burst of static that made everyone in the wheelhouse jump, the harsh sound scraping against their eardrums like sandpaper. But instead of human voices, what emerged was something that might have been speech processed through frequencies that human vocal cords couldn't produce. It sounded almost like chittering transformed into words—clicks and hisses arranged in patterns too structured to be noise. The sound vibrated through the metal panels of the wheelhouse, making the floor beneath their feet hum with an unnatural resonance.

"Sir," Patterson grabbed his arm, her fingernails digging through his uniform sleeve with enough pressure to leave half-moon imprints on his skin, her voice high with panic, the warm puff of her breath against his ear, "are they trying to *communicate* with us?"

The air in the wheelhouse had grown thick and stale, carrying the faint metallic tang of fear and the musty scent of arachnid bodies, like dust and copper pennies mixed together.

Before Mac could answer, the lights went out with a decisive snap that felt eerily intentional rather than mechanical. The sound echoed with finality, like a judge's gavel. Darkness swallowed the wheelhouse whole, bringing with it a silence so profound they could hear the soft, almost imperceptible patter of countless tiny legs moving across surfaces all around them.

Emergency lighting kicked in immediately, bathing the wheelhouse in inferno red. The crimson glow transformed familiar faces into ghoulish masks of terror. But even in the bloodied illumination, Mac could see movement through the windows—spiders on the glass, hundreds of them.

"Sir?" Patterson's voice seemed to come from very far away, hollow and echoing as if traveling through a long, winding tunnel before reaching his ears. "What do we do?"

Mac looked at her, this competent officer who was clearly experiencing genuine panic, and realized that none of his training—naval, maritime, theatrical—had prepared him for a situation where the ship itself had become the enemy. Her face, usually composed and pleasant, now contorted with naked fear in the emergency lighting, sweat beading along her hairline and catching the red glow like droplets of blood.

"Where the hell is that goddamned magician?" Mac bellowed, his Scottish brogue making the curses that much more damning. The ship lurched slightly beneath them, and he grabbed the edge of the console to steady himself. "Patterson, was he there in the dining room this morning? That Spider-Mage charlatan must know more than he's letting on."

"I don't know... I, I... didn't see him," she replied, her eyes darting to the shadows that seemed to writhe and pulse in the corners of the wheelhouse. "What do we do?" she repeated, voice cracking on the final word.

"We try to regain control of our ship," Mac said with a forceful conviction he didn't entirely feel, though even as he spoke the words, he could feel something changing in his own physiology. A tingling in his extremities spread upward from his fingertips like needles flowing through his veins, a subtle alteration in his visual perception that suggested his confident assessment of the situation might be compromised by factors he hadn't yet identified. The control panels before him seemed to undulate slightly, the dials and switches breathing in and out with a life of their own, while the distant chittering sound began to form patterns that almost—impossibly—made sense to him.

When did I get bitten? The thought emerged from nowhere, slicing through Mac's consciousness with alarming clarity, accompanied by the sudden realization that the small puncture wound on his neck, which he'd dismissed as a mere shaving nick that morning, was beginning to burn with an intensity that felt distinctly un-razor-like. The skin around it had tightened, pulling taut across his weathered flesh, throbbing with each beat of his increasingly rapid pulse.

The world tilted slightly beneath his feet, the wheelhouse seeming to contract and expand with his breathing. Colors became more vivid, the green indicator lights on the control panel suddenly glowing with an almost radioactive intensity, the brass fixtures gleaming with impossible warmth. Sounds took on harmonic qualities that human ears shouldn't be able to detect—the distant hum of the engines below decks transformed into a complex symphony of mechanical whispers, while the warble of the spiders evolved into something that resembled language.

And somewhere in the growing chaos of altered perception, Mac began to understand with horrifying clarity that the spiders weren't just taking control of the ship. His fingers quivered as they hovered over the emergency communications panel, his mind struggling to form coherent thoughts through the rapidly spreading venom.

They were taking control. *One bite at a time.* The phrase echoed in his mind with terrible significance as his hand unconsciously drifted toward the holstered service pistol at his hip, his fingers finding the cool metal with an intimacy that felt predetermined, inevitable.

CHAPTER 14

Olivia leaned against the cool, polished railing of the upper deck, the salty air rushing past her face in a brisk caress, a futile attempt to shake off the lingering dread that clung to her like a second skin.

The tang of the ocean filled her nostrils, mingling with the faint scent of sunscreen and the distant aroma of fresh pastries wafting in from the dining room. Yet, the beautiful surroundings felt utterly discordant with the chaos she had just witnessed. The flashes of horror played on a loop in her mind like a twisted film reel, each frame more revolting than the last.

The camera hung heavily in her hands, its weight a stern reminder of the terrifying scene she had been forced to confront. She raised it instinctively, framing the scene before her through the viewfinder, her breath shallow as she focused. The bright sky loomed overhead, an expanse of blue punctuated only by the faintest glimmers of stubborn morning stars, all dimmed by an eerie fog that seemed to rise from the ocean itself—a ghostly shroud, as if it, too, had succumbed to the madness unfolding below.

She replayed the appalling events in the camera, each detail fresh and vivid: Colby White, a quiet man who had mostly kept to himself throughout the cruise, had sat at his table enjoying breakfast, the sun casting a warm glow upon him as he took a bite of his croissant. She steadied her breath, the taste of bile rising in her throat, as she zoomed in, forcing herself to relive each moment, each heartbeat.

Olivia had been seated at the table adjacent to Mr. White, her camera lens discreetly capturing the ambiance of the dining room. The morning sunshine, finding its way through a hole in the ocean fog, poured in through the grand windows, casting a buttery hue over the patrons as they reveled in the nostalgia of the old-fashioned menu. She observed Colby through the viewfinder, barely paying him any attention as he chewed slowly on his flaky, jam-slathered bread, his gaze drifting over the other passengers, their laughter rising and falling like a symphony of carefree mirth, completely oblivious to the darkness that was about to descend upon them.

Through the camera's eye, Olivia watched as Colby's expression morphed into one of bewilderment. His hands flew to his throat, fingers clawing at the skin in a frantic, instinctual gesture. The fear that gripped him was palpable, etched across his features. His eyes, wide and bulging, searched the room for help, reflecting the stark realization that the laughter would soon be replaced by shrieks of horror.

As the seconds ticked by, the transformation of the scene was swift and brutal. The joyous sounds of conversation and clinking cutlery were abruptly silenced, replaced by a jangling stillness as people began to take notice. Olivia's heart pounded in her chest, a staccato rhythm that matched the growing sense of dread enveloping the room. She knew, with a sinking certainty, that the tranquil breakfast setting was about to become a theater of nightmares, and her camera, a mute witness to the unfolding terror. She wanted to do something, but she was frozen with uncertainty.

"Help!" Colby's stifled cry sent ripples of panic through Olivia's entire body. She felt each heartbeat thud like a bongo against her ribs.

A waitress rushed forward, face drawn tight with concentration as she prepared for what came next. Olivia could feel every set of eyes glued to them, the way tension crackled in the air like static before a storm.

"Come on," Olivia whispered under her breath as she watched the tiny moving picture, as if willing Colby to get through it this time, as if she hadn't seen him die just minutes before.

The waitress sprang into action. She wrapped her arms around Colby's slender waist, her fingers digging into the fabric of his vintage attire. With a swift, upward motion, she hoisted him off the ground, her movements precise and fueled by an urgent desperation that suffused the air. With her free hand, she loosened his bowtie. Olivia could hear the sharp, sudden exhale that escaped the savior's lips, a sound that seemed to encapsulate the fear and hope of everyone present. The room fell into a tense hush, every pair of eyes fixed on the unfolding drama, every breath bated in dreadful anticipation.

In the pregnant silence that followed, something unthinkable occurred. From Colby's O-shaped lips, a dark projectile erupted with the force of a cannonball, hurtling into the crowd. The passengers recoiled as one, their faces contorted in shock and revulsion, as if they had been lashed by an invisible whip. A cacophony of gasps ricocheted around the dining room, the sound amplified by the grandeur of the art deco space. People scrambled away from their tables, their chairs clattering to the floor in their haste to escape the unknown menace.

Then, as if an otherworldly tap had been turned, spiders began to spew from Colby's open mouth in a relentless, writhing torrent. The creatures cascaded onto the floor, their small, skeletal bodies glistening under the chandeliers' light. A wave of tiny legs scuttled across the polished wood, a nightmarish flood that defied all rational explanation. The sight was so surreal, so at odds with the world as they knew it, that for a moment, the onlookers could only stare in abject horror.

The spiders, driven by an uncanny instinct, began to converge, their individual skittering sounds merging into a single, ominous rustle. They moved with purpose, their eight legs pistoning and multiple eyes gleaming with a malevolent intelligence that was neither natural nor welcome.

The elegant dining room, once filled with laughter and the clink of silverware, had been transformed into a chamber of horrors, its opulence now a backdrop for a living hell. The reality of their predicament settled upon the passengers like napalm, white-hot with despair and the creeping realization that their floating paradise had become a vessel of death, each shadow a potential lair for the venomous invaders.

Olivia captured it all—the frantic movements, people screaming and jumping onto chairs or scrambling toward any exit they could find. She didn't stop filming even when Colby fell forward, lifeless on the floor amid writhing creatures that scuttled over him without care.

He looked peaceful for just a moment before his slack lips twitched violently; his body convulsed beneath them. The spasms came in waves, each more violent than the last, his limbs jerking with such force that his heels drummed against the polished floor. His eyes bulged unnaturally from their sockets, bloodshot and unseeing as they rolled back to reveal only whites. Foam gathered at the corners of his mouth, tinged with a sickening pink that indicated internal bleeding. The veins in his neck and forehead protruded like twisted ropes beneath his skin, which had taken on an ashen pallor that seemed to drain of color with each passing second.

Those nearest to him backed away in repulsion, their vintage attire meant to evoke bygone glamour, now a macabre contrast to the modern nightmare unfolding before them. The man's bow tie had come completely undone during his seizure, hanging limply around his collar like a defeated flag, while his carefully pomaded hair had become disheveled, strands sticking to his clammy forehead.

The convulsions continued relentlessly as tiny dark shapes scurried away from his body, disappearing into the shadows beneath tables and behind the ornate woodwork of the dining room. Their mission complete, the arachnid assassins retreated, leaving their victim to suffer the full effects of their unnaturally potent venom.

Olivia turned away from that table as if stepping back would shield her from what had just transpired. She lowered the camera slightly but kept filming, capturing people shouting over one another as they turned on each other, accusations flying like daggers across the opulent dining room. Her fingers slipped against the viewfinder, but some compulsion kept her recording, documenting the swift descent into chaos as the poisonous panic spread faster than the spiders themselves.

"It was you! You brought this on us!" A man shouted at another who stood frozen in shock. His face had contorted into an ugly visage of fear and fury, spittle flying from his lips as he jabbed an accusatory finger. His period-perfect fedora had been knocked askew, and his carefully waxed mustache was coming loose.

"No! I didn't do anything!" The accused man stumbled back against a wall lined with portholes that offered no solace now, only reminders of how trapped they were amidst this spiraling ordeal. His complexion had gone ashen, eyes darting frantically around the room as if searching for an escape that didn't exist. The brass fixtures of the portholes gleamed coldly behind him, framing circular views of endless ocean that seemed to taunt everyone aboard with their isolation.

"It's that magician! He brought those spiders onboard." A woman in a satin caftan shouted as she pointed toward the door that led to the stage. "The Amazing Spider-Mage—what did you expect with a name like that? He's responsible for this!"

The fracas intensified as more passengers joined in, their period costumes now disheveled, transforming the elegant breakfast into something that resembled a mob scene. Coffee mugs and crystal juice glasses toppled from tables, shattering against the floor as people pushed and shoved. Someone knocked over a silver candelabra, sending flames dancing dangerously close to the velvet curtains as the crowd's hysteria built to a fever pitch that matched the dying man's convulsions.

Olivia felt sweat trickle down her back as she clutched tightly to the camera for some semblance of control amid chaos.

She needed fresh air, some distance from all this madness, and bolted up to the upper deck where shadows enveloped everything except for ghostly shapes below swarming toward safety or salvation—or something darker lurking just out of sight.

On deck, wind whipped through her hair and pulled at her clothes while sunlight shimmered across waves lapping at the hull like whispers filled with secrets long buried beneath murky depths. The vast expanse of ocean stretched endlessly before her, deceptively serene against the horror unfolding within the *Pacific Dream*'s ornate confines. Salt spray misted her face, momentarily washing away the lingering sensation of panic that clung to her skin like cobwebs.

She heard footsteps, deliberate and measured, crunching against the polished teak. Someone had followed her. Her heart lurched painfully in her chest as the sound paused, then resumed. Closer now. The silence between each step stretched like an eternity, each footfall landing with terrible precision. Was it a passenger seeking refuge, or something more sinister? The hair on her neck bristled with warning as shadows shifted unnaturally at the edge of her vision. She dared not turn around immediately, frozen by the terrible possibility of what—or who—might be stalking her across the abandoned deck.

Olivia let out a sigh of relief.

It was the First Officer, Patricia Patterson, her crisp, spotless uniform a stark contrast to the chaos below decks. "Hi-de-ho!" the woman saluted with practiced charm, maintaining the 1940s character that now seemed grotesquely inappropriate. "What happened, doll?"

Olivia couldn't speak.

"Someone said you filmed it?" Patricia pressed. "The whole ghastly business?" Her eyes betrayed genuine concern beneath the affected vernacular.

Olivia nodded, throat too constricted with emotion to form words, and silently held the camera up so the officer could see the video. Her fingers were clumsy as she navigated back to the footage, revealing the horrific scene that had unfolded moments before: bodies convulsing, spiders skittering across skin, the unmistakable moment when life drained from a man's eyes.

Patricia's face went pale, the carefully applied rouge standing out starkly against her suddenly ashen complexion. She put her hands on the camera, manicured fingers gripping the device with unexpected force. "I need to take this. Show it to the captain," she insisted. "This isn't some shipboard entertainment gone wrong—this is... something else entirely."

Instinctively protecting her content, Olivia jerked back with unexpected force. "No—wait—" The camera slipped from her hands and clattered across the deck, spinning wildly on the polished surface, capturing fragmented images of sky and sea and panicked faces.

The boat lurched violently, riding a massive wave that seemed to rise from nowhere, and the camera slid inexorably toward the edge. Both women lunged for it simultaneously, fingers grasping at empty air as the device slipped through the ornate railing into the sea with a distant, significant splash, taking with it the only evidence of what had truly happened below.

Patricia got to her feet and straightened her uniform, the veneer of deference completely gone. "I'll alert the captain immediately. Don't leave the deck." She turned on her heel and marched away, her footsteps echoing with purpose across the wooden planks.

Olivia gripped the railing, knuckles blanched against the cold brass. She leaned over, scanning the churning waters below. The sun, fighting through banks of fog, caught on something—a flash of metal? Her heart leapt. Maybe the camera strap had caught on an outcropping or decorative molding along the hull.

"Please, please, please," she whispered, stretching farther over the edge. The content couldn't be lost. Not now. Not when she was up to a million followers.

The ship rolled gently beneath her feet as she leaned out, squinting against the glare. There it was again—a glint of something reflective dancing between the waves. If she could just see better...

A tickle on her calf, light as a feather, sent a shiver up her spine. Olivia froze, the sensation triggering an instinctual dread that radiated from her core to her fingertips.

She looked down.

Against the pale skin of her leg, just above where her black and yellow playsuit ended, sat a small spider. Its body was compact and fuzzy, with distinct forward-facing eyes that seemed to study her with unnerving intelligence. A jumping spider. One of Christopher's, no doubt.

The creature paused, legs shifting slightly as it oriented itself. Those eyes—so many eyes—fixed on her face.

Olivia's breath caught in her throat.

The spider tensed, front legs lifting imperceptibly.

It leapt.

Olivia shrieked, her hand swinging wildly to intercept the arachnid hurtling toward her face. Her palm connected with nothing but air as her momentum carried her forward. The brass railing, slick with morning dew and ocean spray, slid beneath her grip.

Her gut lurched as gravity took hold.

For one suspended moment, Olivia hung in space, the ship's white hull sliding past her field of vision. Her fingers clutched desperately at the air where the railing had been, finding nothing to arrest her fall.

She screamed, the sound torn away by the wind rushing past her ears. The blue-green water rushed up to meet her with terrifying speed.

The impact knocked the breath from her lungs with a dull, hollow thud. Ice-cold water enveloped her, the shock of it paralyzing her muscles as thousands of needles seemed to pierce her skin simultaneously. Her vintage fabric, so stylish on deck, now dragged her down like anchors, the once-light material becoming a sodden prison against her limbs. Salt water flooded her nose and mouth as she gasped involuntarily, burning her sinuses and coating her tongue with a harsh, briny taste that made her gag.

Olivia kicked frantically, fighting to reach the surface, her water-logged tennis shoes scraping against nothing but more endless ocean. Her ears popped painfully under pressure before her head finally broke through the waves with a rushing sound, and she gulped air, her throat raw as she screamed again, louder this time, the sound tearing from her lungs. "Help! HELP ME! SOMEBODY, PLEASE!" Her plea broke as the wind carried it away, the roar of the ocean nearly drowning her desperate cries.

Her voice echoed across the empty expanse. The *Pacific Dream* continued its stately progress, oblivious to her plight. No heads appeared at the railing, no alarms sounded. Everyone was below decks, dealing with the horror she'd just escaped.

A massive wave crashed over her head with the force of a freight train, sending Olivia tumbling beneath the surface again. The salt water churned and twisted her body like a rag doll in a washing machine, disorienting her completely as her sodden clothing wrapped around her limbs like seaweed. She fought desperately against the current, her lungs burning for air, her arms and legs flailing in panic as she clawed her way back toward the distant shimmer of light above. After what felt like an eternity, she broke through to the surface, spluttering and choking, expelling seawater from her nose and mouth in violent, painful heaves.

Something touched her face then—not water, not the sting of salt or spray, but something solid. Something with purpose. Something with legs.

The jumping spider, no larger than a dime but somehow impossibly present, clung to her eyelid with preternatural tenacity. Its tiny body remained completely dry despite the churning ocean all around them, defying all laws of nature and physics. Eight beady eyes, arranged in perfect symmetry, stared directly into her pupil with an intelligence that no arachnid should possess. Its front legs were raised delicately, almost daintily, as if in formal greeting or perhaps in a gesture of ultimate triumph.

Olivia's scream died in her throat as another wave crashed over her. The last thing she saw was those multiple eyes, studying her with cold curiosity as the water closed over her head, pulling her down into the vast, uncaring deep.

The spider remained, impossibly, clinging to her eyeball as darkness swallowed her whole.

CHAPTER 15

C leo had spent three years perfecting the art of reading people's desperation, but standing in what had once been the *Pacific Dream's* elegant *Golden Parlor*, she found herself confronting varieties of human panic that transcended her professional experience. The room had become an impromptu war council where the veneer of old-school civility had gone completely, revealing the primitive survival instincts that lurked beneath every passenger's carefully curated cruise persona.

Funny, she thought with the dark humor that had kept her sane through decades of disappointment, *how quickly people abandon their fantasies when reality starts biting back.*

Just moments earlier, Cleo sat cross-legged on the floor of her opulent suite, surrounded by scattered papers covered in half-formed incantations and hasty sketches of arcane symbols. The grimoire lay open before her, its yellowed pages revealing nothing new despite her desperate searching.

Her fingers traced the worn leather binding as memories of yesterday flooded back.

The Spider-Mage's stage confidence had crumbled as he paced, his hands shaking whenever he glanced at the glass enclosures that once housed his eight-legged performers. The way the spiders had returned to their cages after their first disappearance, arranging themselves in perfect geometric patterns, watching with an unsettling combined intelligence, had shattered something fundamental in him.

"They're not just multiplying," he'd whispered to her through tight lips. "They're evolving."

Roger Blacksmith, the retired entomologist who'd been aboard for his fiftieth wedding anniversary, had examined the specimens with academic detachment that seemed almost offensive given the circumstances.

"Impossible," he'd muttered. "Spiders are solitary predators, not hive-minded creatures."

"It's the spell," Cleo had admitted, her voice cracking. She turned to Roger. "I did this."

Christopher's face had darkened then, not with anger but with a grief so profound it made her chest ache. He'd sunk into an armchair, eyes fixed on some distant point.

"Maybe it wasn't just you," Christopher had sighed. "I have a dark shadow on my soul." He'd paused, then said, "My brother Danny was seven when it happened. We were exploring our grandparents' attic." Christopher's voice had grown flat and hollow. "Black Widow's nest. I knew there were spiders in there; I'd seen one earlier. But I forgot to warn him."

Cleo remembered how his fingers had twisted together, knuckles bloodless.

"The venom... it was too much for his little body. I watched him die, inch by inch, over three days. That's why I started collecting them, training them. Controlling them." A bitter laugh had escaped him. "Some control I have now."

Roger had cleared his throat awkwardly. "If this truly is... supernatural in origin, then perhaps the solution must be as well. What exactly did your ritual involve?"

Cleo closed her eyes now, trying to recall every detail she'd shared with them. The words spoken in anger, jealousy coating her tongue like the remnants of a bitter pill.

"Reversal spells typically require symmetry," she'd told them. "The components used must be inverted or purified. But I just made up this incantation... I didn't think it would actually do anything. I don't even remember exactly what I said."

Cleo's gaze drifted to the small pile of items she'd gathered: a piece of Christopher's costume, a lock of her own hair, candle stubs from the ship's dining room. Pathetically inadequate tools for undoing catastrophe.

She needed her phone. Needed to research proper counterspells. Needed to contact real practitioners. But the phones remained locked in the ship's vault, surrounded by writhing masses of venomous guardians.

"Think, Cleo," she muttered, pressing her palms against her temples. The spell had activated during a full moon. Did that matter? She'd channeled jealousy and rage. Was that something she could tap into now?

The answer was here somewhere, hidden in plain sight like a spider in the corner of a room, waiting for the right moment to drop.

A scream shattered Cleo's concentration, high-pitched and primal. Not the performative shriek of someone startled by a spider sighting, but the raw sound of genuine terror.

She abandoned her makeshift altar, stumbling toward her cabin door. She slipped into her shoes and slammed the door behind her. The ship's hallway lights blinked, casting nervous shapes across the faded art deco carpet. The air felt thick with humidity and something else—a musty, almost metallic scent she couldn't place.

"Get it off! GET IT OFF!" A man's voice, brittle with panic.

Cleo's feet moved instinctively toward the commotion. The ship listed slightly to port, making her brace against the wall. Beneath her palm, she felt a faint vibration, rhythmic, like thousands of tiny legs moving in unison somewhere within the bulkhead.

More voices joined the first, shouting, cursing, and the unmistakable sound of furniture being overturned. Something shattered. Glass? Metal?

Christopher and Roger joined Cleo in the hallway.

"East wing," Christopher said, pointing toward a fresh volley of screams. "Something's happening."

"We need to split up," Cleo suggested, surprising herself with her steady voice. "Cover more ground."

"Engine room for me," Roger nodded. "If they've gotten into the machinery..."

Cleo swallowed hard. "I'll head toward that ruckus."

Christopher touched her arm. "Okay. I'll check the ballroom. If my guess is right, the ventilation shafts there connect to most of the ship."

They exchanged glances. No goodbyes, no good lucks, just silent acknowledgment that they might not all return.

The corridor ahead remained empty, but a crowd had gathered around a corner, their backs to her. Between shifting shoulders and heads, Cleo caught glimpses of frantic movement. The ship's intercom system crackled to life, then died with an ominous pop.

The crowd parted momentarily, and Cleo's breath caught in her throat.

The Lichtenstein twins were having what could generously be called a philosophical disagreement near the main bar, their usual brotherly bickering elevated to something approaching genuine hostility by the particular stress that came from being trapped in a floating nightmare with no clear exit strategy.

"We have to get to the lifeboats," Arthur was insisting, his wheelchair positioned strategically between his brother and the room's various exits. "Whatever's happening here, we can't fight it. We need to evacuate. Now!"

Arnold, standing behind his brother's chair, shook his head with stubborn determination. "The lifeboats are compromised," he said. "I saw the webs myself. They're not just blocking the exits—they're *guarding* them. As if whatever's controlling these things doesn't want us to leave."

"So what's your brilliant alternative?" Arthur snapped, spinning his wheels to face his brother directly. "We stay here and wait for them to pick us off one by one? We're performers, Arnold, not action heroes. We do illusions, not actual magic."

Illusions versus magic, Cleo thought, recognizing the distinction that had haunted her own transformation. *The difference between pretending to touch the impossible and actually succeeding.*

"Maybe there's still equipment we can use," Arthur continued, clearly seeking practical solutions. "Stage effects, pyrotechnics, anything that might give us an advantage. I'll bet they have all that stuff backstage, if we can reach it."

"That's suicide," Arthur said flatly. "Those corridors are crawling with—"

"Okay, then. We'll get the captain and get him to send up SOS flares."

"He was bitten, you know that. Dr. Hand said..."

Arthur was interrupted by movement in the shadows near the service entrance. Something small and dark detached itself from what had appeared to be empty wall space, moving with the erratic, jerky patterns that Cleo was learning to associate with huntsman spiders on reconnaissance missions. The creature tiptoed across the ornate molding, its eight legs barely touching the surface, leaving invisible trails of silk that caught the dim emergency lighting when it shifted.

She realized Arthur saw it too, his eye catching the movement with a gasp. His face—once animated for audiences of thousands—now contorted with germinal fear. He reached toward the shadow, perhaps thinking he could brush away what he hoped was merely a trick of light, his fingers trembling with a slight palsy.

The spider moved faster than human reflexes could track, a blur of motion that ended with Arthur jerking his hand back, a small mound already beginning to swell on his palm. Two tiny punctures, perfectly spaced, wept clear fluid that shimmered unnaturally in the half-light of the chaotic bar.

"Fuck," he whispered, staring at the bite mark with the particular fascination that came from witnessing one's own death sentence. The color drained from his face, the red flush on his cheeks ghoulish against his suddenly pasty skin. "Oh, fuck."

Two minutes, Cleo thought, her hand instinctively clutching the crystal pendant at her throat, remembering Christopher's detailed descriptions of huntsman venom effects during their conversations in his cabin. *Maybe three before the hallucinations start. Less if the spell has enhanced their potency. God, what have I done?*

Arnold was already moving, positioning himself beside his brother's wheelchair with the protective instincts that had kept them working together through decades of professional challenges and personal setbacks, and one horrible tragedy. *No, make that two.*

Arnold's fingers gripped the handles of the chair with intensity, as if he could somehow anchor his twin to reality through sheer force of will. But there was nothing he could do now except watch the venom work its way through Arthur's system, transforming him from family to liability in the space of heartbeats.

"Listen to me," Arthur said, his voice taking on the particular urgency of someone trying to communicate critical information before a window of opportunity closed permanently. He grabbed his twin's wrist, his grip already unnaturally strong. "Whatever happens, don't trust what I tell you after the poison kicks in. Don't trust anyone who's been bitten. We're not ourselves anymore." His pupils began to dilate, the irises nearly disappearing as the venom reached his central nervous system.

At least some people understand the stakes, Cleo thought grimly, adjusting her turban with trembling fingers as she backed away from the twins. The weight of her fraudulent identity seemed trivial compared to the transformation now overtaking Arthur. *Though understanding and surviving are entirely different challenges. And I'm the one who started this.*

Around her, the *Golden Parlor* was devolving into something that would have horrified the cruise line's authenticity consultants—passengers abandoning their 1940s personas completely, crew members dropping their theatrical vernacular in favor of modern profanity, the careful illusion of wartime nostalgia replaced by genuine terror that transcended any historical period.

Cleo slipped away from the tragic scene unfolding between the twins, unable to watch another transformation she'd unwittingly caused. The ship's corridors felt strangely silent as she navigated toward the next room, where she could have sworn she heard a hearty Scottish brogue.

She pushed open the heavy double doors and froze. The once-glamorous space had become a cathedral of silk, gossamer threads glistening in the dim light. The *Pacific Dream*'s *Grand Ballroom* had been transformed from a glamorous homage to wartime elegance into something from humanity's earliest nightmares. Massive webbing stretched from chandelier to balustrade, creating translucent highways that pulsed with movement. Egg sacs bulged from corners, their thin membranes revealing the silhouettes of thousands of developing spiders.

Cleo's throat tightened as she stepped over a carpet of dead arachnids, casualties of whatever internal conflict the hive mind was waging. Their exoskeletons crunched beneath her feet, brittle and hollow. The air hung thick with a musty, acrid smell that coated the back of her throat.

"Captain Abercrombie?" she called, her voice swallowed by the webbing's strange acoustic properties. She neither heard nor saw him, and his absence spoke volumes.

The room was not empty, though. Passengers clustered together, some crying. Stewards and other *Pacific Dream* employees looked dazed.

From across the room, Matt Craig's voice cut through the growing chaos with the particular authority of a man accustomed to being heard in corporate boardrooms and private clubs where money translated directly into social dominion.

"This is ridiculous," he announced, his expensive suit somehow still spotless despite the ongoing horror. "We're treating this like some kind of natural disaster when it's obviously the result of sabotage."

He gestured toward Christopher, who was slumped with hollow-eyed exhaustion that indicated his entire worldview had collapsed in the space of hours. He stood motionless by a window near the stage where he'd performed just days earlier. His expression was vacant, eyes fixed on something only he could see. A thin line of dried blood traced from his ear down his neck, disappearing beneath his collar. The master of arachnids looked utterly defeated, a marionette whose strings had been let slack. The spiders had taken something from him. Something beyond physical harm.

"That man brought these creatures on board," Craig continued, his voice taking on a prosecutorial tone. "His performance animals, his theatrical nonsense—he's responsible for everything that's happened. And she—" He pointed at Cleo with the particular contempt reserved for people whose existence offended his understanding of proper social order. "—she's been encouraging it with her mystical garbage."

Scapegoating, Cleo recognized with weary familiarity. After all, she was someone who'd spent years being blamed for other people's problems. *Find someone different, someone performing instead of conforming, and make them responsible for whatever's going wrong. But of course,* she thought wryly, *he's not wrong.*

"I say we throw them overboard," Craig continued, his suggestion carrying the casual cruelty of someone who'd spent his career treating human resources as expendable commodities. "Cut our losses, eliminate the source of contamination, and focus on survival."

Okay, now he's wrong, Cleo mused with a shudder, watching the faces around the room as Craig's suggestion found purchase in minds that had been pushed beyond rational thought. *How eagerly people embrace barbarism when they're scared enough.*

But before anyone could respond to Craig's proposal, a sound echoed through the ship that made everyone freeze. It was the unmistakable crack of gunfire, followed immediately by the more ominous sound of metal tearing and water rushing into spaces where it didn't belong.

Captain Abercrombie, Cleo realized with horror. *Bite symptoms. He's been bitten, he's hallucinating, and he has access to firearms!*

The ship's intercom crackled to life, but instead of the captain's usual authoritative tone, what emerged was something that sounded like multiple voices speaking in unison—Captain Abercrombie's words, but layered with harmonics that suggested another consciousness was influencing his communication.

"All passengers and crew," the voice said, carrying undertones that made Cleo's teeth ache, "remain in your current positions. Do not attempt to access restricted areas. Do not attempt to communicate with outside authorities. We are... I am... the situation is under control."

He's fighting it, Cleo realized. *Part of him is still human, still trying to maintain command. But something else is speaking through him.*

The sound of rushing water was becoming more pronounced, and the ship's subtle list to starboard suggested that whatever damage had been done was significant enough to affect the vessel's stability. Not immediately catastrophic, but the kind of progressive flooding that would eventually become everyone's problem.

We're not just trapped, Cleo thought. *We're on a sinking ship controlled by creatures that don't want us to escape.*

Through the chaos of mounting panic and deteriorating circumstances, she found herself looking at Christopher Webb, the man whose spiders had become the vector for her accidental awakening of something vast and terrible, the performer whose own deep-seated psychological wounds had somehow resonated with her own hidden damage.

For a moment, she saw him calculating distances, evaluating exits, clearly considering Craig's earlier suggestion about throwing the performers overboard. Not out of malice, but out of the simple survival mathematics that occurred when people realized they might have to choose between their principles and their lives.

He's thinking about abandoning me, she realized without surprise or judgment. *Probably the wise choice. I'm the one who caused this. I'm the liability.*

But even as she watched him weigh his options, something in his expression shifted. The facade fell away, revealing something more complicated than simple self-preservation. Guilt, responsibility, and perhaps recognition that they were bound together now by more than circumstance.

He can't do it, she understood. *Whatever else he is, he's not someone who abandons people to save himself. Even when it's the logical choice.*

Christopher moved toward her through the increasingly chaotic crowd, his face set with determination. It seemed to her he'd made a decision that probably wasn't smart but felt unavoidably necessary.

"We need to find somewhere secure," he said quietly through clenched teeth, his voice pitched for her ears alone. "Somewhere we can figure out how to reverse what you started."

What I started. The words carried weight that went beyond simple blame. She had started this. Not intentionally, not with malicious purpose, but with careless arrogance. And they'd already tried. She'd tried. But the spirits had abandoned her. Or maybe they were laughing at her.

Emma Glopstein, telephone psychic from Metairie, trying to play with forces she didn't understand, she thought with the brutal self-honesty that crisis demanded. *And now people are dying because I wanted to win a stupid game of romantic rivalry.*

But maybe, Cleo thought as she followed Christopher toward whatever uncertain sanctuary he'd identified, *that's the most honest thing that's happened on this ship since we left port. Maybe it takes genuine horror to strip away the performance and reveal what people really are underneath.*

The question was whether what lay underneath would be enough to survive what was coming next.

Behind them, Arthur Lichtenstein was beginning to speak in voices that weren't entirely his own, his wheelchair spinning in circles as he described geometric patterns that existed only in his poisoned perception. Arnold stayed beside him, listening to Arthur's fevered revelations with the dedication of a brother who understood that love sometimes meant witnessing deterioration without being able to prevent it.

The center cannot hold, Cleo thought, remembering half-forgotten poetry from her brief college years. *Things fall apart. The best lack all conviction, while the worst are full of passionate intensity.*

But perhaps, she reflected as she and Christopher disappeared into the ship's increasingly web-infested corridors, the worst thing wasn't passionate intensity. What if it was discovering that you'd been performing your entire life, and the only time you'd ever touched real power was when you'd used it to destroy everything you'd been pretending to protect?

CHAPTER 16

Arnold's fingers ached from gripping the handles of his brother's wheelchair. Adrenaline had given him strength he didn't know he possessed, but now his muscles trembled with fatigue as he navigated the listing corridors of the *Pacific Dream*.

"Just a little further, Arthur," he murmured, though his brother had stopped responding coherently minutes ago.

The ship's emergency lighting cast sickly amber apparitions across the walls. Each intersection required careful scrutiny—spiders had claimed certain passages completely, their webs forming translucent barriers that pulsed with life. Arnold chose his route based on which corridors showed the least webbing, though the distinction was becoming academic. The entire vessel was being consumed, or so it seemed.

Arthur's head lolled forward, then snapped back. "The patterns... they're talking to me, Arnie. Geometric certainties. Eight-fold symmetry. The perfect web."

Arnie. He hadn't heard that nickname since adolescence. "Save your strength," Arnold said, swallowing the fear that threatened to choke him. He'd seen the bite mark on Arthur's wrist—angry red, with black tendrils spreading outward like squid's ink.

"Need to get you somewhere quiet," Arnold added, though he wasn't sure if he was speaking to reassure Arthur or himself.

The lifeboat deck seemed logical. Open air might be safer than the increasingly claustrophobic interior. If Arthur was... if the worst happened, Arnold couldn't bear the thought of strangers watching. They'd spent their entire lives performing for audiences. Death, at least, should be private.

The final door to the exterior deck was partially blocked by fallen debris. Arnold braced himself against the wall and pushed with his shoulder until the gap widened enough to maneuver the wheelchair through.

Bracing air hit his face, but brought no relief. The night was moonless in the thick cloud cover, the darkness absolute except for the ship's emergency lights that created pools of illumination across the deck. The Pacific heaved beneath them, waves crashing against the hull with percussive force. Spray lashed upward, soaking Arnold's pant legs as he wheeled Arthur toward where the lifeboats hung.

"Jesus Christ," he whispered.

The lifeboats, their last possible escape, were completely engulfed. Webs stretched across each davit and cradle, creating cocoon-like structures that undulated in the wind. The webbing wasn't the delicate gossamer of normal spiders; these strands were rope-thick, with an unsettling pearlescent sheen that caught the emergency lights.

Worse, something human-shaped hung suspended between two of the boats, swaying gently with the ship's motion like some grotesque pendulum. Arnold squinted through the darkness, straining to make out details, then immediately wished he hadn't. A crew member—the distinctive white uniform now gray with thick, glistening webbing—was wrapped in layers of silk, cocooned like a fly in a spider's larder. Only the face remained partially visible through the translucent shroud. The man's eyes were open, unblinking, bulging with terror and reflecting the dim emergency lights, his mouth frozen in a silent scream that would never find voice. Dark stains had spread across the webbing near his neck, evidence of where the venom had entered his system. Small shapes, barely visible in the gloom, moved methodically across the suspended form, reinforcing their macabre preservation work with fresh strands of silk.

"They're efficient predators," Arthur said with sudden clarity, his voice eerily calm. "They don't waste. They store. They preserve."

Arnold knelt beside the wheelchair, turning it so he could see his brother's face. Arthur's skin had taken on a waxy pallor, and sweat sheened his forehead despite the brisk wind. His pupils were still massively dilated, with something moving behind them that wasn't entirely Arthur.

"You're going to be okay," Arnold lied. "We just need to—"

"Don't," Arthur interrupted, gripping Arnold's wrist with urgent strength. "Don't waste time with comforting fiction. I can feel them, Arnie. Inside me. Rewriting."

A soft pattering sound drew Arnold's attention to the deck. Dark shapes moved across the metal surface... dozens of spiders advancing toward them with unnatural coordination, in formation that reminded Arnold of stage blocking, each creature maintaining precise spacing from its neighbors.

"They're beautiful," Arthur whispered, watching the approaching arachnids with something like reverence. "Do you see it? The pattern they're making?"

Arnold didn't answer. He positioned himself between the spiders and the wheelchair, though he knew the gesture was futile. What could he, an elderly man, possibly do against creatures that had already disabled an entire ship?

"We've spent our whole lives creating illusions," Arthur continued, his voice taking on a dreamy quality. "Making people see what isn't there. But this, *this* is real magic. They're remaking the world, thread by thread."

A particularly large spider—a huntsman, Arnold thought, though it seemed impossibly big—detached from the group and scuttled forward. Arnold kicked at it instinctively. The creature dodged with liquid grace, then rose on its back legs in what looked unmistakably like a threat display.

"Don't," Arthur said sharply. "They'll kill you if you resist."

"And if I don't resist?" Arnold asked, not taking his eyes off the spider.

"Then they'll show you wonders," Arthur replied, but the voice didn't sound entirely like his brother anymore. Something else was speaking through him, using familiar vocal cords to shape unfamiliar concepts.

The ship lurched suddenly, the list becoming more pronounced. Water sloshed across the deck, momentarily scattering the spiders. Arnold grabbed the wheelchair handles to stop Arthur from sliding away.

"You should go," Arthur said, momentary lucidity returning to his eyes. "Find the others. I'm already... changing."

"I'm not leaving you," Arnold insisted.

Arthur's laugh was hollow. "Always the protective big brother. Even though I'm only younger by seven minutes."

"Seven minutes is seven minutes," Arnold replied automatically, their lifelong exchange suddenly precious in its familiarity.

The moment of connection shattered as Arthur's body convulsed. His back arched impossibly, head thrown back in silent agony. When he relaxed, something different looked out through his eyes. Something ancient and patient and utterly inhuman.

"The convergence is beginning," Arthur said, his voice overlaid with a chittering quality that made Arnold's skin crawl. "The web tightens. The pattern completes."

The spiders resumed their advance, more purposeful now. Arnold backed up until the wheelchair bumped against the railing. The sea churned below, black and hungry.

"Arthur," Arnold pleaded, "if you're still in there—"

"Arthur is becoming something magnificent," his brother replied. "As we all will. The transformation has already begun."

The huntsman spider leapt gracefully through the air, its long legs extended outward like some grotesque starfish, before landing with surprising delicacy on Arthur's lap. Its body, the size of a small dog, settled onto the damp fabric of Arthur's trousers, eight gleaming eyes reflecting the dim emergency lighting overhead. Instead of exhibiting the natural human revulsion, instead of brushing the creature away with panicked hands, Arthur regarded it with an expression approaching tenderness. His fingers, pale and trembling, the veins beneath his skin more pronounced than they had been just moments ago, reached out to stroke the spider's bristled back with gentle, almost reverent motions.

"They only want connection," he whispered, his voice carrying an eerie serenity that contrasted sharply with the bedlam surrounding them. A thin strand of saliva connected his lower lip to his chin, glistening in the half-light. "To bring us all into the pattern. The beautiful, infinite pattern." His eyes, now clouded with that alien intelligence, fixed on Arnold's face with unsettling intensity. "Isn't that what everyone wants, in the end? To be part of something larger? Something eternal?" His fingers continued their rhythmic stroking as three smaller spiders emerged from his sleeve, traversing the landscape of his wrist with purposeful movements.

The ship groaned beneath them as more water flooded the lower decks, the metal hull creaking with a deep, mournful sound that vibrated through Arnold's wheelchair and up his spine. Salt spray misted his face as the vessel listed slightly to port. Arnold's nostrils filled with the acrid scent of corroding metal and the unmistakable musty odor of the spiders, thousands of them, their united presence creating a sickly-sweet, almost fungal smell that repulsed him.

Arnold realized with sudden, gut-wrenching clarity that they were facing multiple extinction events simultaneously—drowning in the rising, frigid Pacific waters, predation by the unnaturally intelligent arachnids whose scampering legs he could hear approaching from every shadow, or whatever transformation his brother was undergoing before his very eyes.

Dear God, he thought, his weary heart hammering painfully against his ribs, *how do you choose between terrible deaths?* His palms were slick as they gripped the wheelchair armrests, knuckles tight with tension. The taste of fear, metallic and sharp, glazed his tongue as he watched another spider crawl up his brother's arm without Arthur showing the slightest discomfort.

"Which will it be for me?" he wondered silently, his mind racing with horrific possibilities. "Will I feel the water fill my lungs, or will I become like Arthur—hollowed out and filled with something... else?" A tremor ran through his aged body that had nothing to do with the ship's movement.

And in that moment, watching the brother who had been his other half for seventy-three years slip away into something unrecognizable, Arnold felt more alone than he had in his entire life.

A shudder passed through Arthur's body. His spine straightened, eyes cleared, and for one precious moment, he was fully himself again, the brother Arnold had known for seven decades plus three.

"Arnold," Arthur whispered, voice stripped of that strange chittering. "You need to let me go."

"What?" Arnold's fingers tightened on the wheelchair handles.

"I'm fighting it, but not for long." Arthur's words came in pained gasps. The huntsman spider on his lap froze, as if sensing rebellion. "They're in my head. Thousands of voices. Becoming one voice. *My* voice."

Arnold knelt before his twin, their faces inches apart. In the darkness, he could see the war raging behind Arthur's eyes—moments of clarity battling the encroaching otherness.

"There has to be another way," Arnold pleaded, his voice breaking. "We've always found another way."

Arthur seized Arnold's wrist, his grip uncomfortably tight. "Not this time, Arnie." A tear trailed down his pallid cheek. "I don't want to become... whatever they're making me. I don't want to be used to hurt anyone else."

The ship groaned beneath them, listing further. Seawater sloshed across the deck, soaking Arnold's knees where he knelt. The cold bit through his trousers, numbing his skin.

"Please," Arthur whispered. "Let me go while I'm still me."

The spiders around them had stopped their advance, as if confused by the resistance in their chosen vessel. Arnold could hear their legs skittering against metal, an impatient, angry sound like rain on a tin roof.

"I can't," Arnold choked out.

"You can." Arthur's smile was gentle, the same smile he'd worn when they'd nailed their first synchronized illusion at age twelve. "The Amazing Lichtensteins always knew how to make the perfect exit."

A sob tore from Arnold's throat. The salt spray mingled with his tears, both tasting of loss on his lips. The wind whipped around them, carrying the scent of brine and decay, while distant thunder rolled across the waves. The entire world seemed to be mourning what was about to happen.

"I love you, Arthur."

"Love you too, little brother."

"Seven minutes," they said in unison, a lifetime of shared humor distilled into two words.

Arnold released the wheelchair handles and stepped back. His hands felt impossibly empty.

Arthur nodded once, then, with a strength that belied his condition, spun his wheelchair around and pushed toward where the deck sloped most severely. The spiders on his lap and shoulders seemed to realize what was happening. They began moving frantically, weaving strands as if to secure him to the chair.

"Always wanted to do a solo act," Arthur called over his shoulder, his voice almost lost in the wind. "Guess I finally get my chance."

The wheelchair picked up speed as it rolled down the incline. Arnold watched, heart shattering, as his brother made his final journey. At the last moment, Arthur turned to look back, his face peaceful, himself again.

As if orchestrated by some cosmic stagehand, a massive wave rose alongside the ship, higher than should have been possible in the otherwise calm sea. It crested just as Arthur reached the railing, breaking over the deck in a wall of frothing white.

Arnold felt the impact through the deck plates, heard the crash of water against metal. The wave receded as quickly as it had come, dragging with it Arthur's empty wheelchair, spinning into the darkness below.

"Goodbye," Arnold whispered, standing alone as water streamed from his sodden clothes.

The spiders that had been advancing on them scattered in apparent confusion, their coordinated movement temporarily disrupted. Without Arthur to serve as their vessel, they seemed momentarily directionless.

Arnold stared into the black void where his brother had disappeared. For seventy-three years, they had shared every moment, every triumph, every failure. Now half of him was gone, swallowed by the merciless Pacific.

Yet in his grief, Arnold found a strange, terrible comfort: Arthur had died as himself.

CHAPTER 17

D r. Fiona Hand had always prided herself on maintaining professional composure under pressure—a skill honed through years of CDC crisis management where panic was a luxury that could cost lives. But watching Rashida Bell emerge from the ship's maintenance closet armed with industrial-strength bug spray and a crowbar, her expression set with the grim determination of someone who'd decided that journalism and survival weren't mutually exclusive skill sets, Fiona found herself recalibrating her assumptions about who would emerge as heroes in genuinely impossible circumstances.

"Right," Rashida announced, hefting the crowbar with surprising competence, "I've covered war zones, natural disasters, and three different corporate scandals involving toxic waste. Killer spiders are just Tuesday with more legs."

Dark humor as psychological armor, Fiona noted automatically, though she had to admit the woman's practical approach was more reassuring than the theatrical hysteria that had consumed most of the other passengers.

They'd established a makeshift command center in the ship's library, which was one of the few areas that seemed relatively spider-free, possibly because the creatures found nothing tactically useful in collections of vintage nautical literature and 1940s romance novels. The warm wooden shelves and reading lamps cast a deceptively cozy glow over what had become their last bastion of rationality amidst the spreading chaos.

Roger Blacksmith sat at the central table, surrounded by open books and hastily scrawled notes, his wire-rimmed glasses sliding down his nose as he hunched over his work. The tabletop was littered with coffee cups, torn pages, and hastily sketched diagrams of arachnid anatomy. "The reproductive patterns make no biological sense," he was saying, his academic excitement barely contained despite their circumstances, fingers drumming nervously on a leather-bound encyclopedia. "Normal spider reproduction involves egg sacs, gestation periods measured in weeks or months, limited offspring per cycle. What we're observing suggests exponential multiplication, with each generation larger, more aggressive, more coordinated than the last. It defies everything we know about arachnid development."

Coordinated. The word that had been lurking at the edges of Fiona's medical observations finally found its proper context. She'd been thinking in terms of individual pathology: parasites, neurotoxins, environmental factors that might explain behavioral anomalies. But Roger's entomological perspective was indicating something far more disturbing.

"You're talking about collective intelligence," she said slowly, the pieces clicking together with the particular satisfaction that came from solving diagnostic puzzles. Her mind flashed back to CDC research models on swarm behavior. "Not just individual spiders acting strangely, but multiple organisms operating as components of a larger system. Like cells in a single organism rather than individual predators."

"Precisely." Roger's eyes lit up with enthusiasm. He seemed proud that his retired expertise had suddenly become critically relevant. He pushed aside a stack of papers to reveal a diagram showing interconnected webs. "Think about ant colonies, bee hives—social insects that surrender individual autonomy to serve group purposes. But spiders are typically solitary predators. They don't naturally exhibit hive behaviors. They compete rather than cooperate. They cannibalize rather than collaborate. This is unprecedented in arachnology."

Unless something artificial is driving the coordination, Fiona thought, remembering Cleo's spell, Christopher's descriptions of his performers' lock-step movements, the geometric patterns that were appearing throughout the ship with such panache. She recalled the perfect hexagonal formations of webbing they'd discovered in the ventilation system, too regular to be natural, too purposeful to be random. The medical part of her brain rebelled against the supernatural explanation, but the evidence was becoming harder to dismiss.

"What about the multiplication process itself?" she asked, leaning forward across the table. The ship creaked ominously around them, as if listening. "The rate of reproduction we're witnessing... is there any natural precedent? Anything in the scientific literature that could explain how they're propagating so rapidly?" She tapped her pen against her notepad, the rhythmic sound oddly comforting in the quiet.

Roger shook his head grimly. "None. But there are theoretical frameworks in evolutionary biology—punctuated equilibrium, adaptive radiation—that suggest organisms can undergo rapid transformations when exposed to sufficient selective pressure. If something were artificially accelerating evolutionary processes..."

Magical selective pressure, Fiona completed the thought that Roger's scientific training wouldn't allow him to voice directly. *Su-*

pernatural intervention forcing biological systems to adapt at impossible speeds.

From across the library, a voice interrupted their theoretical discussion with the sharp edge of practical desperation.

"This is all very academic," Cleo Laveau interjected, "but we're not dealing with natural evolution. We're dealing with something I unleashed, and I think I know how to stop it."

She moved toward their table with the particular urgency of someone carrying information they weren't sure would be believed or accepted. Her makeup had smeared, her period-appropriate costume was torn, and her eyes held the haunted quality that came from accepting responsibility for catastrophic mistakes.

"The incantation I used," she continued, her voice dropping to the confessional whisper that people used when admitting to crimes they couldn't take back, "it wasn't just random words. I realize now that I wasn't in control. It had to be part of a specific ritual, an unveiling ceremony that opens doorways between what is and what could be. If I perform the same ritual in reverse, speak the words backward, undo the pattern I created..."

"Absolutely not," Rashida interrupted, her innate skepticism cutting through mystical explanations with pragmatic brutality. "You've already proven that you don't understand the forces you're playing with. How do we know reversing the spell won't make things worse?"

Valid concern, Fiona thought, though part of her medical training was intrigued by the possibility. *If magical intervention caused the problem, magical intervention might solve it. But the risk factors are impossible to calculate.*

"Because it's my fault," Cleo said, her voice breaking. "I cast the spell out of jealousy, out of petty anger, without understanding what I was really doing. People are dying because I wanted to win some stupid romantic competition."

As if on cue, Christopher Webb appeared in the library doorway, his performer's presence diminished but not entirely extinguished by the ongoing horrors. Blood speckled the cuffs of his once-immaculate shirt, and dark circles shadowed his eyes like ghastly stage makeup. He'd been moving through the ship like a ghost, documenting the spread of creatures that had once been his partners in entertainment, accepting responsibility that wasn't entirely his while carrying guilt that was all too familiar. A weight he'd carried since childhood when another spider had taken someone he loved.

"She's right," he said quietly. "This started with her spell, and it's connected to forces that exist outside normal causality. The spiders—my spiders—they're not behaving according to any natural pattern I've ever witnessed in all my years of working with them. If there's a way to reverse it..."

"If there's a way to make it worse, you mean," Roger cut in. "We're dealing with organisms that have developed interwoven intelligence, tactical coordination, and reproductive capabilities that defy biological precedent. I've watched them communicate across impossible distances. Adding more magical variables to the equation seems like throwing gasoline on a fire that's already burning out of control." Roger's voice cracked. "My wife Karen is still locked in our cabin, terrified of anything that moves." His fingers drummed against the table. "I promised I'd come back for her, but the corridor to our deck is completely overrun."

He was interrupted by a sound that made everyone in the library freeze. It was the synchronized tapping that had become the spiders' signature communication method, but louder now, more complex, coming from multiple directions simultaneously.

They know where we are, Fiona realized. *They're coordinating an approach.*

Through the library's portholes, she could see geometric web patterns spreading across the glass. Not chance spider architecture, but symbolic arrangements that made her temples throb. The intricate silken designs formed complex, repeating structures that resembled numerical equations or perhaps a primitive alphabet. In some places, the webs connected in perfect hexagonal formations; in others, they spiraled outward with precise spacing between each strand. What disturbed Fiona most wasn't just their unnatural precision, but how quickly they appeared, as if dozens of arachnids were working in perfect synchronicity, their eight legs weaving with machine-like efficiency. The creatures weren't just intelligent; they were developing their own form of written communication, a multifaceted system of symbols and patterns that seemed designed to convey specific information between members of their rapidly evolving hive mind. Watching the meticulous construction continue across every available surface of glass, Fiona felt a chill of scientific fascination mingled with a sense of existential dread.

Language, she thought with the wonder that accompanied genuinely unprecedented discoveries. *They're developing language in real time.*

Rashida was already moving toward the library's exit, crowbar raised, bug spray ready. "Academic debate is officially over," she announced. "We can argue about magical solutions after we survive the next ten minutes."

But as the others began preparing for what was clearly going to be another desperate struggle for survival, Fiona found herself watching Christopher and Cleo with the particular attention she'd learned to pay to interpersonal dynamics during crisis situations.

Guilt and responsibility creating emotional bonds, she noted. *Shared trauma accelerating intimacy. Classic psychological pattern.*

She followed them surreptitiously as they moved toward the library's balcony, ostensibly to evaluate escape routes, but clearly seeking privacy for conversations that couldn't happen in front of the group. The ocean stretched endlessly beyond the ship's rails, beautiful and indifferent, offering no solutions to problems that existed entirely within the *Pacific Dream's* increasingly compromised hull. The setting sun painted their silhouettes in amber light that belied the horror unfolding within the vessel's corridors.

"This isn't all your fault," Christopher was saying, his voice carrying the gentle authority of someone who understood psychological self-destruction from personal experience. His silver strands caught the fading sunlight, and his fingers absently traced one of the spider tattoos on his wrist. "You cast a spell you didn't expect to work. I've been dancing with these creatures for years, knowing they could kill me. We're both responsible, and we're both victims. Neither of us could have predicted... this."

Mutual absolution, Fiona observed from her position in the doorway, noting how Christopher's normally rigid posture had softened in Cleo's presence. *Probably psychologically necessary, though not entirely accurate in terms of causal responsibility. Classic displacement of guilt through shared narrative reconstruction.*

"I wanted to hurt you," Cleo confessed, her normally theatrical voice stripped of its performative quality. She twisted one of her crystal pendants nervously between her fingers as she spoke. "When Eleanor was flirting with you, when you seemed to be considering her offer, I wanted to... to show you that I had power you couldn't ignore. It was petty and stupid and now people are dead because I couldn't handle rejection like an adult."

Christopher moved closer to her, his proximity suggesting intimacy that transcended the practical considerations of their shared crisis. The wind tousled his hair as he reached for her hand, their fingers intertwining with a familiarity that seemed incongruous amid chaos. When he kissed her—gently, tentatively, with the particular tenderness that people showed each other when they thought they might be about to die—Fiona found herself witnessing something that felt both inevitable and surprising. The kiss was framed against the darkening horizon, a moment of humanity against the backdrop of monstrous transformation.

Attraction accelerated by extremity, she thought with clinical objectivity, cataloging the physiological signs of their connection. *Though possibly genuine connection revealed by circumstances that strip away social performance. The trauma bond forming between them could be either destructive or constructive depending on outcome variables.*

The kiss lasted only moments, but it carried weight that seemed to settle something between them. Not absolution, exactly, but acknowledgment that whatever happened next, they would face it as allies rather than strangers thrown together by circumstance. As they pulled apart, their breath mingled in the cooling evening air, and Fiona noticed how Cleo's hand lingered on Christopher's chest, directly over the playing card tattoo visible beneath his partially unbuttoned shirt. The Queen of Hearts.

Psychological resilience through emotional bonding, Fiona noted.

From inside the library, Roger's voice carried new urgency: "They're not just coordinating anymore. They're problem-solving. The patterns they're creating; they're testing structural weak points, evaluating defensive positions. This isn't hunting behavior. This is siege warfare."

Hive mind achieving tactical sophistication, Fiona thought, turning away from the balcony scene to focus on the more immediate crisis. *Each individual spider serving as a neuron in a distributed intelligence that's learning to think strategically. We are so screwed.*

And somewhere in the ship's web-infested corridors, thousands of creatures that had been designed by nature as simple predators were discovering what it meant to be part of something larger than themselves—something that could plan, anticipate, and adapt with the joint wisdom of minds that were no longer quite individual, no longer quite arachnid, but not entirely of this world either. The spiders moved in synchronicity, their eight-legged bodies flowing like dark liquid through ventilation shafts, behind wall panels, and across ceilings. What had once been mindless hunters were now coordinated battalions, communicating through imperceptible vibrations and chemical signals that Fiona could only begin to comprehend.

In some sections of the ship—the darkest, most remote corners—she suspected they had constructed elaborate three-dimensional webs that weren't merely traps but information networks, each strand a conduit for transmitting intelligence about human movements, structural vulnerabilities, and tactical opportunities. Even the silk itself seemed to have evolved, becoming stronger and more adhesive by the hour, as if the spell had accelerated millions of years of natural selection into mere days.

We're witnessing the birth of a new form of consciousness, Fiona realized with awe. *And it's trying to kill us.* Her grappling mind couldn't help but marvel at the phenomenon even as her survival instinct screamed warnings. The spiders had transcended their genetic limitations, achieving something that shouldn't be possible outside of science fiction. Collective sentience emerging from thousands of tiny minds working in concert.

The question was whether human ingenuity, magical intervention, or simple stubborn survival instinct would prove stronger than intelligence backed by evolutionary acceleration and an apparently unlimited capacity for reproductive expansion. Fiona had seen Christopher's most deadly specimens—the lightning-fast Australian huntsman that could outrun a human, the venomous Chinese bird spider whose bite could kill within hours, the nearly invisible Chilean recluse whose toxin dissolved flesh, the Wraparound whose flattened body with highly camouflaged, bark-like carapace could hide in plain sight, and the fuzzy, blue-fanged jumping spider, able to leap many times its body length—all now operating not as individual threats but as specialized units in an organized army.

In the dim emergency lighting, she could see webs beginning to form intricate patterns that resembled neural networks, as if the ship itself was being transformed into the physical substrate for this emerging consciousness. The most terrifying aspect wasn't their numbers or even their venom, but the calculated patience with which they were systematically cutting off escape routes and isolating pockets of survivors. They were learning from each encounter, adapting their strategies based on human responses, becoming more efficient with each passing hour.

Will we survive? Time to find out, Fiona thought, watching Rashida prepare for what would undoubtedly be the next phase of their increasingly desperate struggle for survival.

CHAPTER 18

Standing in what remained of the ship's upper deck lounge, watching a group of cruise passengers and crew members plan an assault on a cargo hold that had been transformed into something resembling a spider cathedral, Rashida Bell found herself cataloging the psychological markers that separated rational risk assessment from the kind of magnificent self-destruction that made for either great journalism or impressive obituaries.

Probably both, she thought, hefting her crowbar with grim satisfaction.

The once-filtered air was chokingly thick with humidity and the acrid scent of fear, pressing against Rashida's lungs with each labored breath. The once-pristine, vintage-themed décor, with its art deco curves and polished brass, which had so delighted Old Hollywood and war-era enthusiasts aboard, now lay marred by elaborate webbing that glistened menacingly in the flickering emergency lighting, transforming elegant fixtures into grotesque parodies of their former elegance. Silken strands hung from crystal chandeliers like perverse party streamers, catching the intermittent red glow in ways that made them appear wet with blood rather than spider secretions. But the substantial weight of the cold metal in her hands was reassuring; the crowbar's solid presence was a tangible connection to reality in a situation that'd spiraled so violently beyond the boundaries of the rational world she'd always inhabited and documented with professional detachment.

At least they had something resembling a plan, however desperate it might be. But it was just the three of them now, a fact that made Rashida's stomach churn with both dread and a strange sense of purpose.

Roger had left several minutes ago, his face tight with worry as he'd muttered something about returning to Karen in their stateroom—a choice Rashida couldn't fault him for, even as she questioned his chances of making it there alive.

Meanwhile, Dr. Hand was determined to find and somehow neutralize the captain before his increasingly erratic behavior endangered the survivors remaining on the lower decks. She was actively trying to figure out how to get to the cargo hold, where she had backup medical supplies, including potent sedatives.

"The cargo hold access is three decks down," Dr. Hand was explaining, her medical training lending deliberate detachment to what was essentially a suicide mission briefing. "We'll need to move through sections of the ship that are heavily infested, past defensive positions that seem to have been established with tactical sophistication." The doctor's hands moved with deft assurance as she traced her route on a crumpled ship schematic, her fingers lingering over the areas where they'd encountered the densest concentrations of spiders.

Tactical sophistication, Rashida repeated silently. *Because apparently we're now dealing with spiders that understand how we think.* She'd seen the evidence herself—the way the creatures seemed to anticipate their movements, cutting off escape routes and herding survivors into traps.

Rashida's eye caught movement from something large and stagger-
ing. A giant spider? No... Arnold Lichtenstein stood in the doorway,
soaked, shivering, and shaking. The absence of his twin brother spoke
volumes. His vintage suit, once dapper in keeping with the cruise's
classy theme, hung in tatters from his thin frame. Water dripped from
his white hair, creating small puddles on the carpeted floor beneath
him, evidence of some desperate journey through the ship's flooded
sections.

"I'll create a distraction, Dr. Hand," he said quietly, his voice
weighted with the heaviness of an irreversible decision. "Arthur would
have wanted... would have insisted that we try to save as many people
as possible." His hands trembled, but his gaze remained steady, fixed
on some point beyond the immediate horror of their situation.

The surviving twin, Rashida thought, remembering the horrific
deterioration they'd witnessed as Arthur's bite symptoms progressed
from hallucination to complete psychological dissolution. *Now ready
to join his brother in whatever passes for heroism when you're trapped
on a drifting spider colony.* She'd interviewed the brothers just yesterday—or was it the day before?—for a fluff lifestyle piece on elderly
travelers embracing adventure cruising. The irony of the word "adventure" wasn't lost on her.

"Arnold, no," Dr. Hand protested with the automatic objection
that medical professionals offered when presented with voluntary
martyrdom. "We can find another way. There has to be another approach that doesn't require—" Her voice pitched slightly higher, betraying the exhaustion that they all felt after fighting, running, and
watching their fellow passengers succumb to venom that transformed
victims before killing them.

"Sacrifice?" Arnold gave a sad smile. The word hung in the air
between them, heavy with implication. His eyes, rheumy but deter-

mined, swept across the survivors, lingering briefly on each face as though memorizing them for whatever came next.

An unlikely action hero, Rashida thought, though she had to admit the old man's logic was unassailable. *Sometimes the best contribution you can make is knowing when you're expendable. That's a good line. If I survive to write the story, I can use that.* She tightened her grip on the crowbar, feeling the metal bite into her palm, and wondered what her own contribution would ultimately be to this ever-unfolding calamity.

Christopher and Cleo were conferring near the windows, their conversation carrying a particular intensity. The kiss Rashida had glimpsed earlier had apparently settled something between them.

"The reversal ritual," Cleo was saying, her voice carrying confidence that hadn't been there during her earlier confessions, "it's not just about speaking words backward. It's about reconnecting with the spiritual forces that were activated by the original spell." She gulped. "At least, I hope so."

"But," Christopher replied, "if you're wrong about the spiritual connection, if the spell has evolved beyond what you originally act ivated..."

"Then we die anyway," Cleo finished with the fatalist honesty that extreme situations demanded. "But at least we die trying to fix what I broke instead of hiding from it."

Fair point, Rashida acknowledged. *Though I'd prefer dying long after writing a Pulitzer Prize-winning exposé about impossible biological phenomena.*

The sound of orderly tapping echoed through the ship's walls, the spiders' communication network coordinating something that sounded increasingly like battalion preparation. Whatever was directing their behavior had apparently decided that the human survivors represented a problem requiring a comprehensive solution.

They're planning something, Rashida realized with the pattern recognition skills that had served her well during investigations of corporate malfeasance and political corruption. *This is organized elimination.*

"We need to move now," Dr. Hand announced with medical authority that brooked no argument. "Before they finish whatever they're weaving."

Arnold Lichtenstein stood with the careful dignity of a man whose arthritis had been temporarily overruled by adrenaline and purpose. "Give me ten minutes to reach the main stairwell. When you hear the commotion, move fast. Don't stop, don't look back, and don't waste the opportunity."

Ten minutes, Rashida thought. *Long enough for a doomed man to walk into a swarm of supernaturally enhanced predators and create enough chaos to give the rest of us a fighting chance.*

But really, what will that do? she wondered. *It's not like we have anywhere to run. But maybe it'll buy us some time to get to the safes, to our phones, to the comm systems. No, they had to get back to the terrariums... that's what the clairvoyant had said. But could she be trusted?*

As Arnold left the lounge with the measured pace of someone who'd accepted his fate, Rashida found herself experiencing the particular emotional complexity that came from witnessing genuine self-sacrifice. She'd covered enough disasters to recognize courage when she saw it, but this felt different. More personal, more immediate, less abstract than observing heroism from journalistic distance.

This one's going in the memorial section, she thought, already composing the paragraph that would capture Arnold's final contribution to humanity's ongoing survival project.

The ten minutes passed with the subjective speed of geological time. Each second stretched into eternity, marked only by the shallow breathing of survivors and the distant skittering of eight-legged predators probing through the ship's corridors. Rashida found herself counting heartbeats, each one a small victory against the encroaching horror. When the sounds of Arnold's distraction finally echoed through the ship—shouting, the crash of overturned furniture, a chandelier crashing to a hardwood dancefloor, followed by the unmistakable cacophony of hundreds of tiny legs rushing toward fresh prey—Rashida felt something settle in her chest that was equal parts admiration and grief.

Good death, she thought with the respect that professional observers accorded to heroes who chose meaning over safety. *The kind that makes the story worth telling. The kind editors put on front pages and readers remember decades later. The kind I'd want, if it came to that.*

Dr. Hand checked her medical bag one last time, her fingers lingering on a syringe filled with the strongest antivenin she'd managed to concoct from the ship's limited supplies. Her uniform was stained with muck and her once-immaculate bun had come undone, sending wisps of dark blonde hair across her face.

"This won't hold them off for long," she said, meeting each of their eyes in turn. "But it might buy you enough time." She wished Rashida, Christopher, and Cleo luck, her workplace demeanor peeling away just enough to reveal the fear underneath, then she followed in Arnold's footsteps toward the lower decks, her white shoes clicking against the floor.

The trio turned and moved through the ship's corridors with the purposeful efficiency of people who understood that hesitation meant death. They hurried through hallways recklessly, only one goal in mind.

Christopher Webb's suite, when they finally reached it, defied every reasonable expectation of what spider infestation should look like. The door still hung partially open, revealing not the chaotic mess of silk and egg sacs one might expect, but something far more disturbing. Instead of random webbing and chaotic reproduction, what they found was more architecture—geometric, purposeful structures that suggested not just intelligence but aesthetic sensibility. Concentric circles connected by radial threads formed perfect mandalas across the ceiling. Spiraling columns descended to the floor, creating a forest of silken pillars that gleamed with an opalescent sheen never found in nature.

They're building something, Rashida realized with the awe that accompanied witnessing genuinely unprecedented phenomena. *Not just multiplying, but creating. Constructing something that serves purposes we can't even imagine.*

At the center of the web cathedral, Christopher's original terrariums sat like altars in some Gigeresque temple, their glass surfaces covered with patterns that boggled the mind—symbols that seemed to shift and move when viewed peripherally, revealing depths that shouldn't exist in two-dimensional space. The spiders weren't just using them as breeding sites, they were treating them as sacred objects, focal points for whatever collective cohesion was emerging from their preternatural evolution.

"We need Eleanor," Christopher muttered, scanning the intricate web structures with mounting anxiety. His hair hung limply around his face, and his vintage threads were torn at the sleeve where a jumping spider had nearly caught him. "These patterns. They're not just premeditated shapes. I can see the figures of two women and a man. They're weaving our likenesses into their architecture."

Rashida watched the illusionist's hands move at his sides, the magician's fingers moving as if practicing invisible sleight-of-hand, cards and coins dancing through phantom routines. *A self-soothing mechanism*, she realized. Something to ground himself when reality became too slippery, when the line between illusion and monstrosity blurred beyond recognition.

"I haven't seen her since the flooding started," Cleo whispered, her voice only just audible over the distant trilling that pulsed through the ship's infrastructure like some terrible heartbeat. Her thick mascara had run further, leaving dark tracks down her pale cheeks. "You don't think she's—"

"Don't," Christopher cut her off, his voice a sharp retort. "We can't afford to think that way."

Rashida understood their desperation. Eleanor Hargrove was the missing third point in their triangle, the final element needed to complete whatever ritual might undo Cleo's accidental working.

"I think you have it, Christopher. The reversal ritual needs all three of us," Cleo insisted, her fingers tracing symbols in the air that mirrored the web patterns, leaving faint trails of blue light that hung momentarily before fading. "I can feel the energies, but I can't interpret what they've become. It's like trying to read a language that's evolving as I watch."

Our unlikely trinity, Rashida thought, gripping her makeshift weapon tighter. *The magician, the medium, and the maneater. And now we're missing a third of our defense. Classic horror movie scenario—the moment you think you've found a solution, the universe throws another impossible obstacle in your path. At least we don't have to try and start a car.*

Their moment was interrupted by sounds from the ship's PA system. Captain Abercrombie's voice, distorted by whatever hallucinogenic venom was still coursing through his system, announced his intention to "clear the contaminated areas" with what sounded like improvised explosive devices. His words slurred together, punctuated by bursts of maniacal laughter that echoed through the empty corridors like the soundtrack to a nightmare.

The captain's lost it completely, Rashida realized. Their already impossible situation had just acquired additional complications. *And he has access to the ship's emergency flares.*

The explosion, when it came, shook the entire vessel with the particular violence that screamed structural damage beyond routine repair. But it was followed by something worse: the sound of more flooding, of compartments that were supposed to remain watertight being opened to the Pacific Ocean's inexorable pressure.

Christopher looked wan, and his eyes were wide with barely contained panic. "I'll find Eleanor. She can't be far. Cleo, can you do something—anything—to hold these spiders off until I get back?"

"I don't know about her," Rashida snapped. "But I can!"

She swept her crowbar in a wide arc, the metal whistling through the air before connecting with a sickening crunch against another spider, smashing its bulbous body against the wall. Dark ichor splattered across the vintage wallpaper, adding to the grotesque Jackson Pollock already forming there.

The damn things were retreating, but not fast enough for Rashida's comfort. She counted six—no, seven—of the larger specimens still lurking in the corners of Christopher's once-luxurious suite, their movements more erratic now, but no less menacing. Their legs twitched with unnatural coordination, as if receiving instructions from some unseen conductor.

The magician nodded once in grim acknowledgment before speeding out the cabin door, his tall, thin frame disappearing into the corridor with surprising agility for a man who probably had no idea where he was going.

Cleo watched him go, her heavily made-up face crumpling like an abandoned child's. Her false eyelashes, now askew from the chaos, fluttered as her light brown eyes filled with tears.

"Keep going," Rashida urged Cleo, who quickly regained her composure and stood in the center of the room, arms extended, fingers splayed. The psychic's eyes were rolled back now, showing only sclera, her body swaying slightly as she continued her incantation. Her dyed black hair had come loose from beneath her turban, cascading around her shoulders like a protective cloak.

Cleo's voice deepened to an unsettling register that seemed impossible for her frame to produce. The words themselves were an incomprehensible mixture of mangled Latin, Creole, and something far older that made the fine hairs on Rashida's arms stand at attention. With each syllable, the temperature in the room dropped perceptibly, and the remaining spiders seemed to recoil, their harmonized movements becoming increasingly erratic.

Rashida straightened her grip on the crowbar, its metal surface now slick with spider gore and her own perspiration. She'd come aboard to write a scathing review of this ridiculous throwback cruise, and maybe a couple of puff pieces for her freelance outlets, not to face death by arachnid apocalypse. Yet here she was, standing guard for a woman she'd dismissed as a fraud, watching in astonishment as Cleo's amateur witchcraft actually seemed to be working against the eight-limbed chimeras surrounding them.

The woman was actually doing something. Rashida had built a career on skepticism, but she couldn't deny the evidence before her eyes. With each phrase Cleo uttered, more spiders fled, pouring into air vents or scuttling beneath the door in undulating waves of chitinous bodies.

Water sloshed against the doorway, rising steadily. Whatever the captain had done with those flares had compromised another section of the ship. The Pacific Dream was taking on water at an accelerating rate, tilting slightly to port.

"This ship is going down," Rashida said, keeping her voice level. "Whatever you're doing, do it faster."

Cleo's response was unintelligible. Not English, not even the Louisiana French she'd been using earlier, but something older that made the air vibrate uncomfortably.

The overhead speakers crackled to life, Captain Abercrombie's voice distorted by both the damaged system and whatever hallucinogenic venom was coursing through his veins.

"All hands... abandon ship! The Germans have launched... torpedoes from their U-boats!" His voice dropped to a conspiratorial whisper that still managed to carry through the entire audio system. "They're disguised as spiders. Clever bastards. I see through their tricks."

Rashida flinched as cold water began seeping under the door, darkening the carpet around their feet. "We're running out of time."

"I can't complete it," Cleo gasped suddenly, her voice returning to normal as she stumbled backward. "The ritual needs both the original caster and the original vessel." She pointed at the terrariums. "Christopher and Eleanor need to be here. And we need all the spiders that were in those containers originally."

"Well, that's just perfect," Rashida muttered, smashing another spider that ventured too close. "There must be thousands of those things all over the ship by now. How are we supposed to know which ones are the originals?"

"I can feel them," Cleo said, pressing her palm against her forehead. "They're... different. Stronger. Like the parents of all the others."

The ship groaned, metal twisting somewhere deep in its structure. The floor tilted another few degrees.

"Attention passengers!" the captain's voice boomed again. "The enemy has breached our hull! Man the lifeboats! Women and children first!" A pause, then quietly: "No, not the children. The children have eight legs. They're in disguise."

Rashida met Cleo's eyes. "He's getting worse."

"So is the ship," Cleo agreed, steadying herself against a dresser as the floor shifted again.

Water was now flowing steadily under the door, soaking their shoes. The lights flickered as emergency systems struggled against the dual assault of flooding and arachnid sabotage.

"Can you hold these ones off?" Rashida asked, gesturing at the remaining spiders with her crowbar. "I should go after Christopher before we're all underwater."

"I can maintain a barrier," Cleo nodded, her hands tracing symbols in the air that seemed to shimmer momentarily. "But hurry. The energy I tapped into is fading. Whatever window we have to reverse this is closing fast."

Rashida lowered her crowbar. "If I'm not back in ten minutes..."

"We'll all be dead anyway," Cleo finished with grim stoicism.

As Rashida reached for the door handle, the ship lurched violently. Something massive had given way below decks. The overhead speakers emitted a high-pitched squeal before the captain's voice returned, singing an off-key rendition of "Rule, Britannia" that echoed eerily through the flooding corridors.

Not how I expected to die, Rashida thought as she pulled the door open, facing the flooded hallway beyond. *Definitely not how I expected to believe in magic.*

She stepped into the rising water, weapon raised, and moved toward whatever time they had left.

CHAPTER 19

S omewhere in the ship's flooded lower decks, Captain Abercrombie was having a conversation with crew members who might or might not have been entirely human anymore, planning repairs to damage that might or might not have been accidental, serving a chain of command that was becoming more united and less individual with each passing hour. Horror and fear helixed around one another, twisting and spinning as parallel knells of inevitable kismet.

Captain Abercrombie braced himself against the corridor wall, his uniform now torn and stained with something dark that might have been blood or engine oil. The row of brass buttons was dulled with something viscous, and he'd lost his shoes somewhere along the way.

"Steady as she goes, men," he muttered to the empty hallway. "We'll weather this squall yet."

The ship listed slightly to port—or was that just his balance failing? Mac couldn't be certain anymore. The venom worked its way through his system, reshaping reality with each heartbeat.

"Damage report," he barked at a cluster of spiders congregating in the corner. They rearranged themselves into what looked like a naval formation. Mac nodded appreciatively.

"Good lads. Best crew I've ever had."

Water sloshed around his ankles. The flooding from the hull breach was spreading faster than he'd calculated. But that was part of the plan, wasn't it? Mac tried to remember why he'd fired his service pistol and set off the flares. Something about saboteurs. Yes, that passenger had been trying to scuttle his beautiful ship.

"Can't have that," he muttered, pulling his captain's hat lower. "The *Pacific Dream* stays afloat on my watch."

The spiders skittered ahead of him, leading the way toward the engine room. Mac followed, convinced they were his loyal engineers. Their eight-legged gait reminded him of synchronized sailors during inspection. Perfect formation. Perfect obedience.

A distant scream echoed through the corridors. Mac ignored it. Just the wind in the rigging, he reasoned. Or perhaps a siren call. Weren't there mermaids in these waters? The ship's map in his mind had become fantastical, territories marked with "Here Be Monsters" in elegant script.

"Captain! Captain Abercrombie!"

Someone was calling him from the darkness ahead. Mac squinted, trying to focus. A woman's silhouette wavered in his vision, multiplying into eight identical forms before coalescing back into one.

"The flooding's reached D-deck! We need to seal the bulkheads!"

Mac smiled benevolently. "No need for alarm, miss. The water's our friend."

"What? Captain, you're not making sense—"

"The spiders don't like water," he explained patiently, as if to a child. "Naval strategy, you see. Flood the lower compartments, drive the enemy upward where we can contain them."

But even as he spoke, Mac watched in fascination as spiders skated across the water's surface, their tiny legs creating impossible tension. Beautiful. Like a ballet.

"They're not the enemy, though, are they?" he whispered to himself. "They're the crew now. My crew."

The woman's face contorted in horror. Mac couldn't remember her name. Was she even real? The venom pulsed behind his eyes, transforming her features into something cartilaginous and familiar.

"We need to get you to Dr. Hand," she insisted, reaching for his arm.

Mac jerked away, drawing his pistol. "Stand down, sailor! That's an order!"

He fired a warning shot, but his aim was compromised. The bullet struck a pipe overhead. Steam hissed into the corridor, and more water began to pour through.

"Perfect," Mac nodded approvingly. "Just as planned."

The woman fled, shouting for help. Mac turned back to his arachnid crew, who seemed to be multiplying before his eyes. Thousands of them now, covering the walls, ceiling, flowing like a living river alongside the water.

Mac stumbled forward through the corridor, water sloshing around his calves. The ship groaned beneath him, listing more noticeably now. His arachnid crew skittered alongside, their synchronized movements mesmerizing in the dim, strobe lighting.

"Steady as she goes," he muttered, pressing one hand against the wall to maintain balance. "We'll outrun these German devils yet."

The sound of splashing water ahead caught his attention. Mac squinted into the murky corridor, his venom-addled vision transforming the approaching figure into something both human and not.

Eight limbs? No, just two arms gesturing emphatically as the man waded through the rising water.

"Captain Abercrombie, sir! Thank heavens I've found you!" The voice was crisp, the cadence perfectly matched to their 1940s charade. Denver Wheaton approached, his steward's uniform still remarkably spotless despite the chaos. "The situation topside is most dire, sir. Jerry's got us surrounded, dropping eight-legged paratroopers by the dozens!"

Mac's brow furrowed. Something about Denver's unwavering commitment to character struck him as suspicious. The spiders around Mac's feet paused, their mutual attention focused on the steward.

"Wheaton," Mac growled, eyes narrowing. "You've been compromised."

Denver's smile never faltered. "Begging your pardon, sir, but I'm fit as a fiddle and ready to serve! Though I must say, you're looking a bit under the weather. Perhaps a medicinal brandy is in order?"

Mac raised his pistol, aiming it squarely at Denver's chest. "Drop the act, Wheaton. The Krauts have gotten to you."

Denver's eyes widened, but his period-perfect demeanor remained intact. "I say, Captain, that's quite a serious accusation! And if you don't mind my saying so, that sidearm appears to be pointed in a most unfortunate direction."

"They sent you to infiltrate my crew," Mac hissed, the venom twisting his thoughts into paranoid delusions. "To sabotage my ship from within."

The spiders began to advance toward Denver, forming a semicircle behind Mac like obedient soldiers awaiting orders.

"Captain, I believe you may be suffering from battle fatigue," Denver said, backing away slowly, water rippling around his knees. "Dr.

Hand has been searching for you. Perhaps we should find her straight-away, what do you say?"

"Dr. Hand is compromised, too," Mac snarled. "You're all com-promised. All except my new crew." He gestured to the spiders with his free hand. "Loyal to the end, these lads."

Denver's eyes darted between Mac's face and the gun, then to the mass of spiders. His expression remained locked in that perfect old-school professional courtesy, but his jaw was clenched and his lips went tight beneath his mustache.

"Well, sir, if you'll excuse my frankness, it appears you've gone completely off your nut," Denver said, still maintaining his period dialect despite the gun aimed at him. "Those eight-legged fiends aren't your allies. They're the enemy! The genuine article! They've got you bamboozled, Captain!"

Mac fired, jerking the muzzle up at the last moment, and the bullet whizzed past Denver's ear and embedded itself in the wall behind him. The corridor echoed with the report, water rippling from the sound wave.

"Next one goes between your eyes, spy," Mac growled. "The spiders showed me the truth. You're working with the enemy."

Denver ducked behind a partially closed watertight door. "I must respectfully disagree with your assessment, sir! And might I add that firing upon your crew violates several maritime regulations!"

Mac fired again, the bullet punching through the metal door inches from where Denver had taken cover. The spiders surged forward, flowing around Mac's legs like a living tide.

"They're not the enemy," Mac shouted, advancing through the water. "They're the salvation! They'll cleanse this ship of traitors like you!"

Denver peered around the edge of the door, his face pale but his voice steady. "Captain, this simply won't do! I've served under you for three cruises now, and I must say your behavior is most irregular! Perhaps we could discuss this over tea like civilized gentlemen?"

Mac emptied his clip at the door, bullets pinging off metal. Denver seized the opportunity during the reload, splashing through the water and diving into a perpendicular corridor.

"You can run, but my crew will find you!" Mac bellowed, fumbling with a fresh magazine. His hands shook violently, the venom's effect intensifying with his agitation. "We'll cleanse this ship stem to stern!"

Denver's voice echoed back from somewhere in the darkness. "I shall alert the proper authorities about your condition, sir! No hard feelings! Chin up and all that!"

Mac roared in frustration as the spiders streamed past him, pursuing Denver through the flooded corridors of the dying ship.

"Set course for the main ballroom," he commanded. "All hands topside. We'll make our final stand where the dancing is."

The spiders flooded forward, and Mac followed, certain they were leading him to victory. The ship groaned around him, water rising steadily, but Captain Abercrombie walked with the confidence of a man who believed he still controlled his vessel, unaware that he had become merely another vessel himself.

Mac staggered through the half-flooded corridor, the water slopping around his knees, cold as a Scottish winter. The emergency lights cast red shadows that danced along the walls, transforming familiar passages into unfamiliar territory. "Set course for the starboard bow," he called out to no one in particular. "All hands to battle stations!"

The spiders marching alongside him—hundreds of them—paused in perfect unison, as if considering his orders. Mac nodded approvingly. Such discipline! Even the Royal Navy couldn't boast of crew so perfectly synchronized, so utterly devoted to their commander's will.

"That's right, lads," he murmured, adjusting his captain's hat which sat askew on his head. "We'll outflank the enemy yet."

The ship groaned around him, metal twisting somewhere deep in its structure. Or perhaps it was singing? Yes, that was it: the Pacific Dream was serenading him with the sweet music of stressed bulkheads and flooding compartments. A lullaby of impending doom that somehow made perfect sense to his mixed-up mind.

"Beautiful," he whispered, tears welling in his bloodshot eyes. "Absolutely beautiful."

The bite on his forearm had swollen grotesquely, angry red lines spreading outward like a roadmap to madness. Each pulse of his heart pushed the poison deeper, reshaping reality with every beat. The world around him seemed to breathe, walls expanding and contracting in rhythm with his own labored breathing.

"Captain Abercrombie!"

A voice called out from the shadows ahead. Mac squinted, trying to focus on the figure that wavered in his distorted vision. The silhouette split into eight identical forms before merging back into one—a woman in what might have been a doctor's uniform, though in his perception it looked more like a wedding dress made of cobwebs.

"Dr. Hand," he said, recognizing her despite his delirium. "Come to join the inspection, have you? The crew's performance is exemplary today."

"Jesus Christ," she whispered, taking in his disheveled appearance and the mass of spiders flowing around his feet like black waves. "How long since you were bitten?"

Mac chuckled, the sound bubbling up from his chest like champagne from a shaken bottle. "Bitten? Nonsense. Just a training exer-

cise. War games, you understand. Preparing for the German U-boats."
He tapped the side of his nose conspiratorially. "They're disguised as
spiders now. Clever bastards."

Fiona approached cautiously, her hands raised in a gesture of peace.
The spiders parted around her feet, maintaining a perfect circle of
empty space. In Mac's warped viewpoint, she seemed to glow with an
ethereal light, her white clothing catching the emergency lighting and
transforming it into a halo.

"An angel," he murmured. "Have I died, then? Is this judgment
day?"

"You're not dead yet," Fiona said, her voice cutting through his
hallucination with unexpected clarity. "But you will be if we don't get
that venom neutralized."

She reached slowly into her medical bag, movements measured to
avoid startling him. Mac watched with detached fascination as she
withdrew a syringe filled with amber liquid.

"What's that?" he asked, suddenly suspicious. "German truth
serum? I'll tell you nothing! Name, rank, and serial number only!"

"It's antivenin," Fiona explained, inching closer. "I synthesized it
from samples I collected. It might help counteract the neurotoxic
effects."

Mac's hand moved to his service pistol with alarming speed. "Stand
down, spy! I'll not be poisoned by enemy agents!"

The gun wavered in his trembling hand, pointing somewhere
in Fiona's general direction. Water continued to rise around them,
now reaching mid-thigh, making his movements sluggish and unpredictable.

"Listen to me, Captain," Fiona said, her voice taking on the particular tone that medical professionals reserved for patients in crisis.

"You've been compromised. The venom is affecting your perception. What you're seeing isn't real."

"Not real?" Mac glanced down at the spiders, which had formed a defensive perimeter around him. "My crew? The finest sailors in His Majesty's Navy?"

"They're not your crew," Fiona insisted. "They're controlling you. Using you. You fired on your own ship, Captain. You put a hole in the hull. We're sinking because of what they made you do."

Something in her words penetrated the fog of his delusion. Mac blinked rapidly, momentarily glimpsing reality through the haze of hallucination. The corridor wasn't filled with loyal sailors but with arachnids whose synchronized movements suggested not military discipline but extraterrestrial intelligence.

"My God," he whispered, horror dawning in his eyes. "What have I done?"

The moment of clarity was fleeting. The spiders sensed his wavering loyalty and streamed forward, climbing his legs with renewed purpose. Mac screamed as they swarmed over him, their tiny legs pricking against his skin like hundreds of needles.

"Get them off!" he cried, dropping his gun to frantically brush at his uniform. "Get them off me!"

Fiona lunged forward, syringe raised. "Hold still!"

The spiders formed a living barrier between them, rising up in a wave that threatened to engulf the doctor. But Fiona had come prepared. From her pocket, she produced a small aerosol can of vintage shellac hairspray. She squirted in a wide arc, creating a path through the swarming mass.

The creatures retreated from the chemical assault, their coordinated movements momentarily disrupted. Fiona seized her opportunity, closing the distance to Mac and plunging the syringe into his arm just above the bite.

"I'm sorry," she said as she depressed the plunger. "This is going to hurt."

The effect was instantaneous and agonizing. Mac howled as the liquid fire spread through his veins, burning away the venom's influence with brutal efficiency. He collapsed to his knees in the rising water, convulsing as the antivenin waged chemical warfare against the supernatural toxin.

The spiders scattered in apparent confusion, their hive mind losing control of its human vessel. They flowed away down the corridor, disappearing into vents and crevices with unnatural speed.

Mac's vision cleared gradually, reality reasserting itself in painful increments. The singing bulkheads became creaking metal. The loyal crew dissolved into fragmented memory. The flooding corridor remained, however, all too real and rapidly becoming a death trap.

"We need to move," Fiona said urgently, helping him to his feet. "This section is going to be completely underwater in minutes."

Mac nodded, his mind still foggy but increasingly his own. "The passengers... the crew..."

"Most are gathered in the main ballroom," Fiona explained, supporting his weight as they waded through the waist-high water. "Christopher and Cleo are trying to reverse whatever started this. I've gotten word that Bonita's organizing a group to reach the lifeboats. But I'm afraid they're webbed over... I've never seen anything like it."

"I think I shot someone," Mac said, the memory surfacing with sickening clarity. "One of the crew. He was trying to... trying to..."

"He was trying to blast through a bulkhead to reach the communications room," Fiona finished for him. "You thought he was sabotaging the ship."

Shame washed over Mac, more bitter than the seawater soaking his uniform. "How many dead because of me?"

"You weren't yourself," Fiona said firmly. "The venom affects the brain's perception centers. Creates hallucinations, paranoia, suggestibility. They were using you as a weapon."

They reached a stairwell leading upward, away from the flooding. Mac paused, looking back at the corridor that was rapidly disappearing beneath the rising water.

"My ship," he said softly. "She's dying."

"But her captain isn't," Fiona replied, tugging him toward the stairs. "Not if I can help it. Come on, Mac. Your crew needs you. The real you."

Mac straightened his shoulders, military discipline reasserting itself despite his weakened state. With each step away from the flooded corridor, his mind cleared further. The antivenin continued its work, burning away the last vestiges of the hive mind's influence.

By the time they reached the upper deck, Captain Alastair Abercrombie was himself again—battered, exhausted, and haunted by what he'd done under the venom's influence, but determined to save whatever lives remained under his command.

"Where to, Doctor?" he asked, his voice regaining its natural authority.

"The ballroom," Fiona said, pointing toward the ship's center. "That's where everyone's gathering for a last stand."

Mac nodded grimly. "Then that's where we're needed most."

Together they moved through the perishing ship, racing against rising water and time itself, toward whatever fate awaited them in the heart of the *Pacific Dream*.

Chapter 20

The memory of the fateful night she'd uttered that damnable curse burned through Cleo's mind as she stumbled down the corridor toward Christopher's cabin. Her rage had been a living thing, coiling around her heart.

"Stupid, stupid, stupid," Cleo muttered now as she led their small group back toward Christopher's quarters. The emergency lighting cast shifting contours along the walls, and every creak of the ship made them freeze.

Christopher kept close behind her, his breathing shallow. Eleanor—who had somehow survived by barricading herself in a coat closet—followed with wide, mascara-smeared eyes. Rashida brought up the rear, now clutching a makeshift flamethrower fashioned from a can of bug spray and a lighter.

Cleo hadn't expected to find Eleanor alive, let alone convince her to join their desperate mission. They'd stumbled upon her by accident. Cleo and Christopher had been searching for her, but had nearly given up when they heard whimpering from a nearby closet.

"It could be a trap," Christopher had whispered, but Cleo felt something distinctly human about the sounds.

When they'd pried open the door, Eleanor shrieked, wielding a broken wine bottle. Her designer dress was torn, her carefully styled hair a tangled mess, and her eyes wild with terror. She clutched a Dior handbag to her breast like it was a shield.

"Stay back!" Eleanor had hissed. "I know what you two did. This is *your* fault!"

"Eleanor, we need your help," Cleo said, keeping her distance. "I can fix this, but I need the three people who were involved in my spell."

"Why would I trust you? You're the witch who caused this!"

Christopher stepped forward. "Because we're your only chance. Everyone else on this deck is dead."

Eleanor's mascara-streaked face crumpled. "Everyone?"

"Everyone we've found," Cleo admitted. "But we have a plan."

What finally convinced Eleanor wasn't trust but survival instinct. When a skittering sound came from the ventilation shaft above them, she'd practically leapt into the hallway.

"Fine. But if we survive this, I'm making sure everyone knows what you did."

They'd been making their way toward the cargo hold when Rashida found them. She'd appeared from a service corridor, covered in spider bites but somehow still fighting. The flamethrower in her hands had clearly seen use, as the acrid smell of burned chitin surrounded her.

"Found you," Rashida had panted, leaning against the wall. "Come on, we have to go back to Christopher's cabin." Then she started off, indicating that everyone should follow her.

"You're sure this will work?" Christopher whispered, falling into step beside Cleo.

"No," Cleo admitted. "But I feel something pulling me. Like a leash around my throat. We have to get those terrariums."

They rounded the corner to Christopher's cabin. The door was now splintered at the hinges. Inside, where his elaborate terrariums had once stood in neat rows, was a carnage of glass shards, spilled substrate, and twisted metal frames.

"They're gone," Christopher said, voice hollow.

A sound from the bathroom made them all jump. Rashida pushed past them, weapon raised, and kicked open the door.

There stood Rashida—another Rashida—surrounded by hundreds of tiny corpses. The smell of scorched chitin filled the air. This second Rashida's arms were covered in bites, her clothes torn and bloody, but her eyes blazed with triumph.

"Your spiders," she said, swaying slightly. "Killed every last one."

Christopher rushed forward, face twisted in horror. "Those were rare specimens, and we need the original five for the reversal of Cleo's curse."

"That were trying to kill us," Rashida snapped, then collapsed against the wall. "They locked me in here."

The Rashida at the door raised her can of bug spray. "We need to torch her."

Cleo's blood turned to ice. "You're not Rashida."

The woman slumped against the doorjamb, smiling, her face rippling slightly. "So, you really are psychic."

Before any of them could move, the false Rashida's form melted, collapsing into thousands of tiny spiders that scattered across the floor. Eleanor screamed as they surged toward the door.

"The terrariums!" Cleo shouted, grabbing Christopher's arm. "We need the pieces they left behind!"

Christopher hesitated only a moment before nodding. They gathered what remained while Rashida—the real Rashida—leapt from her bathroom prison and swung her tire iron at spiders that came too close.

"The cargo hold," Cleo said, that supernatural pull growing stronger. "That's where this needs to end."

They fought their way through the ship, Rashida clearing paths with her tire iron, using it like a machete to slice through the jungle of writhing masses. Eleanor proved surprisingly useful, her designer handbag wielded like a weapon against anything that moved.

The deeper they descended, the stronger Cleo felt the connection like invisible threads tightening around her wrists, her throat, pulling her toward something ancient and hungry that she'd accidentally awakened.

"I can feel it," she muttered as they approached the cargo hold doors. "Whatever's down there knows we're coming."

Christopher still clutched the terrarium shards to his chest. "Then let's not keep it waiting."

The stairwell leading up from the lower decks felt endless. Cleo's legs burned with each step, her lungs struggling against the thick, humid air. Behind her, Christopher's labored breathing kept rhythm with Eleanor's occasional whimpers. Rashida took up the rear, her weapon held at the ready.

As they reached the promenade deck, Cleo raised her hand, stopping abruptly. The others bumped into her like dominoes.

"What is it?" Christopher whispered.

Cleo pressed a finger to her lips. Through the partially open doors of the grand ballroom, voices drifted out. Actual human voices—not screams of terror, but conversation.

She inched forward, peering through the gap. The sight made her breath catch. Captain Abercrombie stood at the center of a small group, his uniform torn and bloodied, but his eyes clear. The deranged, venom-induced madness that had possessed him earlier was gone. Dr. Hand was bandaging Karen Blacksmith's arm while Denver was distributing water bottles.

"The captain's alive," she whispered, turning back to the others. "And he's... normal."

Christopher moved beside her, his eyes widening. "How? He was completely gone. I saw him shooting at shadows."

"The venom must be wearing off," Rashida suggested. "Maybe when we started the reversal process?"

Eleanor pushed forward. "We should join them. Safety in numbers."

"No." Cleo pulled her back from the doorway. "We can't."

"Are you insane?" Eleanor hissed. "There are people in there. Living people!"

"If we tell them what we're doing, they'll try to stop us," Cleo explained, her voice low and urgent. "They'll want to evacuate, to get everyone to safety first. But the ritual has to happen now, while the connection is still strong."

Christopher nodded. "She's right. I can feel it too. Whatever's down there is... waiting for us."

Eleanor's face paled beneath her smudged makeup. She reluctantly stepped back from the doorway.

"We move silently," Cleo instructed. "Hug the wall. If they see us..."

"They won't," Christopher assured her, slipping into the practiced stealth of a stage performer.

They crept past the ballroom entrance, freezing when Denver's voice rose above the others.

"—checking the lower decks again. There might be more survivors."

Cleo's heart hammered against her ribs. If Denver came looking, they'd be discovered. She caught Christopher's eye, nodding toward the service corridor ahead. They needed to move faster.

The group slipped around the corner just as footsteps approached the ballroom doors. Cleo pressed her back against the wall, feeling the pull of something primordial and terrible drawing her downward, toward the room where this nightmare would end, one way or another.

The doors to the cargo hold stood partially open, darkness pulsing beyond them like a necrotic heartbeat. Cleo took a deep breath and stepped forward, drawn by forces she'd unleashed but never truly understood until now.

This is what real power looks like, she thought with the mixture of awe and terror that accompanied witnessing the impossible made manifest. *This is what I accidentally called into existence.*

The webbing formed geometric patterns that hurt to look at directly, mathematical precision that suggested intelligence far more sophisticated than anything evolution should have produced in the space of days. At the center of it all were Christopher's original terrariums. Now that they were broken, something vast and grotesque had taken shape. It was beautiful in the way that AI artistry was beautiful, utterly wrong by human aesthetic standards, but possessed of its own terrible logic. Hundreds, perhaps thousands of spiders had somehow fused into a single organism that retained individual components while achieving collective purpose. Eyes—far too many eyes—tracked their descent into the hold with intelligence that felt ancient despite being just days old.

The hive queen, Cleo realized with the particular clarity that came from recognizing her own handiwork transformed beyond recognition. *What kind of monster have I created?*

Staying beside Cleo, Christopher moved with the particular grace of a man whose performance training had unwittingly prepared him for situations that existed outside normal experience.

But she could see the strain in his posture, the way his hands wobbled with the effort of maintaining control over instincts that were screaming at him to run. *He's terrified,* she realized. *But he's staying anyway. Because of guilt, because of responsibility, because of whatever passed between us on the balcony.*

"The reversal incantation," she said, her voice steadier than she had any right to expect, "needs to be performed at the epicenter of the original spell. Where the spiritual energy is most concentrated." *Which is approximately three feet from something that looks like it could eat us all without turning a hair,* she added silently.

Christopher nodded. "What do you need me to do?"

"Place those fragments of terrarium as close as you can to the five pieces there," she replied. *Easier said than done.*

Cristopher swallowed hard and did as he was told. His fingers were sliced in multiple places, thin rivulets of blood trickling down the jagged edges of what had once housed his prized collection. The shattered containers, meticulously crafted to maintain precise humidity and temperature controls for his exotic performers, now served only as makeshift magical weapons against the very creatures they were designed to protect. His eyes, once filled with accusation toward the self-proclaimed psychic, now reflected something entirely different: a commitment to their shared survival.

Cleo felt something shift in her consciousness. Not her familiar self-doubt, but something older, deeper, more authentically connected to forces she'd only been pretending to understand. Emma Glopstein had spent thirty-seven years pretending to commune with forces beyond human understanding, but deep inside the *Pacific Dream's* cargo hold, she found herself face-to-face with something that made her decades of theatrical mysticism look like children's party tricks.

O spirits, she whispered silently, reaching for the spiritual guidance that had always felt like imagination but was beginning to feel like something embedded into her DNA. *Help me fix what I've broken.*

The response came not in words but in knowledge. In sudden, complete understanding of what the reversal ritual actually required. Not just spoken incantation, but genuine spiritual communion. Not performance of mystical authority, but authentic surrender to forces that existed beyond human control.

I have to stop being Emma pretending to be Cleo, she realized with the particular clarity that accompanied genuine spiritual revelation. *I have to become whatever I actually am underneath all the pretending.*

The hive queen stirred as they approached, its interlocked cognizance apparently recognizing the threat they represented. Cleo felt the vibration through the soles of her shoes before she saw the movement; a subtle trembling that sent icy prickles skating across her skin. The musty, acrid smell of the creatures filled her nostrils, an alien scent that triggered something in her limbic brain.

They know why we're here, Cleo thought, beginning the incantation even as creatures swarmed around their feet. *They understand that we're trying to undo their existence.*

The attack, when it came, was seemingly endless waves of individual spiders flowing toward them in patterns that suggested more than simple predatory instinct. Their tiny legs made a soft, horrifying patter against the metal floor. Like rain, but deliberate and hungry.

Eleanor screamed and huddled to the ground, folding herself into as small a target as possible, her trembling hands desperately trying to shield her face and ears from the relentless onslaught. The once-elegant fishtail evening dress she wore tangled around her legs as she crouched, its vintage fabric offering no protection against the fiends surrounding them. Her terrified whimpers escaped between her fingers as wave after wave of arachnids scuttled across the metal flooring around her.

Rashida froze in horror, her body locked in place as if she herself had been envenomed. Her wide eyes tracked the impossible movement of hundreds—no, thousands—of spiders flowing across the floor like a living carpet. The blood drained from her face, leaving her dark complexion ashen against the vibrant red of her smeared but period-appropriate lipstick. Her chest barely moved as she held her breath, afraid that even the slightest motion might trigger something even worse.

The attacking spiders, mere inches from overwhelming them completely, suddenly scurried away as if repelled by an invisible barrier. They retreated in perfect synchronization, their tiny legs repositioning in eerie unison as they flowed back toward their queen like a receding tide. Their unified movement betrayed confusion and hesitation, clearly confounded by some unseen force emanating from Christopher and Cleo's united presence, a power neither of them fully understood but which momentarily held the horde at bay.

CHAPTER 21

L ouisiana French poured from Cleo's lips with fluency that astonished her—not the carefully memorized phrases she'd been using for performance purposes, but words that seemed to emerge from genetic memory, ancestral knowledge that had been waiting decades for authentic expression.

"Que les liens soient brisés comme ils ont été forgés. Que la volonté collective redevienne individuelle. Que ce qui a été éveillé retourne au sommeil éternel."

Let the bonds be broken as they were forged. Let the collective will become individual again. Let what has been awakened return to eternal sleep.

But the ritual required more than words. It demanded sacrifice, genuine risk, the kind of authentic magical working that couldn't be achieved through theatrical performance.

The hive queen sensed the building spiritual energy and responded with increasing aggression, sending wave after wave of attackers toward them with dexterity that spoke to wisdom that transcended anything natural evolution should have produced. The massive, pulsating entity at the center of the web network quivered with malevolent awareness, its compound eyes reflecting a sinister shared goal. Each movement of its grotesquely fused limbs triggered precise responses from its minions, deploying them in tactical formations that no natural arachnid could conceive. These were pincer movements, diversionary attacks, and sacrificial waves designed to exhaust their human prey.

We're not going to make it, Cleo thought as spiders swarmed over her legs, their bites delivering venom that was already beginning to affect her perception. *There are too many of them, and they're too coordinated.*

The sensation of countless tiny legs crawling across her skin sent tidal waves of primal terror rushing through her body. The venom worked quickly, making the edges of her vision blur and the ship's ornate 1940s-inspired décor warp and twist in impossible ways. She prepared to die.

That was when Christopher did something that surprised her.

Instead of fighting the attacking spiders or trying to help with the incantation, he stepped into the center of the swarm and began to perform—not the elaborate stage magic he'd built his career on, but something simpler, more fundamental. Sleight of hand so pure and perfect that it transcended entertainment and morphed into genuine mysticism. His fingers moved with flair, creating patterns in the air that seemed to bend light itself. The vintage cufflinks hanging from threads on his tattered attire caught the emergency lighting, sending hypnotic flashes across the chamber as he wove reality and illusion together with movements that contained no deception, only the raw, honest manipulation of attention and perception that formed the foundation of all magical arts.

Misdirection, Cleo realized as she watched him make objects appear and disappear with movements that seemed to tear at the very fabric of their beings. *He's using performance to create genuine magic.*

The hive queen's attention shifted toward Christopher's impromptu show, its amalgamated intelligence apparently fascinated by the display of controlled impossibility. Individual spiders stopped their attacks, gathering instead to observe this human who seemed to be rewriting the laws of physics with nothing more than skilled fingers and seamless timing.

Cleo felt Rashida's intense gaze from the edge of the chamber, her journalist's instinct apparently undimmed even in the face of horror. The woman stood with her back pressed against a bulkhead, seemingly composing the narrative in her mind. If they survived, Cleo had a feeling their story would fly off the shelves and be shared millions of times.

As Christopher's hands wove their hypnotic patterns, drawing the hive queen's attention, a figure emerged from the shadows.

Eleanor Hargrove, her composure regained, moved with purposeful steps toward them.

The influencer positioned herself equidistant from Christopher and Cleo, completing a triangle around the pulsating mass of the hive queen. Without explanation or hesitation, she raised her hands in perfect mimicry of their ritual postures.

Power surged through the space between them. Not the manufactured energy of Cleo's performances or Eleanor's carefully curated social presence, but something authentic and ancient. Three points forming a circuit, channeling energies that transcended individual intention.

The spiders froze in unison as the trinity locked into place.

They're distracted, Cleo understood. *Christopher and Eleanor are giving me the space I need to complete the ritual.*

She raised her voice, pouring everything she had—Emma's desperation, Cleo's accumulated theatrical power, and something deeper that might have been genuine spiritual authority—into the final phrases of the reversal incantation.

"Par le sang de mes ancêtres, par la sagesse des esprits, par la force de la volonté juste—que ce sort soit défait!"

By the blood of my ancestors, by the wisdom of spirits, by the force of righteous will—let this spell be undone!

The effect was immediate and stupefying.

The hive queen convulsed, its fused body beginning to separate with wet, tearing sounds that suggested organic architecture collapsing from within. Individual spiders that had been components of the collective consciousness suddenly found themselves alone in their own minds, confused and disoriented by the abrupt severing of neural connections they'd never possessed naturally. Legs twitched spasmodically while abdomens pulsed with uncoordinated rhythms, a grotesque symphony of arachnid panic playing out across the cargo hold's slick, corrugated metal floor.

It's working, Cleo thought with triumph that was immediately overwhelmed by visceral horror as she surveyed the consequences of her magical intervention unfold in real time. Her stomach lurched as the mass before them continued its gruesome disintegration, the reversal spell tearing apart connections that should never have existed in nature.

The hive queen's death was not clean or quick. She exploded outward in a cascade of biological fragments of spider parts, web material, and substances that didn't seem to belong to any recognizable taxonomy. Chitinous exoskeletons erupted and split, revealing iridescent fluids that steamed when they hit the cold metal flooring. The sound was indescribable, somewhere between breaking glass and screaming metal, with harmonic undertones that suggested intelligence experiencing dissolution on a level that human consciousness couldn't fully process. The air filled with a sickly sweet odor reminiscent of burnt caramel and formaldehyde, making Cleo gag as she maintained her position in the ritual triangle.

Around them, the smaller spiders began falling from the walls and ceiling in clumps, their supernatural cohesion dissolving as the queen's influence waned. They landed with soft pattering sounds, like macabre rainfall against the ship's hard surfaces, their legs curling inward in death's final embrace.

The individual spiders died in waves, their mystical vitality draining away as the shared purpose that had been sustaining them collapsed. But their deaths weren't random. No, they fell in patterns that suggested the hive mind's final moments were being used to communicate something, to leave a message written in the arrangement of thousands of tiny corpses.

What are they trying to tell us? Cleo wondered, even as relief flooded through her system. *What kind of final wisdom does a dying intelligence want to share?*

But there was no time to analyze the spiders' posthumous communication. The ship was still flooding, still listing to starboard with the progressive inevitability of physics asserting itself over human engineering. Whatever they'd accomplished in the cargo hold, they still needed to survive long enough to escape the *Pacific Dream* before it decided to become their tomb.

We did it, she thought, looking at Christopher with something that might have been love or might have been shared trauma or might have been recognition of the strange alchemy that had allowed a failed

magician and a fraudulent psychic to perform genuine magic when
everything else had been stripped away.

We actually did it. Real magic.

Cleo's knees gave way as she watched the final transformation unfold before her. Thousands of spider corpses didn't just decompose,
they evaporated like morning mist under a rising sun, leaving behind
only the faintest shimmer on the metal floor. The air cleared of its
putrid stench, replaced by the familiar smell of salt water and the ship's
polished wood.

"Look," she whispered, her voice hoarse from the ritual.

There on the floor, impossibly intact, sat Christopher's five original
terrariums. Each glass enclosure stood perfectly arranged as if they'd
never been disturbed and as if the nightmare of the past days had been
nothing but an elaborate hallucination.

The Australian huntsman perched on its eucalyptus branch, legs
spread in that distinctive ready position that had so delighted audiences. Next to it, the Wraparound spider clung to the curved bark
Christopher had specially selected to showcase its unique camo hunting style. The Chinese bird spider's terrarium contained the miniature
rock formation that Christopher claimed resembled the mountains
of Yunnan Province. The Chilean recluse remained partially hidden
in its preferred shadow, visible only as a silhouette against the sandy
substrate. And the North American jumping spider stood alert on its
tiny platform, seeming to watch Cleo with those oversized eyes that
gave it an almost cute, cartoon-like appearance.

Five terrariums. Five spiders. Nothing more.

"They're just... spiders again," Cleo murmured, reaching out a
trembling hand before pulling it back. "Regular spiders."

She studied them with newfound respect and fear. These creatures
had been the core of the hive mind, the original vessels through which

an ancient power had manifested. Now they appeared so ordinary, so contained—yet Cleo would never see them as merely animals again.

"The spell didn't destroy them," she realized. "It restored them."

The symmetry wasn't lost on her. Her jealousy had transformed these performers into monsters; her remorse had returned them to their natural state. The curse had been reversed completely, leaving behind no evidence of the horror except in the memories of survivors.

Cleo felt something shift within her. Not just relief, but understanding. The power she'd accessed wasn't something external to be commanded through theatrical gestures. It had always been there, waiting for her to recognize it.

The question now was whether any of them would survive long enough to process what they'd learned about the spaces where human will intersected with forces that existed beyond rational understanding. The bullet holes were all too real, and the ship was still sinking.

Cleo's legs trembled as she reached for the first terrarium. Her fingertips hesitated at the glass edge, half-expecting the Australian huntsman to launch itself at her face. Instead, it remained motionless on its branch, legs tucked in a resting position.

"They won't hurt us now," Christopher said, his voice carrying a mix of reverence and caution.

Cleo lifted the container, its weight solid and real in her hands. She gathered a second terrarium while Christopher collected the remaining three.

The ship groaned around them, metal protesting as water found new pathways into the hull. A sharp tilt sent Cleo stumbling against Christopher's shoulder.

"We need to move," she said, steadying herself. "This place could go under any minute."

Cleo looked back once at the space where the hive queen had pulsated with malevolent life. Nothing remained but faint iridescent residue, and even that was fading before her eyes.

"Whatever power was here," Christopher murmured, "it's gone now."

Cleo nodded, feeling the absence like a pressure change in her ears. "Let's find the others." She turned to Eleanor and Rashida. "Come on."

The weight of the terrariums felt oddly comforting in Cleo's arms as she made her way back through the ship's winding corridors. Each glass enclosure contained a single spider, docile and ordinary once more, a stark contrast to the demons they'd unleashed. The emergency lighting cast long shadows across the walls, and the distant groan of metal reminded her that their victory was incomplete. The ship was still sinking.

Christopher walked beside her, cradling his terrariums with the reverent care of a father reunited with his children. "I can feel them," he said, glancing down at the glass containers. "I was right. They're just... spiders again. Nothing more."

"Regular spiders with regular spider thoughts," Cleo agreed, adjusting her grip on the terrariums she carried. "Whatever consciousness possessed them is gone."

Behind them, Eleanor and Rashida trudged in exhausted silence. Eleanor's usual selfie-straight posture was slumped, and her gait was a slow shuffle. Rashida still clutched her tire iron, eyes constantly scanning for threats that no longer existed.

The ship listed slightly to port as they climbed the stairs toward the ballroom where the remaining survivors had gathered. Water sloshed noisily around their ankles—a reminder that while they'd defeated one enemy, another was claiming the vessel with methodical inevitability.

"When we were down there," Cleo said hesitantly, "during the ritual... I felt something." She paused, searching for words to describe the inexplicable. "It wasn't just me channeling the reversal spell. There was... guidance."

Christopher glanced at her, his expression softening. "I felt it too. Like invisible hands guiding my movements." He adjusted his grip on the terrariums. "Do you think it was actually spirits? Real ones?"

Cleo nodded slowly. "I've spent years faking connections to the other side, but this was different. This was... authentic." She lowered her voice. "Christopher, do you think one of them might have been Danny?"

He stopped abruptly, his face a complex map of emotions—hope, disbelief, longing. "Danny?"

"The way your hands moved during the ritual, it wasn't just sleight of hand. There was purpose behind it, like someone was working through you." Cleo shifted the terrariums in her arms. "And I kept hearing a child's laughter, just at the edge of my perception. A little boy."

Christopher's eyes glistened in the dim light. "He would have been thirty-nine this year." His voice trembled slightly. "Sometimes I wonder what kind of man he would have become."

"A good one," Cleo said with certainty that surprised even her. "He helped save us all."

"You really believe that?" Christopher asked, vulnerability naked in his expression.

"I do." She met his gaze steadily. "I think he's been with you all along, watching over you. Maybe that's why you've never been bitten, despite working with such dangerous creatures for so many years."

They resumed walking, the silence between them now companionable rather than strained. The distant sound of voices grew louder as they approached the ballroom. Survivors comparing experiences, planning evacuation, and processing trauma through shared narrative.

"I never believed in any of this," Christopher admitted quietly. "The spiritual stuff, the other side, all of it. It was just another form of illusion to me—tricks people play on themselves to feel better about the randomness of existence."

"And now?" Cleo asked.

He looked down at the glass enclosures in his arms. "Now I don't know what to believe. Except that whatever happened down there wasn't just your spell or my sleight of hand. It was something... more."

"That's the thing about magic. *Real* magic," Cleo said, the words feeling right in her mouth for the first time. "It's not about knowing all the answers. It's about being open to possibilities beyond our understanding."

As they neared the ballroom entrance, Eleanor pushed past them, muttering something about needing a shower and therapy. Rashida lingered behind, clearly eavesdropping for material while pretending to adjust her rumpled clothing.

"If Danny was there," Christopher said, his voice barely audible, "I hope he knows I never stopped missing him. That everything I've done with spiders was trying to master what took him from me."

Cleo shifted her terrariums to one arm and placed her free hand on Christopher's shoulder. "He knows. That's why he helped us when we needed it most."

For a moment, they stood together in the dim corridor, surrounded by the evidence of supernatural horror but connected by something that transcended both performance and tragedy. It was genuine understanding born of shared experience.

"Come on," Cleo said gently. "Let's join the others. We have quite a story to tell."

They walked the final distance to the ballroom, carrying their glass enclosures like precious artifacts—five ordinary spiders that had briefly become vessels for something far beyond ordinary understanding, now returned to their natural state through a magic neither of them had fully comprehended before this voyage.

And somewhere, Cleo thought she could still hear the faint echo of a child's eternal laughter, fading into whatever realm existed beyond the boundaries of the known world—a sound of joy rather than malice, of completion rather than loss.

CHAPTER 22

Christopher Webb had performed his final show aboard the *Pacific Dream*, and for once, the applause came in the form of silence. The profound, oceanic quiet that followed catastrophe survived. Standing on the ship's listing deck in the gray dawn light, watching rescue helicopters approach like mechanical angels against a sky that had witnessed the unthinkable, he found himself cataloging the particular breed of exhaustion he felt. His legs were leaden beneath him, muscles quivering with fatigue that seemed to reach into his very marrow. The salt air stung his nostrils, mingling with the acrid smell of burnt electrical wiring and something worse: the lingering fusty scent of thousands of arachnid corpses. No matter that they'd disappeared into the ether, he knew.

Hundreds of survivors, he thought, his mind automatically taking inventory even as his body trembled with the aftershocks of adrenaline withdrawal. *Out of three hundred and fifty-nine souls who'd boarded this floating time capsule with nothing more dangerous on their minds than vintage cocktails and swing dancing... Thank god most of them were still here.* The thought pulsed through his skull with each heartbeat, a mantra of gratitude that felt insufficient against the weight of what they'd experienced. His fingertips tingled with phantom sensations—the memory of spiders crawling across his skin, the texture of Cleo's hand gripping his during the ritual, the sharp edges of broken terrariums.

Rashida Bell had claimed a position near the ship's rail, her journalist instincts finally free to function without the immediate threat of becoming spider food. Her notepad was already filled with frantic scribbles, observations captured in the chaotic aftermath that she knew would seem impossible in the light of day. The scratch of her pen against paper created a hypnotic rhythm that Christopher could sense even across the deck. "This is either going to win me a Pulitzer or get me committed to a psychiatric facility," she announced to no one in particular. "Possibly both."

Eleanor, the young woman whom he'd once found slyly alluring and attractive, was a bedraggled ghost of her former self, huddled beneath an emergency blanket that couldn't hide the tear tracks cutting through the grime on her cheeks. The wool material scratched audibly against her skin as she shivered despite the gathering morning warmth. Christopher had to admire the fact that she'd come through in the end to defeat the spider scourge. But he now understood that she was just a girl who probably couldn't wait to redo her makeup and get back on her social media accounts. Her eyes kept darting in the direction of the recovered safe where their phones were stored, as if digital connection might somehow erase the horrors of the past several hours.

Captain Alastair "Mac" Abercrombie seemed at once dazed and drained, even as he retook command. The bite marks visible along his neck had swollen to angry red welts, pulsing with each heartbeat, and his normally pristine captain's uniform hung in tatters from his frame. The gold buttons caught the morning light, winking like tired eyes. His voice shook as he kept in touch with the oncoming rescue crews and broke protocol by announcing that everyone would now be allowed to access their cellphones from the ship's large safe.

A crew member scrambled to work the combination with several eager passengers in tow, and of course, Eleanor. The metal box creaked open with a sound that made Christopher flinch involuntarily. The spiders that had once guarded it were now nothing more than smears of dust and ichor on the polished deck.

Dr. Fiona Hand stood near the ship's radio equipment, her white uniform blackened with various bodily fluids, both human and arachnid. She seemed relieved that her medical training had finally shifted back to focusing on straightforward human injuries rather than supernatural biological anomalies. She checked the vital signs of a semiconscious crew member, her movements precise despite the fatigue etched into every line of her face. The gentle pressure of her fingers against the patient's wrist created a moment of connection that Christopher envied—the simple human touch that confirmed life continued.

Karen Blacksmith sat in the ship's remaining functional deck chair, her frail frame somehow more resilient than passengers half her age, even with her arm in a provisional sling. The canvas creaked beneath her weight with each gentle sway of the ship. The newly-minted widow stared out at the approaching rescue vessels with glassy eyes that had witnessed too much. Her breathing came in shallow, measured intervals, as if each inhale required conscious effort.

Denver Wheaton was pummeled and sagging, his once-immaculate steward's uniform now torn in a few places, but he still maintained his cheer and his period-correct vernacular. The fabric of his jacket made soft swishing sounds as he moved among the survivors. "Quite the pickle we found ourselves in, sir," he remarked to a shell-shocked passenger, adjusting his crooked tie as if they'd merely weathered a particularly rough storm rather than a supernatural arachnid apocalypse. "But the *Pacific Dream* never disappoints when it comes to memorable voyages, does she not?" His voice carried the artificial brightness that Christopher recognized from his own performances. The show must go on.

The handful of crew members and waitstaff who'd made it through the night huddled near the ship's emergency equipment, their usual professional competence replaced by the thousand-yard stare that followed a rough, unexplainable, unknowable trauma. Their breathing synchronized unconsciously, creating an integrated rhythm that reminded Christopher uncomfortably of the spiders' coordinated movements. They passed around a flask of something strong, the liquid sloshing inside with each shaky exchange, their hands wobbling as they took quick, desperate sips. The sharp smell of whiskey cut through the salt air, grounding them in a familiar vice.

Christopher watched the rescue operation unfold with a mix of disbelief and morbid fascination. The thump-thump of helicopter rotors grew louder, vibrating through his chest cavity like a second heartbeat. Coast Guard personnel in bright orange vests guided dazed passengers into evacuation rafts, their voices carrying commands that seemed to come from another world entirely. The rubber of the rafts squeaked against the ship's hull with each wave, a sound so mundane it felt surreal. The survivors moved like sleepwalkers, clutching at blankets and each other, their faces vacant with confusion rather than horror. Their shoes shuffled across the deck in an uneven chorus, a discordant symphony of shock.

"They don't remember," he murmured, catching Rashida's eye as she helped Karen Blacksmith toward the nearest lifeboat. The realization felt like cold water trickling down his spine. Sadly, Christopher thought, the woman would never remember how her husband had sacrificed himself to save her and many others, using his own body as a shield against the swarming spiders in the grand ballroom before they'd dragged him away into the darkness. The hollow absence beside her seemed to have its own gravity, a void that pulled at Christopher's heart.

Rashida finished her task, then approached, giving him a grim nod. "Mass hallucination, that's what they're saying. Some kind of gas leak affecting the ventilation system." Her voice carried just enough for him to hear over the growing commotion, the words tasting like ash in the air between them.

Christopher ran a hand through his hair, sticky with something weblike that he didn't want to identify. The tacky substance clung to his fingers, making them stick together slightly. "Gas leak. Right." The words felt hollow in his mouth, inadequate vessels for the truth they'd witnessed.

The explanation was spreading among the survivors with the efficiency of the very hive mind they'd destroyed. Passengers nodded along, filling in their own gaps with rational explanations. The murmurs created a background hum of denial that was almost soothing in its predictability. He overheard fragments. Something about food poisoning, equipment malfunction, a rogue wave that had caused the ship to list and spill several hapless passengers into the hungry sea. Nothing about sentient arachnids with a taste for human flesh. The rewriting of reality buzzed in his ears like static.

Across the deck, Cleo stood alone by the railing, her frock torn and stained, her face a mask of complicated guilt warring with relief. The wind whipped her hair around her face, the dark strands dancing like living things. Their eyes met briefly before she looked away, the connection between them almost physical in its intensity. The weight of their shared knowledge hung between them like the remnants of her spell, invisible but undeniably real. He could almost feel the threads of it vibrating in the space that separated them.

Eleanor Hargrove passed by, her just-retrieved phone in hand and snapping selfies, despite everything. The artificial camera shutter sound thrummed through the air with jarring brightness. She paused beside Christopher, her voice low, carrying the aroma of expensive perfume that somehow clung to her despite everything. "Nobody will believe what really happened here. I've already tried telling three different rescue workers." Her words carried a bitter undertone that he could almost taste.

"Maybe that's for the best," he replied, feeling the truth of it settle in his gut like a stone.

"Is it?" Eleanor's perfectly manicured eyebrow arched. "People died, Christopher. Horrible deaths." Her voice went up an octave on the last word, revealing the raw grief beneath her composed exterior.

"And what good would the truth do them now?" He gestured toward the cowering masses of survivors. "Look at their faces. They're already healing." The words tasted like a necessary lie, both tart and sweet on his tongue.

Eleanor shook her head and walked away, her heels clicking against the deck in sharp counterpoint to the softer sounds of rescue operations. Christopher watched her go, leaving him to wonder if forgetting was just another form of magic—perhaps the most merciful kind. The thought settled in his mind like a clinging feather, light but impossible to dislodge.

Christopher's own phone showed dozens of missed calls from his agent, his publicist, various entertainment industry contacts who had no idea that their concerns about booking schedules and performance contracts had been rendered magnificently irrelevant by circumstances that existed entirely outside show business parameters.

The device felt unnaturally heavy in his hand, a tether to a world that suddenly seemed distant and unimportant.

He watched as a Coast Guard officer approached, clipboard in hand, ready to take his statement. The man's boots created a steady rhythm against the deck, each step bringing him closer to questions Christopher wasn't sure how to answer. The pen was poised above the paper, waiting to document a sanitized version of impossibility.

"Sir, can you tell me what happened on the ship?" The officer's voice carried the particular neutrality of someone trained not to react to trauma narratives.

Christopher hesitated, feeling the weight of three sets of eyes on him—Cleo's, Rashida's, Eleanor's—each carrying the burden of an impossible truth. His heart pounded in his ears, drowning out the ambient sounds of rescue as he considered what version of reality he was willing to commit to the official record.

"No. No, I can't," he finally stammered, picking up a discarded wooden champagne crate that now housed all five of his spider terrariums and stepping away.

Cleo still stood apart from the others, not from antisocial impulse but from the particular isolation that came from accepting responsibility for catastrophic mistakes and somehow finding the strength to fix them. Her turban was gone, her dark hair falling in tangled waves around her face, catching the morning light in ways that reminded him of the silken strands they'd encountered in the ship's corridors.

Real power, Christopher thought, recalling the moment in the cargo hold when theatrical mysticism had transformed into genuine magical authority. *She spent years pretending to commune with forces beyond human understanding, and when it finally mattered, discovered she actually could.* The realization humbled him. How many of his own illusions had been just that, mere tricks, when something more profound had been waiting all along?

Yet another approaching vessel, a military cutter that looked reassuringly mundane after the onslaught of supernatural horrors, was close enough now that individual crew members were visible on its deck. Their pressed uniforms and orderly movements represented a return to order that felt both comforting and somehow insufficient. Soon, there would be official debriefings, medical examinations, and psychological evaluations designed to determine whether their organized testimony represented genuine anomalous phenomena or elaborate shared hallucinations. The thought made his gut somersault with a mixture of dread and dark amusement. What would they write in their reports? Gas leak? Mass hysteria? Food poisoning from spoiled shellfish?

As the rescue boat drew alongside the *Pacific Dream*, the sickening scrape of metal against metal sending vibrations through the deck beneath his feet, Christopher found himself walking toward Cleo with a purposefulness that came from recognizing that some conversations couldn't be postponed indefinitely. The distance between them seemed both vast and insignificant—just yards of salt-stained decking that somehow represented the gulf between who they had been before this voyage and whoever they were becoming now. Whatever had passed between them during their shared ordeal needed acknowledgment before they returned to whatever passed for normal life in a world where magic existed but couldn't be publicly discussed.

She looked up at his approach, her smoky liner pooled into gothic shadows around eyes that had seen too much. Her expression carried the complex mixture of gratitude, guilt, and possibility that he'd been feeling since the showdown in the cargo hold. A small cut on her lower lip had crusted over, the wound somehow making her seem more substantial, more real than the polished psychic persona she'd cultivated.

"So," she said with a smile that was equal parts Emma Glopstein's self-deprecating humor and Cleo Laveau's mystical authority, "what does someone do for an encore after accidentally creating a supernatural plague and then magically reversing it?" The hoarseness in her voice betrayed the hours she'd spent screaming incantations against the chittering darkness.

Start over, Christopher thought, watching the wind tease strands of her hair across her face. *Accept that everything you thought you knew about yourself was incomplete, and figure out what comes next.* The thought was terrifying and exhilarating in equal measure, like standing at the edge of a precipice and feeling both the fear of falling and the strange urge to jump into the void.

"I was thinking," he said carefully, his voice rough from smoke and seawater, "that maybe we both need some time to process what we learned about... capabilities we didn't know we possessed." He gestured vaguely at the air between them, as if the invisible webs of their shared experience might become visible if he acknowledged them directly.

But not apart, he added silently, watching her eyes for signs that she understood his unspoken meaning. *Not after what we've shared, what we've survived, what we've discovered about the spaces where performance and reality intersect.* The memory of their hands joined in the darkness of the spider queen's lair, power flowing between them like electricity, made his fingertips tingle with phantom sensation.

"Processing," Cleo repeated with amusement, one eyebrow arching as she wrapped her tattered shawl tighter around her shoulders. "Is that what we're calling it? I was thinking more along the lines of 'complete psychological reconstruction following direct contact with forces that aren't supposed to exist.'" A wisp of hair caught in the corner of her mouth as she spoke, and he resisted the urge to brush it away.

Fair point, Christopher acknowledged, the corner of his own mouth twitching upward. *Though I prefer my version. Sounds less likely to require professional therapeutic intervention.* The shared joke felt like a tiny island of normalcy in an ocean of absurdity.

The Coast Guard crew was preparing boarding procedures, their movements carrying the efficient professionalism of people who dealt with maritime emergencies as a routine occupational hazard. Metal clanged against metal as they secured their vessel to the listing *Pacific Dream*, the sounds echoing across the water like industrial church bells. Soon, there would be safety briefings, medical evaluations, and official reports that would transform their supernatural ordeal into bureaucratic documentation, reducing the impossible to checkboxes on standardized forms.

Back to the world, Christopher thought, watching a seagull circle overhead with enviable freedom. *Back to reality where magic doesn't exist officially, and people who claim to have witnessed it are either delusional or publicity-seeking.* The prospect felt oddly empty, like returning to a stage after discovering that real wonders existed beyond the curtain.

But looking at Cleo—at the woman who'd discovered authentic spiritual power in the space between desperation and responsibility—he found himself thinking that perhaps returning to everyday reality wasn't the most important goal. Her presence beside him felt more substantial than the approaching authorities, more meaningful than whatever explanations they would eventually construct to make sense of the insensible.

After all, he thought, reliving the moment when sleight-of-hand had become genuine mysticism, when theatrical performance had transcended entertainment to become actual magic, *why would anyone want to go back to pretending that impossibility is impossible?* The knowledge sat in his chest like a warm coal, dangerous but illuminating.

"Emma," he said quietly, using her real name deliberately, watching how it landed between them like a private token of truth. "When they finish debriefing us, when the official investigation concludes, when we're released back into civilian life..." He let the sentence hang, suddenly uncertain how to articulate what he wanted to propose.

"Yes?" she asked, though her expression suggested she already knew what he was going to say. A small smile played at the corners of her mouth, the first genuine one he'd seen since they'd stood together in the cargo hold, facing down a nightmare made manifest.

"I think I'd like to learn more about magic. *Real* magic." His voice dropped to barely above a whisper, the words meant only for her. "The kind that exists in the spaces between what people believe and what actually happens when someone with genuine power stops pretending."

Partnership, he thought, watching her eyes widen slightly at his words. *Maybe romance. But regardless, an authentic collaboration between people who'd discovered they could touch forces that existed beyond normal human experience.* The possibility stretched before them like uncharted territory, dicey but compelling.

"I think," Cleo said, her fingers reaching out to brush against his, "I'd like that very much." The touch sent electricity up his arm, a reminder that whatever had awakened between them remained alive, waiting to be explored.

They would return to a world where their shared experience would be classified, dismissed, or rationalized into insignificance, reduced to footnotes in official reports and whispered rumors among cruise industry staff. But whatever came next, they would face it together, no longer pretending to be something they weren't, but becoming something neither of them had imagined possible.

Christopher stepped onto the rescue vessel, his legs unsteady from days on the listing cruise ship. The metal deck vibrated beneath his feet, solid in ways that felt almost shocking after what they'd survived. Cleo's hand found his, warm and affectionate, as they moved away from the *Pacific Dream*'s looming shadow.

A flash of white caught his eye. Then another.

His doves, released days ago when the first spiders had appeared, circled overhead in delicate formation. They descended in graceful spirals, landing on the railing beside him, their feathers pristine against the gray morning.

"Impossible," he whispered, extending his hand. The birds stepped onto his forearm with familiar weight.

Christopher glanced at his spiders, now docile in their containers. The huntsman sat motionless, watching him through compound eyes that seemed almost... peaceful.

A breeze brushed his cheek. Warm, gentle, and carrying a scent he hadn't encountered since childhood. Danny's favorite candy. His brother's presence felt as real as the doves on his arm.

"Did you send them back to me?" Christopher asked the empty air.

Beside him, Cleo smiled knowingly. "Some magic doesn't need spells," she said.

CHAPTER 23

Rashida Bell had written about genocides, corporate cover-ups, and presidential scandals, but nothing in her storied journalism career had prepared her for the particular challenge of documenting a voyage of the damned that couldn't be officially acknowledged to exist. Sitting in her suite at the Four Seasons Seattle, the late afternoon storm clouds casting restless shadows across her king-sized bed, she stared at the cursor blinking hypnotically on her laptop screen and tried to find words that would convey impossibility without sounding like someone who'd suffered a complete psychological break. She'd finished her first draft and her second, but she still felt the ending was lacking something. Her fingertips hovered over the keyboard, tensed—not from fear, but from the frustration of trying to translate cosmic puzzles into solid paragraphs.

"The Pacific Dream: A Study in Maritime Disaster and Mass Psychological Phenomenon," she'd tentatively titled the piece. *Psychological phenomenon.* The euphemism zinged harsh in her mind, a coward's compromise, but still the most daring phrasing her editors might allow. It was the linguistic sleight-of-hand that would let her paper publish something resembling the truth without admitting that real-

ity occasionally rewrote itself in ways that made scientific materialism look quaint. Like a child's crayon drawing next to a Rembrandt.

Six weeks had passed since the Coast Guard had pulled the survivors from a sinking ship that had become a death barge. She'd undergone two weeks of debriefings in sterile government rooms, psychological evaluations with stone-faced doctors, medical examinations that searched for toxins and pathogens that didn't exist, and the kind of polite, persistent questioning from men and women in dark suits that made it clear that certain aspects of her testimony would never make it into official reports. The questions always circled back: "Are you absolutely certain about what you saw?" As if uncertainty might erase the memories of eight-legged horrors swarming across cabin ceilings.

Classified for national security reasons, the official explanation read in impeccable bureaucratic prose. *Ongoing investigation into potential terrorist biological weapons requires information restriction to prevent copycat incidents.* A gas leak that made people lose their minds. *No evidence of any spiders were found on the ship*, Rashida thought with dark amusement, taking a sip of her third glass of wine of the evening. Of course they hadn't found any spiders. The curse had been lifted, reversing whatever hellish multiplication had occurred. The evidence had literally vanished before investigators arrived.

The news coverage had been masterfully managed. Just a tragic maritime accident caused by mechanical failure and subsequent passenger panic. The *Pacific Dream* had suffered catastrophic flooding due to structural damage, resulting in the unfortunate loss of life. Standard template, nothing to suggest that reality had temporarily suspended normal biological laws in favor of something that belonged in a fever dream or midnight horror movie.

Thirteen presumed fatalities, according to the official count, printed in respectable newspapers and repeated on evening news broadcasts. *Missing passengers presumed lost at sea.* Easier to categorize them as missing persons and let insurance companies argue over presumptive death claims than to explain bodies that had been drained of all fluids by unnaturally voracious arachnids.

Pacific Dream Cruise Lines deeply regrets the tragic loss of life, the company's statement had read, crafted by crisis management experts earning six-figure retainers. *We are cooperating fully with federal investigations while implementing enhanced safety protocols to prevent similar incidents.* As if safety protocols could prevent amateur witchcraft gone terribly wrong.

The lawsuits had begun within days, grieving families demanding answers that couldn't be provided, wrongful death claims seeking compensation for losses that transcended financial calculation. Rashida had interviewed some of the families in their living rooms surrounded by photos of the deceased, carefully documenting their pain while omitting the details that would have sounded like elaborate fantasy. Their grief was real, even if the official explanation wasn't.

Olivia Batiste's parents had hired a team of maritime lawyers who specialized in cruise ship negligence cases. They wanted to know why their daughter's body had never been recovered, why the ship's security footage from certain areas had been mysteriously corrupted, why the survivors' accounts contained so many inconsistencies and apparent gaps. Rashida had sat across from them at their kitchen table, notebook open, recorder running, heart breaking.

"She was just taking pictures for her social media," Olivia's mother had sobbed during their interview, clutching a framed portrait of her daughter, young, vibrant, unaware of her fate. "She was only nineteen years old, beautiful, full of life. Her smile would light up the room. How does someone just disappear on a cruise ship? They're saying she fell overboard, but Olivia was careful. She wouldn't have done that."

The mother's eyes had begged Rashida for a different truth than the one she thought she knew.

The Lichtenstein twins had been eulogized in newspapers and on television across the country. Rashida had taken copious notes to incorporate into her piece, wanting to make sure they got their due, even if the prose was mostly fiction. The brothers' final act had no audience except those sworn to silence.

Matt Craig was missing, presumed dead. Rashida knew he was actually dead—she'd seen him cornered in the ship's galley, his expensive suit torn, his cunning finally exhausted as a hail of spiders descended from the ceiling vents.

The survivors had scattered to various forms of psychological sanctuary, each trying to rebuild a worldview that could accommodate what they had witnessed but couldn't quite remember, while publicly maintaining the fiction required by authorities.

Captain Abercrombie retired and was now ensconced in his seaside Scottish home with his wife, a stone cottage perched on craggy cliffs where the North Sea's relentless waves provided a constant reminder of his former life. He'd given Eleanor a brief, tightly controlled interview over tea in his book-lined study, his weathered hands gripping the arms of his chair as he recounted the "mechanical failures" that had plagued the *Pacific Dream*. Her additional attempts to reach him had been met with increasingly firm rejections. First polite emails from his wife, then a terse legal notice from a Glasgow attorney warning against harassment of a man suffering from "post-traumatic stress related to his dignified career."

Dr. Hand had promptly returned to academic medicine, accepting a prestigious research position at Johns Hopkins where she could study infectious disease patterns without truly knowing why she'd developed an almost obsessive interest in concerted intelligence phenomena. Her new colleagues marveled at her innovative approach to swarm behavior in bacterial colonies, unaware that the bad dreams Fiona never remembered featured eight-legged horrors moving with impossible synchronicity across cabin ceilings.

Denver Wheaton was already aboard another cosplay destination cruise—this one set in the "awesome" 1980s—where he greeted passengers in neon windbreakers and perfectly feathered hair as if the *Pacific Dream* had been simply another professional engagement. His personnel file showed no gaps in employment, no psychological evaluations, no trauma counseling. Carlotta Cross was on that same cruise, resuming her duties as cruise director with rote efficiency, organizing "Totally Radical Trivia Nights" and "Miami Vice Cocktail Mixers" with the same meticulous attention to detail she'd once applied to 1940s swing dance competitions.

Karen Blacksmith had quietly donated her Roger's extensive entomology collection to the Smithsonian, including leather-bound journals and research notes that contained disturbingly accurate predictions about arachnid behavioral evolution under selective pressure. The curators had been delighted by the unexpected acquisition, never questioning why a grieving widow would part with her husband's life's work so hastily. She'd moved to a retirement community in Arizona—desert climate, far from any large bodies of water, minimal spider population—where she kept her windows sealed year-round despite the heat and slept with the lights on, a can of industrial-strength insecticide on her nightstand.

Christopher and Cleo—Rashida had started thinking of them as a unit, though their relationship status remained diplomatically undefined—disappeared from public view entirely, vanishing with the same abruptness as the spiders they had once commanded.

Christopher Webb's entertainment career had ended with the finality of a door-slam, his slick management team citing vague "health concerns" and the expected "desire for privacy following traumatic experience" in carefully worded press releases that revealed nothing of substance.

Cleo Laveau's flamboyant cruise ship psychic persona had been similarly retired, her turban-adorned promotional photos quietly removed from *Pacific Dream*'s marketing materials, her scheduled appearances canceled without explanation. The once-bustling waiting list for her shipboard readings had evaporated into thin air, just another unexplained casualty of that fateful voyage.

Rashida suspected both of them had simply moved their activities to venues that didn't require public documentation or scrutiny. Underground performances, perhaps, or private consultations for clients wealthy enough to ensure discretion. She'd heard whispers—nothing concrete, just fragments of rumors—about exclusive gatherings where Christopher performed illusions that defied explanation, and where Cleo's predictions carried the unmistakable weight of genuine prophecy rather than carnival trickery. Places where those who had survived similar brushes with the supernatural could speak freely about their experiences, without fear of ridicule or institutionalization.

Her laptop screen showed seventeen pages of carefully crafted prose that told as much truth as could be published without triggering government intervention. She'd woven the supernatural elements into a narrative about mass hysteria, environmental toxins, and the psychological effects of isolation on cruise ship passengers. Technically accurate, if you were willing to accept that "environmental toxins" could include magical intervention, and "mass hysteria" might encompass supernatural interrelated mind power.

Rashida's gaze drifted to the glossy brochures scattered across the desk, promotional materials she'd collected before boarding. They seemed like artifacts from another life now. "Step Back in Time!" one promised in an embellished, swooping font. "Experience the Glamour of the 1940s at Sea!" She picked up the embarkation photo that had been returned to her with her personal effects, showing a woman in a perfectly tailored burgundy dress with padded shoulders, her hair styled in pin-curls, a string of pearls gleaming at her throat.

The photographer had caught her mid-eye-roll at some comment from the steward, but there was unmistakable amusement in her expression. Her cynicism then had been the comfortable, professional kind, the armor of a journalist who'd seen enough to be skeptical but not enough to be broken.

She ran her finger over the image, remembering how she'd actually enjoyed the transformation, secretly delighting in channeling Lena Horne's elegant confidence, a Black star, shining beacons ahead of her time. Rashida had spent a week hunting vintage shops for the right accessories, telling herself it was just thorough research while privately relishing the thrill of stepping into another era's glamour.

That woman in the photograph didn't know what was coming. Didn't know about webbed corridors or desiccated corpses. Didn't know that skepticism was no shield against the impossible.

Her gaze flicked back to the screen. The editors had already expressed enthusiasm for the piece, calling it "a compelling examination of how crisis situations reveal the psychological fractures in seemingly civilized social structures." The magazine's fact-checkers had verified every detail that could be verified, carefully avoiding the aspects that would have required acknowledging the unknown.

Finally, she had the words to close with. She quickly began to type, worried that she would forget, as so many already had. "The true horror of the *Pacific Dream* wasn't the outbreak itself, but the glimpse it offered into reality's fragile construction. Like passengers on a luxury cruise, we drift through life believing in safety protocols and rational explanations, never suspecting that beneath our comfortable illusions lurks a vast ocean of possibilities that science has yet to fathom. When thirteen souls vanished at sea, they didn't just disappear from passenger manifests, they fell through cracks in our collective understanding, victims of forces that official reports will never acknowledge. Perhaps the most terrifying revelation isn't that monsters exist, but that we've built entire civilizations pretending they don't."

Rashida reread the paragraph twice, nodded with grim satisfaction, and clicked "Send." A Message Not Sent error appeared almost instantly. Damn hotel wifi. Her editor would have to wait until first thing tomorrow. She closed her laptop with a decisive snap, feeling the weight of witness lift from her shoulders. The truth, however disguised, would soon exist in the world. She hadn't been able to save everyone on that ship, but she'd ensured their stories wouldn't dissolve like spider webs after rain.

Publication next month, she thought. *Prize-worthy journalism that manages to document impossible events without technically admitting that impossible events occurred.*

First thing tomorrow, she would fly back to New York, return to her apartment, and resume covering normal human disasters that didn't involve supernatural biological acceleration.

Back to reality, she thought. *Back to stories where the worst that can happen is corruption, incompetence, or ordinary human evil.*

As she began packing her luggage, something made her pause. The suitcase seemed heavier than it should have been, and there was a faint scratching sound coming from somewhere inside the fabric lining, like tiny claws working methodically against the material.

Probably nothing, she told herself, even as goosebumps crawled up her arms in a slow, horrible wave. *A trapped mouse, maybe, or just the sound of my jewelry settling against itself in the side pocket.*

She unzipped the main compartment with a reluctance she couldn't quite justify, revealing the neat arrangement of clothes, electronics, and research materials that had sustained her through weeks of travel, careful investigation, and diplomatic writing. Everything appeared exactly as she'd packed it, nothing obviously disturbed, her blouses still folded with crisp pleats, her voice recorder nestled between her notebooks, her toiletry bag zipped tight in its designated corner.

Paranoia, she diagnosed with hopeful desperation. *Post-traumatic stress manifesting as hypervigilance about impossible recurrence. Classic symptom. I should include it in the sidebar about survivor psychology.*

But as she lifted out her laptop case, something small and dark scuttled across the suitcase's fabric lining. Too fast to identify clearly, but moving with the particular jerky accuracy that she'd learned to associate with spiders conducting reconnaissance. Its legs splayed wide, covering more territory than seemed possible for its size, before disappearing into a seam.

No, she thought, her journalist's objectivity crumbling in the face of implications that she'd spent weeks trying to rationalize away in online therapy sessions and late-night writing binges. *It's dead. The spell was reversed. The hive mind was destroyed. Cleo confirmed it herself. This can't be happening.*

The hotel room's lights flickered—once, twice, then began pulsing in patterns that made her mind throb, alternating between harsh brightness and near-darkness in sequences that seemed to contain information rather than electrical malfunction. Somewhere in the walls, something that sounded very much like systematic tapping began to echo with rhythms that suggested communication, coordination, purpose.

The curse remains, Rashida realized with the particular clarity that accompanied the return of familiar nightmares. *We didn't destroy it. We just... dispersed it. Scattered the pieces to places where they could regroup, evolve, adapt. Like a virus going dormant only to reactivate when conditions are favorable.*

She grabbed her phone from the nightstand, intending to call... someone. Christopher, maybe, or Dr. Hand, anyone who might understand what was happening without dismissing her as traumatized or delusional. But the screen showed only static, electronic interference that pulsed in patterns that matched the tapping in the walls, white noise dancing in geometric formations that no software glitch could explain.

They're jamming communications, she thought. *Learning from their previous experience. Adapting their tactics. Preventing us from organizing a defense like before.*

The scratching sounds were multiplying now, coming from multiple directions simultaneously from inside the air conditioning vent, behind the framed artwork above the bed, within the television cabinet. Each scratch carried its own distinct timbre: the metallic rasp from the vent, the soft scraping against canvas from behind the artwork, and the hollow tapping from within the wooden cabinet. The sounds formed a discordant symphony that raised goosebumps along Rashida's arms and sent ice through her veins.

Second wave, Rashida realized as the lights continued their disturbing pulse patterns, casting moving shadows across walls where nothing should be moving. The air had taken on a musty, almost sweet smell, like rotting fruit mixed with something medicinal that made her nostrils flare in recognition. It was the same distinctive odor that had permeated the lower decks of the *Pacific Dream* just before the incident in the dining hall. The temperature seemed to fluctuate wildly, patches of cold air brushing against her skin like ghostly caresses. *The survivors weren't rescued. We were infected. Carriers. Seeds for a new outbreak that would begin far from any maritime disaster that might attract official attention.*

She reached for her laptop, flipping it open with clumsy fingers but determined intent, aiming to document whatever was about to happen with the same dedication that had carried her through decades of dangerous reporting. If she was going to die, she was damn well going to leave a record of the experience that couldn't be dismissed or explained away. For good measure, she turned on her webcam.

The best stories, she thought as shadows began moving independently of their sources and the hotel room's temperature dropped to something that felt distinctly unnatural, frost forming on the inside of windows despite the summer heat outside, *are always the ones that nobody wants to believe.*

The lights flickered one final time, then went out completely. The computer died too, plunging the room into a darkness so complete it seemed to have heft and texture.

In the darkness that followed, something that might have been an expression of mirth echoed through frequencies that human ears shouldn't be able to process. A chittering, clicking sound that resonated in bone rather than eardrum.

Rashida's knees hit the carpet as darkness swallowed the room. "No no no no," she whispered, crawling backward until her spine hit the wall.

The scratching sounds multiplied, a symphony of tiny claws from every direction. Her fingers scrabbled at her own skin, imagining phantom legs scurrying across her flesh.

I documented everything perfectly. I was thorough. I was OBJEC-TIVE.

A sob tore from her throat as something brushed against her ankle. The darkness wasn't empty anymore. It pulsed with movement, with purpose.

After all, the collective consciousness might have thought, if it thought in ways human minds could comprehend, *we are no longer alone. We are no longer individual. We are collective. We are purpose. We are hunger.*

And we have learned so much.

Her mind unspooled like film from a broken projector. Memories fragmented: Olivia's desiccated corpse floating on waves. Matt Craig shrieking as spiders poured from the vents. The captain's eyes, clouded with venom-induced madness.

"I'm Rashida Bell," she gasped, rocking back and forth. "National Press Club Award nominee. Columbia School of Journalism. I report facts. I REPORT FACTS!"

But facts were dissolving in a reality where curses rewrote biological laws and spiders developed hive minds.

She began to scream as legions of spiders marched up her legs and over her body.

When hotel security finally broke down her door, they found Rashida alone, laughing hysterically, surrounded by pieces of a shattered laptop and torn pages covered in frantic scribbles.

AFTERWORD

There are several more *Nature's Nightmares* books in the works, so if you'd like to be kept in the loop, please visit StaciLayneWilson.com

Special thanks to Linda Rose, my constant reader and error eradicator.

If you liked this book, please kindly rate and review... indie authors depend on word of mouth (or word of fingertips, as the case may be). Thank you!

Staci Layne Wilson enjoys writing about herself in the third person, and playing with her pet dumbo rats. She is an L.A. native who enjoys traffic, wildfires, and earthquakes—but since her move to Las Vegas, she's learned to love 110-degree summers, drive-thru wedding chapels, and casinos that still reek of the Rat Pack's cigars. She has been a professional writer since the age of twelve, when she was hired as a columnist for a national magazine. When she's not writing books, she's making movies (*Cabaret of the Dead, The Ventures: Stars on Guitars, The Second Age of Aquarius,* and *Dark House of the Mannequins*).